THE MEMOIRS

OF A SHY PORNOGRAPHER

THE MEMOIRS
OF A SHY PORNOGRAPHER

What I Came From & The Doors Of The World Are Opened To Me & The First Party I Ever Went To & The First Real Home I Ever Had & My Life As A Private Investigator & The Last Party I Ever Went To & The Story Of My Love & Does The Famous Detective Know That Love In A Mist Is Only The Great White Whale Going Down For The Full Count In That Old Seventh Round & The Deer Are Entering This Beautiful Forest & The Greatest And Most Wonderful Plan On Earth & The House Of The Frowning Heart & A Radiant Temple Stands Above The Waters & What Became Of Me

AN AMUSEMENT BY
KENNETH PATCHEN

INTRODUCTION BY JONATHAN WILLIAMS

A NEW DIRECTIONS BOOK

Copyright 1945 by New Directions Publishing Corporation
Introduction copyright © 1999 by Jonathan Williams

Manufactured in the United States of America
New Directions Books are printed on acid-free paper.
Originally published in cloth by New Directions in 1945, and reissued as New Directions Paperbook 205 in 1983
Published simultaneously in Canada by Penguin Books Canada Limited

Library of Congress Cataloging-in-Publication Data
Patchen, Kenneth, 1911–1972.
The memoirs of a shy pornographer : an amusement / Kenneth Patchen ; introduction by Jonathan Williams.
p. cm.
ISBN 978-0-8112-1411-7
I. Title.
PS3531.A764M46   1999
813'.54—dc21
                                98-37235
                                    CIP

10 9 8 7 6 5 4 3 2

New Directions Books are published for James Laughlin
by New Directions Publishing Corporation,
80 Eighth Avenue, New York 10011

FOR MIRIAM

CONTENTS

INTRODUCTION

HOW BOUT A CUPPA EASY-ON-THE-CANNED-COW JUICE CAWFEE, KEN, AND THEN TELL THE NICE PEOPLE WHY YOU HAVE YOUR SHUFFLIN' SHAMUS, BIG ALF BUDD, COME FROM BIVALVE, NEW JERSEY, WHEN HE SHOULD HAVE COME FROM PLUMBSOCK, LOVELA-DIES, PENNY POT, OR SUCCASUNNA. SUCCASUNNA'S ONLY TWO MILES FROM BUDD LAKE, FOR CREEP'S SAKE! BUT, HEY, BIG ALF SHOULD REALLY HAVE COME FROM YET ANOTHER MUCHO COSMIC DUMP LIKE: HUMPTULIPS, WASHINGTON; MONKEY'S EYE-BROW, KENTUCKY; OR (WOW!) ODD, WEST VIRGINIA. THE GUY NEEDS SOME REAL SURREAL CLASS. KEN, ARE YOU LISTENING? I'M NOT.

I read *Memoirs of a Shy Pornographer* exactly 50 years ago. (I didn't know at the time that J. Laughlin's right hand was on the cover, a fact of no particular cosmic import, but still nice to know.)

It's funny what you remember. I remember Harry the Habit very clearly. (His habit is inking up his bare bottom and leaving his prints, which look like a drawing of two halves of a giant pear, on people's ceilings, draperies, and toilet seats.)

And I remember the little man with half a beard. "If you're wonder-ing why I grow a beard only on one side it's to accommodate my two personalities—I'm a true schizo—Rudolph likes to be clean-shaven, Timothy prefers a beard. Simple, isn't it?" His library was the thing. "I reached out and took down a book. It was *The Girl of the Limberlost* by Gene Stratton Porter. I took down another. It was a book by Gene Stratton Porter called *The Girl of the Limberlost*. The third one I took out was *The Girl of the Limberlost* by Gene Stratton Porter. So was the fourth, and the fifth...." "You see," Timothy/Rudolph said, "I thought it would be much more sensible to have one book we really liked than a lot of books we just felt luke-warm about."

"She had nothing on except an American Indian with long green feathers in his war-bonnet"—who could forget that, bub (or Budd)?

And the way the book ends. Its wit reminds me of the finale of Haydn's Farewell Symphony, or the last movement of Carl Nielsen's delirious Sixth Symphony. Knockout!

In my time I have owned the manuscripts of KP's *The Journal of Albion Moonlight* and *Sleepers Awake*. I took dictation of *Fables & Other Little Tales* from KP in Old Lyme, Connecticut in 1950, and later published it as one of the first Jargon Society Books. So, I've been wandering around in the prose texts a long time. The more prolix the man gets, the less I get it. His range, for me, is very limited, like the blues. Simple, passionate, honest to god. Patchen has written 40 to 50 world-class poems. I mean, nobody is any better. He was the master of the shaggy-dog poem, the rope-a-dope poem, the wise-guy poem, the soft-shuffle poem. As I have noted elsewhere, if there had been a movie called *Patchen on the Trail of Beings So Hideous That The Air Weeps Blood*, the only guy who could play him would have been Robert Mitchum—a leonine hunk with a slow, stentorian vocal delivery. Patchen delivers the screwball, the slider, the circle change, the spitter, and even Satchel Paige's unique, patented ephus pitch. After four or five of those, you've had it, you're heading for the dugout, you've been toyed with and are never quite the same again.

What interests me most is the context the stew-pot Memoirs comes out of. This is American Apple-Pie Surrealism and this is more about movies and the radio than it is literature, as in France or Germany. The Marx Brothers and the Three Stooges roamed our hick, corn-fed imaginations. I would be willing to bet a wooden nickel that a primary source for *Memoirs* was a totally wacko movie called *Million Dollar Legs* (1932). It got shown with things like *The Blood of a Poet*, by Jean Cocteau, in art-movie houses on Eighth Street in Greenwich Village. Again, fifty years ago.

Memory is dim, etc., but the Blessed Internet informs me that in *Million Dollar Legs* W.C. Fields is the President of Klopstokia, a Far-Away Country. Chief Exports: Goats and Nuts. Chief Imports: Goats and Nuts.

Chief Inhabitants: Goats and Nuts. Other worthies in this nutbag are Jack Oakie, Hugh Herbert, and Ben Turpin, plus Susan Fleming (later the wife of Harpo Marx). All the Klopstokian men are named George and all the women Angela. Patchenesque—yessiree bob.

And then he takes us into the world of radio soap opera: "Oxydol's Own Ma Perkins," and her pal Shuffle Shofer, or was it Shuffle Chauffeur? "Gosh all hemlock" is what they so often say in Rushville Center, poor devils. And then I seem to be reminded of "Our Gal Sunday," The Story That Asks the Question: Can This Girl From a Little Mining Town in the West Find Happiness as the Wife of Lord Henry Brinthrop, England's Richest, Most Handsome Lord? Well, the answer is: no way, dudes. Anyway. I will almost spare you further adumbrations of Vic and Sade, The Couple Half Way Down the Next Block, or Fibber McGee and Molly. Or Dagwood and Blondie. Or Bogart, Cagney, and the tough-guy lingo of Edward G. Robinson. Yet what about the Duke of Paducah ("Run for the roundhouse, Nelly, the brakeman can't corner you there!"). Bob "Bazooka" Burns, Joe ("Wanna buy a duck?") Penner, and Jerry Collona (How *do* you *do*)? And wait, just one damn minute, "The Catfish" on *Amos and Andy*. Patchen ate his Wheaties and meditated on the good works of *The Shadow* and *Jack Armstrong, the All-American Goy*. These were antediluvian times.

Another thing that interests me is how embarrassing it is for he-man Americans to be poets. Our private eye, Alf Budd, is always running into fairies who whisper "puft, puft" into his ear. Hetero he-men always seem to think they are automatic objects of lust for every faggot in the land. Actually, most of them are real turn-offs. They belong in the garage tinkering with the car; or down at the bowling alley; or at Bible Study class; or having a few brewskies with their a--h--- buddies down at the tavern. Make it a Budd! She-men write poems; or shamans (or berdaches), if you happen to be Native American.

Charles Ives was particularly tiresome about sissies. He ranted and raved about them (yet, most of his audience consisted of Congregational Church women, where a few sissies might have been welcome, actually) and yelled about "Rollo" and other limp-wristed citizens. Kenneth Rexroth said, famously, that poets were little boys who couldn't play baseball or ride bicycles. So, the regular guys got them down in the vacant lot and rubbed sand on their thing. Eventually, they turned to art! Ives was the captain of his New Haven prep-school football team that beat the Yale freshmen. Patchen played football in the Pennsylvania/Ohio rust-belt where big bohunks and polacks did just that and little else. He had a football scholarship to the University of Wisconsin, which is where he first injured his back and had to drop out. He was enrolled in the experimental college organized by Professor Alexander Meiklejohn.

How blank it all was back in those dim days of your yore. On the radio Mr. and Mrs. America were presented with exactly two manifestations of a poet. Ernie Kovacs had one named Percy Dovetonsils. Fred Allen on *Allen's Alley* had Falstaff Openshaw. One of his epic two-liners I still cherish. It went:

"Mother's looking a perfect stranger,
since she caught her face in the record changer."

Homer Capehart, an American Senator, invented this device for changing 78 rpms—a fact of little consequence to Murcan dudes of the present. This was American Poetry, in those kinder, gentler, dumber days. Dumber than now? Just about.

• • •

That's a pretty interesting list of old jazz 78s that KP lays out for us on page 56. About half of it is out of nowhere, but the real half is dynamite. I wonder if the late composer/violinist/archivist, Bill Russell, was his guide? And that makes me wonder about the extraordinary shape-shifting that goes on *Memoirs*. I'm a Scotch whisky drinker meself, lads and lasses, so I'm very ignorant of the modern chemical stuff. Patchen might have sniffed a little Ovaltine, but that's about it. What makes me wonder about his hallucinatory world is the very recent discovery of an enzyme named Melatonin. My painter friend, Jim McGarrell, is a user of Melatonin. It's great for putting you into a deep sleep, and it produces some amazing, phantasmagorical, endless dreams. Jim was a protégé of

Bill Russell, and did some very important recordings of New Orleans music in the early 1950s. The Barnes Bocage Big Five CD on American Music label would have been a Patchen favorite—if he'd ever heard it. Anyway, I dream in this fashion. One instance: huge dinosaurs playing saxophones on little islands in an orange lake (Lago di Garda, perhaps), while in the northern background, the Dolomites, and fierce lightning over the blue/black mountains. Melatonin is produced naturally in the body. Maybe, in KP's case, it produced buckets full? Huh? This is the correct place to quote Basil Bunting's definitive statement: "There is absolutely no excuse for literary criticism."

America has never been as good as its billing. Look at Ives, look at Stevens: Yankee-inventor insurance executives, known to one tenth of one per cent of the population. Don't even think about Whitman, who had to set in type and publish his own book, and then write the only favorable reviews (except for R. W. Emerson). Or Hartley or Ryder or Bill Traylor. Plenty of meat in Murka, but no potatoes!

So, what I am saying is, read the *Memoirs* and recognize that times have changed. We are much crazier than those mildly wacko folks back in the Blank Forest or the Roosevelt Days. We are only "kind of" here. In Patchenland early-blooming paranoia is never out of season.

Ok, Mr. Budd, follow the yel-lowbri-ckroad. Only a sleuth whose middle name's middle name is Leander has a fat, or a thin, chance on a quest like yours. Christ be with us—or, at least, be in the same ball park. Your creator, Mr. Patchen, was a great natural ballplayer. He weren't borned like you and me. Like Babe Ruth, he came down out of the Tree of Heaven. They both struck out a lot, but when they hit one, it stayed hit.

Jonathan Williams

WHAT I CAME FROM

Dear Unknown Friend

My name is Budd. I was born in Bivalve, New Jersey, on March 15, 1905. In my nineteenth year I went to work in a factory at 650–1 Gastor Street, near Welman Dinker's Square, Manhattan, N.Y., where I worked in continuous employment until the second Thursday of a recent October. My sister, Mabelle Frances, has two children, a little girl ten years of age, named Karlanne, and a boy of eleven, who is called Medrid. We live in a four-room apartment at the corner of Visalia and Fairwood in the Borough of Brooklyn. Our street door is on Fairwood.

Mabelle Frances, born on June 26, 1910, also in Bivalve—but not in the same house—has reddish hair, worn in one large and two smaller buns, tan eyes, rather thick ankles, and weighs 108 pounds.

Medrid has a scar running from just over his left eyebrow down almost to his weak chin—fattish hands, weight 147½.

Karlanne is fairly small for her age, favors no one in the family, and has a nasty little playmate with the name Michael who has campaign buttons pinned all over her dress.

Leroy Shelby, Mabelle Frances' husband, walked out of the house one day and never came back. Eight years ago—May 2, 1936, to be exact. Leroy had little formal education, going on part-time in a shoestore at fourteen, and when he disappeared he was on regular but in a different location. He was then making 21.50—3.25 less than I made though his hours were longer and mine only a five day to his six.

Our parents were fatally injured by an automobile when we were three and eight. They had been shopping in Millville and were on their way back to the jitney-stop when an air-cooled Franklin of that period pinned them against the steel window-guard of a pawnshop. It was a little after four on a Saturday afternoon. We learned when we were old enough to understand that our father's head was smashed in two, his right leg torn off at the hip, and most of his chest ripped out; mother, more fortunate, had her trouble mainly inside, dying fifty-six hours later without losing consciousness.

One thing we thought of a lot as children was that they hadn't even been able to breathe their last in Bivalve, which, we knew, they would have wanted to do.

Sis and I were raised by a Mr. and Mrs. Ed Hall. He worked in the mills around that section and his wife, a native of the Tennessee hills, spent a lot of her waking hours around the house frying levee-welly cakes, the batter for which she stirred by foot. That was the only proper way to do it, suh, she always said. I have vivid memories of her sitting crouched over on a chair in the kitchen, both her rather shapeless feet pumping up and down in a thick, liver-colored mass which overflowed the rim of an old wooden tub. I am sure that if I tasted a levee-welly right now, all that time would fill my subconsciousness and I'd see again through memory's eye the long red hairs sticking out of Mr. Hall's nose.

They had four children of their own—Chalice, a girl; Hegger, a boy; Mildreen, another girl; and Wilhelmina, called Will, who wore men's pants and smoked a pipe at thirteen. I loved Chalice, and Hegger loved Mabelle Frances.

Hegger is now district organizer of a Russian political association in Pottsville, Pa. Golden haired Chalice drowned in a small creek on March 12, 1921. We were born five days apart. She was given respiration by artificial means, but did not respond to it. Many years passed before I went skating again.

Medrid and I slept together on a studio couch in the front room. Karlanne and her mother had their own bedroom on the street side.

When Leroy went, my sister started to do dress-making. The little room off the kitchen was supposed to be used for fittings, but mostly nobody bothered to. At times it was very embarrassing. For me.

I don't like to think much about my life before it happened —before I wrote *Spill of Desire*, or, as I called it first, *The Spool of Destiny*—but I should say something about the factory.

We wound linen gauze around armatures, wrapping them just right and putting three dabs of glue on each. Neddy and 'Budge' Shadron worked with me. I never knew Neddy's other name. He spent all his spare time reading everything he could get his hands on about Anthony B. Comstock. For quite a while we called Shadron 'Big Bill' but then he stopped talking about Tilden's game for Donald B.'s.

We had a boy who moved the spools on and off the benches and brought around the basins of water we washed the glue off our hands with. I think he was Brazilian or Spanish because there was an accent around the word he said and his hair was worn long in front of his ears and came down over his red cape at the back. He never used more than that one word—which I can't print in a family book of this sort. He was really an old boy, forty or so.

There was a reddish stain near the mirror in the Men's Room, and often as I stood in front of it it seemed to get smaller and tighter—like an eye looking at me. Once or twice I wanted to tell Neddy or 'Budge' about it, but somehow the right time never came up.

I knew what Buchanan, the boy, would have said if I told him—and I didn't want that word near the eye.

One of the things I didn't like was Medrid's drinking so much water just at bedtime.

A girl stopped me once and said:
"Are you afraid, too?"
This took place in front of *Ludmore's Notions And Hard-To-Find-Goods* on 8th Avenue near 23rd Street. I was admiring a tiny glass angel with red wings and a little yellow polka-dot nightie that stood between a tiger made of green wood and a lamplighter in an old-fashioned coat with big pockets with the paint chipped off his right hand—yet very nice for the mantel.

However, what I collected was the mud from the running boards of trucks. I'd look at the license plate and after scraping off a nice piece get my tag with the date and the state's name on it. In this way I gradually had mud from every state in the Union except S. Dakota, Wyoming, Nevada and W. Virginia.

I discovered that the drivers are inclined to be suspicious and even crude at times.

On the basis of beginning at two years old, I have eaten 14,196 breakfasts, 14,084 lunches—(four months once I tried three carrots and an apple, which hardly counts) and 14,194 suppers. I have traveled 109,200 subway miles getting to work and back. I have worn out 361 pairs of socks, 46 of pants, 83 of shorts, 35 of shoes, 102 shirts, 9 sets of rubbers, and five pairs of slippers. I have had 6 overcoats, 1 topcoat, 5 "good" suits, 34 neckties, 6 pairs of sleeve holders, 7 of Paris garters, and 2 hats, one dark gray, and one bright yellow.

I have used 83 tubes of Colgate toothpaste, 16 Prophylactic brushes, 348 Herald Square blades, 3 Gillette de Luxe safety-razors, 9 combs, 2 Ogilvie hairbrushes, 1 Fuller Long Bristle, 121 bottles Tiger Lily hair tonic, 94 of Indian Maiden (herb), 48 of Wild Root, 25 of Kreml, 14 of Glovers, 246 of Listerine, 92 of witch hazel, and 6 of Murine.

(From my Diary)

May 10, 1936. Well here it is eight days since Leroy left the scene. Much crying and dashing around. . . . So spend evenings in the DeKalb Branch Library, Bushwick and DeKalb Avenues.

The librarian, a Miss Wedrabitt, seems to be a very interesting woman.

May 17. Man I met in Reading Room is not as cultured as I thought. Caught him putting my watch in his pocket as he asked me if I followed the *New Republic* editorials.

Sept. 24, 1937. Sunday. M.F. and I quarrelled because she

still insists on bathing the children together in the same tub despite their advanced age.

Bit into piece of fat on my second veal chop.

Not a very good Sept. 24th.

Nov. 30. Mrs. Mulligan forgot her lending library book last night and since it was so late when we discovered it I didn't return it then—but having nothing better to do started to read it.

Dec. 2. The book is *The Case of the Velvet Claws* by an Erle Stanley Gardner.

On Chapter Seven and a New Pacific is opening up in front of me.

Jan. 10, 1938. I have read all Mr. Gardner's works.

March 6. Rereading *The Cases*. M.F. said this morning at breakfast:

"Who is this hussy, Albert?"

I fixed my steady, penetrating gaze upon her.

"What are you talking about?" I asked coolly.

"You know very well what I'm talking about, and stop looking at me like a sick chicken," she answered evasively.

Later I found out I'd been calling her Della—though she hasn't much in common with Miss Street.

Jan. 11. Overheard in the park this noon:

"All primitive people have it. Did you ever hear of an Arab who didn't live in the present tents?"

There is a building on Madison in the fifties where 400 elevator boys live in a large room in the basement unknown to the superintendent, despite the fact that two old darkies go down there every night and teach them tap-dancing.

A man they call The Diver told me about it. He walks with

a little shuffle and both his ears are sort of puffy. A salvage worker, I think.

July 22, 1939. Miss Wedrabitt has been transferred to the Brownsville Branch—a long walk for me and the neighborhood has people in it like the two who stopped me last night:

"In the market for a mouse, Budd?" (Never saw them before.)

"You will pardon me," I said, trying to walk around them.

"A hard one to please, hunh? What flavor you like? We got 'em chinky, dark meat, red tops, bow legs, hump backs—"

"What do you do with these unusual mice?" I said to humor them.

"A foxy grandpaw, hunh?" one said.

"I got him lamped as an Eagle Scout," the other one said.

Then they said some other things I won't repeat.

Sept. 2. I have become a friend of an old man who is considered rather strange, walking about the street in his bare feet and a long white beard with a sign on his chest reading:

Where Will You Be When Jesus Comes, Brother?

I see now it was a mistake to ask him for supper. M.F. got very snippy after he left at four in the morning.

For three weeks he rang our bell every time we were ready to sit down at the table and I got a lot of unpleasant looks for it.

Dec. 17. It was snowing when I got out of work today and I thought it would be nice to imagine a big snake crawling along the street—so right away I saw one poking his nose into the upper storeys of houses and lashing his tail around. Then he turned to look at me and his tail whipped out and cracked me in the leg.

When I took off my pants for bed I was surprised to find a bruise on my left leg about 3 inches from the knee cap.

May 2, 1940. I was sort of day-dreaming this morning after I woke up—imagining it was ten below zero and a lot of ice on the sidewalk. I got out of the house without M.F. seeing me, and though I had my overcoat buttoned-up to my ears I nearly froze and fell down three times.

A lot of small boys followed me for blocks—watching me blow steam out on my breath.

Oct. 8, 1941. The Diver told me today that there never really was a Benjamin Harrison who came after Cleveland as the President. According to his information, seven bell hops in Akron thought up the whole thing and had themselves elected by getting an old bum off the street to pretend he was Harrison. They moved into The White House and sold off most of the states west of the Mississippi to two millionaire jockeys who wanted to turn the whole thing into a big race track, but their plan fell through because any horses they brought out from New York got so homesick they all died.

But the hops had the money and when the old man lost the next election they went to Egypt and spent most of it air-conditioning the pyramids so they could live sort of like a hotel there.

Dec. 7. I wonder why evil people get more power than good people. Wish I never had to go out until this is all over because they may decide to kill me too.

I won't talk about it if I can help it.

Michael has switched from buttons to collecting pictures of Robert ('Bob') Hope.

Received six advertising pieces in the mail this morning about varicose veins, trusses, relief from hemorrhoid distress, and so forth—the biggest amount of mail I've ever had on one single day. But where did they hear of me and think I am in trouble of that kind?

I average six Xmas cards and about five with greetings from

mountains and the seashore in the summertime. And once I got a ten pound keg of codfish sent me by mistake, which I have no taste for because of boniness.

My nearsight is worse but it would be terrible if I stumbled with them on so won't risk glasses.

Dec. 31. I resolve—Not to forget to put my rubbers, overcoat, muffler, suitcoat and socks all in one place near the bed at night because it upsets M.F. when I go off without them. Not to take Perry Mason with me to lunch anymore since when reading don't eat and was even three minutes late getting back on the bench one day. Not to always let everybody stop me in the street to talk because these people have nothing better to do than get me all excited and happy—(Mistake to let them try on my hat because they lay their eggs in your hair and can hurt the scalp.Or ever give out our address. And stop carrying cigarettes to hand them since M.F. might find a package and think I had begun their use, besides making them angry offering them Chesterfields when they want Camels . . .). Not to expect a nervous child like Karlanne to realize she shouldn't mark up my books and even tear sixteen pages out of *The Sulky Girl*—and not try anymore to hypnotize her because I hardly knew what I was doing all the rest of the week. And not suggest using string in front of Medrid again. Or hide the Hopes where I did. To stop wondering what the spools we wrap are used for. To understand you can't keep supper waiting while somebody wastes time in front of a pet shop or half an hour helping an old lady across the street because the doctor gave her too much medicine for her cold and have her follow you back when you turn around for a minute, and use bad language.

Not to have more than one "vision" a day.

To pray every night for everybody in the world.

Jan. 6, 1942. I have a secret, dear Diary.
I am writing a book! A regular book!

Jan. 7. M.F. thinks I am writing letters to *The Eagle* again—which I used to do a lot of about stray cats and children leaving balls on the stairway.

Feb. 4. It is odd that I have never had a dream in my whole life. I have always been able to sleep solid through any noise of the sewing machine or when Karlanne wakes up with a nightmare or the steam pipe broke. Excellent elimination despite what Serutan says.

The Diver gave me a little rubber bag to keep my fountain pen in.

April 27. I have finished *The Spool of Destiny!*

April 28. The man I misjudged of trying to take my watch in the DeKalb knows my secret.

He said he was a good personal friend of William Morrow, and I let him have it to read since it happens he is in the business of Author's Agent at only 50% and the Copyright made out to him.

Skujellifeddy, his name, has a nervous way of looking around from so many business responsibilities and his hair is the healthiest I've ever seen—besides the little man who is always with him seems to have confidence in him.

The Agent's friend is about 35, thin wrists, fawn spats, yellow shirt with purple stripes, apricot necktie, silver belt-buckle with the head of some baseball player on it, a sort of pink-orange coat, deep green pants, and has a retiring manner.

His name is George Arliss, the same as an actor. He always carries around a small dead mole which he fondles with his thumb in a dreamy way.

I have a feeling that something is going to happen.

THE DOORS OF THE WORLD ARE OPENED TO ME

The next time I saw Skujellifeddy McGranehan he was pretty excited.

"Your book," he said.

"Terrific," George Arliss explained.

"You mean you really like it!" I said, hardly daring to believe my ears.

"It's going," the Agent said, turning another page of *The Nation.*

"Places," his friend said. He had the mole out on the table and was shoving gently at the back of its head. "Enormous possibilities," he continued.

"Have you seen Mr. Morrow?" I asked.

"Who Morrow?" Mr. McGranehan inquired, picking up *Partisan Review*.

"Why, he published Mr. Gardner. . . ."

"Who Gardner?"

"That mystery fellow," George Arliss said.

"Erle Stanley Gardner," I said, beginning to feel a sense of foreboding.

"Look here, Budd," the Agent said.

"The brass tacks," George Arliss said.

"It's sweet."

"Skujellifeddy means it's as pure as the old drivelling snow. . . ."

"Let me shoot the biz, George, hunh?"

"Lead on, Mac."

"We hadda make a couple changes, Budd."

"What sort of changes?"

"Oh, nothing much."

"Make that two ohs," George Arliss said mysteriously.

"Stop mussing that G——ned mole, George."

"Ah, I didn't mean nothin', Skujellifeddy."

"What sort of changes?" I repeated.

Mr. McGranehan tore out about half the pages in *P.R.* before he spoke. I was expecting Miss Wedrabitt to come over any minute.

"Nice Hank James article," he said. "Budd, this is it. Why does a man like a woman?"

"Why, I suppose because—"

"Because they're different," George Arliss said. He had the mole turned over and seemed to be studying its stomach.

"And that's why they're going to like you, Budd," Mr. Mc-Granehan said. "You're different, see. An innocent, see. Not dry behind yet, see. Ever had a wet dream, Budd?"

"I never dream at all," I informed him.

"Ride with it," George Arliss said.

"People are fed up, see. A new kick, thrill, sensation, see. And that's where you come in, Budd."

"Is it really that good?" I asked, hardly daring to believe my ears again.

"Good? Next to this St. Francis taught the birds bad habits, see. That's why you're a monster."

"What . . . ?"

"Let him come to you," George Arliss said.

"After we fixed it a little. . . ."

"Pardon me for interrupting, Mr. McGranehan," I said. "But I'm all in the dark about this."

"See," George Arliss said.

"We made it like raping your mother. You take a little girl and squeeze her eyeballs out, see."

"Wait until he leads again," George Arliss advised.

"So we have the love tale of a moral leper, of a man who lifts the trailing vestments of the unblemished nun . . . and what does he see, Budd!"

"Why, *Mr.* McGranehan," George Arliss said.

"G—— it, George."

"All right. All right."

"So you spit in the face of all that men hold dear, Budd," Mr. McGranehan explained. "You tear aside the veil, see. You wear the face of an angel, but a black wolf lurks underneath . . . a wolf with his teeth in the throat of all that is decent and wholesome since the world began."

"Woof. Woof," George Arliss said.

"So we've had to send it out of the country, Budd."

"But why?" I cried.

"Any fool knows you can't leave out words like that in the States."

"What words . . . ?"

"Like * * * * and * * * * and * * * * and * * * * and

* * * * and * * * *," George Arliss said. "And * * * *, too."

I wanted to cry but I finally managed to say, "But what has leaving out such awful words got to do with my book?"

"Because they've been left out, Budd, see."

"Put it all on the tray, Skujellifeddy," George Arliss said. "I've got to go out and look up a fresh one."

His mole did look pretty frayed-like by now.

"You remember on the first page this here Barry Chasen makes with the puss to this Chaleen dame?"

"He means when he busses her," George Arliss elaborated.

"Well, he don't no more, see."

Mr. McGranehan was looking through the *New Republic*.

"Always save it for last," he said. Then he continued: "We put another word in for kiss."

"What word?" I asked.

"* * * *," George Arliss said, sliding his used-up mole into the magazine rack.

"And it's Snavely now, Gregor Snavely," Mr. McGranehan volunteered.

"Jes' ain't no mo' po' Barry Chasen in thar," the mole-fancier said.

" 'Stead of this Chal-something, we got Maggy Daline, more sinned against than sinning."

"But if you leave out words why won't people think they're nice ones instead of bad?" I asked at last, wondering if perhaps I had not abrogated certain rights in this matter so vital to me.

" 'Why people?' you mean," George Arliss said.

"You'll have them undressing each other in the streets," Mr. McGranehan said, adding pensively: "At six skins a throw."

Just then an old lady reached down for a magazine, and she must have touched the mole because she gave a little shriek.

"Help yourself, sister," George Arliss said. "The thrill's all gone out of that one for me."

2

As is their habit, the weeks passed. Monday was followed by Tuesday, Wednesday was right there ahead of Thursday, etc.; and in my soul all was flux and turmoil too.

I hate to think how I waited; how I even forgot to brush my hair on one occasion; how my patience wore so thin I snatched Medrid's sixth glass of water out of his fat little fist one night at bedtime; how I didn't even complain much when Michael got into my drawer and pulverized my specimens from Mich., Va., Vt., and Cal. before I could grab her arm and give it a slight fracture; how I put only two dabs of glue on several spools; how one morning I started out of the house with only my shorts on under my overcoat—please don't make me dwell on it!

I couldn't even keep my mind on my Gardners.

Then one day when I got home from work it was there waiting for me!

My fingers shook so bad I could hardly get the wrapping off the package which had a lot of foreign stamps on it.

And it hardly looked like a book at all! Just faded blue paper for a cover and nothing printed on it. Inside it said: *Executed by non-union labour at San Vincente de Castillos, Uruguay, Anno Domini 1943.* And on the next pg. there it was:

SPILL OF DESIRE

by

Albert Fish Budd

Well I sat down and read it right through. Mabelle Frances had taken the children to the movies after supper and it was like fate that nobody was there to bother me. I was unhappy at first having so many words left out, but after while it seemed like all the words I'd had there were there anyway and Barry and Chaleen hadn't had their names changed either. I cried when he laid her on the couch after the shock of her finding out that the window-washer had seen her putting her hair up; and when they discover that Barry Chasen's own mother has committed the murder I felt so proud I almost thought for one little second I'd tell Mabelle Frances all about it. But she'd just start worrying I'd neglect my job or think it was pretty funny my book didn't look like a book at all and had to be printed in some foreign country with words left out of it. I even thought I might tell her that down there they don't have the type for some of the letters we use but she'd only say So why not in Bklyn.? they got all the types.

So I hid it under my side of the mattress.

Even their putting a new title on it, Agents are a strange class of people; but if they had troubled to ask me, I could have told them that my middle name is Hubert Leander Cauldwaller.

3

Six weeks later I was moving into a place of my own; a woman had sent me ten thousand dollars in fifty dollar bills just straight mail with a note inside with so many words like George Arliss said that I only read the first two sentences and if there'd been an address to send it back to I would have, but she said I'll surely meet you around somewhere at a party; and I got 74 other letters with the same kind of wording and a total of five hundred and sixty-seven dollars and eighty cents in them; so I waited two weeks and quit my job, giving five thousand to Mabelle Frances and three hundred to the Animal Rescue. My sister got the idea that the old lady I helped across the street had left it to me in her will, so I let her go on thinking it.

I have a nice room in the same building where The Diver lives and they're all very pleasant to me—teaching me to play Poker and a game where you move around three shells to guess where the bean is.

Now I can do anything in the world I want to.

A little later, after I have rested a bit and got used to it, I'm going to realize one of my fondest dreams:

To become a Private Investigator, with my own Office and everything.

It's wonderful to be free and happy, and have money.

THE FIRST PARTY I EVER WENT TO

Mr. McGranehan and I met in the Automat near Columbus Circle, from whence we repaired to an apartment on West End Ave. It was beautiful, all subdued rugs and lights in the wall and soft Muzak providing an appropriate background to the conversation of the forty or fifty celebrities who were already present.

"George will be along after while," My Agent said, as he grabbed his coat back from the maid. "He has to see a man about a little dog he's after."

"That's nice he likes animals," I said, noticing in time that

I was starting to wrap my muffler round and round the hat-tree. Lucky I didn't have any glue with me.

"Pronounce that with the 'b'," Mr. McGranehan said.

Since I didn't know what to say I didn't say anything; but after we had started down a long hall behind another maid, I said:

"May I call you Skujellifeddy? Mr. McGranehan's sort of awkward."

"Ten minutes a la Garbo with her and she wouldn't think so," he said, and I could have sworn he was speaking more to the maid than to me because she started to move her hips in such a manner that they touched the walls on either side of her.

"Make mine for percolator," he said.

And then we were entering a huge room with a grand piano and three palm trees. The lights were casting a lavender glow and somebody was working in a little garden off to one side. She had on overalls with a low-cut front; sand-colored.

I felt a moist hand on my arm and found myself staring into the face of a very large woman who was carrying what looked to be a flute. Skujellifeddy was over at a little bench-like thing with a lot of bottles and glasses on it. In the instant I looked over he drank two glasses full of some dark liquid.

"Oh, you must be Mr. Budd," the big lady said. "I'm your hostess. Just lower it anywhere; the place's yours."

I thanked her as she turned away; then she called back over her shoulder:

"We must —— sometime. Don't let me forget."

I found a chair and sat down. Two men at once sprawled out at my feet. They were both a little too heavy and smelled of onions.

"Picasso is too evasive," one of them said, squinting up at me.

I didn't know what he meant but I didn't want to get off on the wrong foot.

"I'm sorry to hear it," I said.

"Take Utrillo," the other one said.

"Or Braque," the other one said.

I thought I felt a hand on the front of my pants so I got up and went over and sat down in another chair.

"The fly," a man said.

I knew it wasn't the season for them but I looked around anyway.

Then I felt a little cool there and buttoned it.

"What'll you have?" he asked me.

"Have?" I said.

"To drink."

"Oh, I don't drink."

"Never?"

"Not in my whole life."

"Hey, Grudmore!" he called.

Another man came over with a young woman holding on to his arm.

"This fellow doesn't drink," Mr. Grudmore's friend explained.

"What do you do?" the young lady asked.

I tried hard to remember what My Agent had called the type of book mine was. The word wasn't in my dictionary— sort of a long one. . . .

Then I remembered:

"I write pornography."

"Oh you do," she said.

"Yes, Miss," I said.

"Yes, *Miss*," Mr. Grudmore repeated.

"Nobody'd ever guess it to look at you," the other man remarked.

Mr. McGranehan came over then and said to me:

"What're they doing to you, kid?"

He staggered and his glass kept spilling over on the nice
soft rug.

"Tells us he's a smutty," Mr. Grudmore said.

"You smutty the —— out of here and leave him alone," My
Agent said with a show of anger.

They muttered a few inaudibles and went over to watch the
woman working in the garden.

"Why don't you run along home, boy?" Mr. McGranehan
said, drinking as he spoke. It dribbled down his chin.

"I'd really like to stay, Skujellifeddy—listen to the people
talk and all that," I said. "It's all very exciting to me."

"I'm liable make like a light any minute," he said, trying
to sit on a chair but sinking all the way to the floor instead.
"This damn modernistic furniture!" I got up to help him but
he pushed me off. His hair looked like a beautiful bush in the
lavender light.

"Look, Stevie," he continued, "I'm no good, see. Don't
speak to me on street, see. All right, accuse me. Try to get my
guts. I don't want no part of—"

Then he started to snore.

I saw George Arliss just coming in the door. He had on a
sailor suit now and a girl about ten years of age was with him.
They walked into one of the bedrooms.

"Puft, puft," a slender man of indeterminate years said
near me.

He seemed to like saying it because he said it several times
more before he moved away.

All smiles a man I hadn't noticed before came over to me
with his hand stretched out. As I shook it he whispered:

"Play up to me. Pretend you know me. I'm trying to throw
a spy off the track. FBI stuff." Then he said in a very loud
voice:

"Charlie! You old baboon. Imagine bumping into you
here."

A lot of people were looking over at us.

"How long's it been now anyway?"

"Quite a while," I managed to murmur.

"You precious old goat!" And he pushed my shoulder so I almost fell out of the chair. "Remember how we used to masturbate together up in the principal's office? Why, you old—"

Just then the phone rang and he walked over and picked up the earpiece.

"Hel-lo. Who? Yes, this is Dexter." He lowered his voice, speaking very tenderly. "No, I won't, honey. The police are here. Now, now, don't get all excited. I had to do it. I tell you I simply had to do it. The only bad thing was the blood. Everywhere—on the walls, on the ceiling— They're coming for me now. 'Bye, baby."

Mr. McGranehan opened one eye, then he opened the other and reached for a bottle on a little low table. He drank a long time from it.

"Freddie," he said to me, "we've gone through a lot together. Am I right? Nights in the desert, stars like canned pears hangin' in the old sky— Am I right?" He drank some more.

A very pretty young lady in a light blue dress sat down on the arm of my chair. There was a lovely smell about her.

My Agent started to sing *Home on the Range*. He stopped in the center of a word and frowned very hard at me. His right eye he'd get open, then it'd shut.

"Any objection, pal?" he asked. " 'Cause if there is, let me tell you that's our President's favorite ditty."

He began to sing some more of it but fell asleep in the middle of where the antelopes play.

"I don't believe I know you," the young lady said. "My name is Cora Marie, Cora Marie Suchard."

I told her mine but it had no reaction on her, which made me more at ease for some reason.

"Where are you from, Mr. Budd?" she asked.

I told her that too.

"What an odd name. I'd think it would have depressed you."

"Oh, no. Bivalve is a beautiful city. You see, just as the river turns—"

"May I call you Albert?"

"Why, yes, please do."

"And will you call me Cora Marie?"

"Yes . . . Miss Cora Marie."

"Aren't we sweet!"

I wanted to say you are but somehow couldn't.

"You were telling me about Groundvalve—"

"Bivalve," I corrected her.

"Bivalve," she took the correction. "Was your father rich too, Mr. Budd—I mean Albert?"

"We were never hungry."

"How fortunate. Do you mind if I sit on your knee?" she asked, sliding onto it. The soft way she felt, I thought my heart would stop; but I couldn't help wondering how that 'too' after rich had got in there.

"Am I being forward, Albert?" she whispered. I could smell something in her hair that made me want to pray.

"I suppose it's all right," I said.

My Agent woke up and looked over at us:

"With two heads they're growing, yet," he said.

George Arliss, back in his own clothes, walked over and pushed Mr. McGranehan with his foot.

"The boys are all set, Chief," he said.

Skujellifeddy tried to sit up, getting hold of Miss Suchard's leg as he did so. Right away he seemed to revive and he started to move his hand upwards.

"None of that," his friend said, lifting him to his feet. "No time for it. The joint's all cased and we gotta be on our way."

"Louie out there?" My Agent said, trying to get down on the floor again.

"Sure. Louie, Moe the Muggle, Turkey Snot Jack, Feverish Sam— Sure, Chief, they're all out there."

"Is Melchior out there?"

"No, Chief."

"No Lauritz, eh?"

"No Lauritz."

"Is Vanny out there?"

"Cornelius?"

"Sure, Cornelius."

"Nope, Chief."

"At the Stork, hunh?"

" '21.' "

"22."

"23."

"But Louie's there?"

"Louie's there all right, Chief."

"Right on deck, hunh?"

"Right on deck."

"How's his wife?"

"She's swell."

"And Sarah? How's Sarah?"

"Who's Sarah?"

"Louie's wife."

"Oh, she's swell too, Chief."

Mr. McGranehan's head suddenly toppled over and George Arliss slung him up on his shoulder and walked off with him to a bedroom. I didn't see whether it was the same one he'd been in before because Miss Suchard distracted me by saying:

"Are you really in love with me, Albert? Isn't it possible for one to be too precipitate in a thing like this?"

Then before I could say anything she was crying and she got up and started away.

I caught up with her and said:

"What's the matter?"

She turned around and faced me, not crying anymore but looking angry.

"I'll tell you what's the matter. I know who you are. I thought you must be a nasty old . . . old man. And you're not at all. That's what's the matter." Then she took my hand. "You're really good, aren't you? You see, I never met anybody who was good before. I read your book—all the girls were snickering about it at school—I go to Vassar—and when I read it it occurred to me that maybe . . . well, it wasn't quite like that—I had a dream about your book, and in my dream it was the most beautiful and innocent story I'd ever heard—" She turned quickly. "I need a drink." We went across the room to the bench with the glasses and bottles on it. "You?" she asked, picking up a shaker.

"I'm sorry, but I don't drink," I said.

"A pity," she said. "I can think of nothing I'd rather do than get stinko with a nice old man." I guess she saw my face then. "I'm sorry, Mr. Budd. Really I'm sorry."

"Why are you so unhappy?" I asked.

"Am I?"

"Yes."

"Well, then, I suppose I am."

"But why? You're young and—"

"I'm beautiful."

"So why then?"

"So why then h—l."

I thought maybe I'd better go back to my chair.

"Wait a minute," she said, putting her hand on my arm. "I want to say something to you, and then I want you to do me a favor. Is it a deal?"

I said that it was a deal.

She filled her glass again and said:

"I don't know what I want. I don't know what I like. I don't know what I believe in—if I do believe in anything. My father *was* rich, even if yours wasn't. He had money, that is. He was a selfish, domineering, stupid boor—but a boor with money is never a boor in the true sense of the word. Other women— God help their souls! if it hadn't been for them my mother would have killed herself long ago. And my kid brother and I would have killed him. Oh, what the h—l . . . . I'm just working up to a disgusting drunk— But you let yourself in for it by not getting rid of me in the first place. And you were on the level about that Bivalve stuff? You really, honest to God do love that place, don't you? Well, maybe it is beautiful . . . maybe some day I'll let you take me there—" She caught her breath quickly; looked at me in a funny way, and said very quietly:

"I don't want to live anymore, Mr. Budd."

I didn't know what to do or to say.

"Look around this room," she said in a steadier voice.

And although I hadn't planned to bring such things into my book, I can't help it now—sort of for her sake. For the room was full, of course, with soldiers and women in different kinds of uniform.

"Jesus! aren't they pretty!" she said. "Doesn't it make you proud? This is what all the books I've read and all the paintings I've looked at and all the music I've listened to means. Is that it? Is that really it? Does it all add up to this?"

"I don't believe in killing anybody," I said.

"There's no other way of saying it, is there?" she said softly. "The rest is all a lie."

I could hear the pip-pip of the flute off in another room. A drunken man had crawled into the little V-shaped garden and was vomiting all over the feet of the woman who had been digging there.

"It's too bad he can't bleed to death in there, isn't it? That would really complete the picture," she said.

"I'd like very much to see you again, Miss Suchard," I said.

"I'm leaving for Florida tomorrow morning," she answered. "My brother's there. I used to watch him play football. But I won't again . . . you can't play without legs, or at least not very well." Then she said quickly:

"I made up the Suchard."

"And the Cora Marie?"

"I didn't make that up."

"My middle name isn't really Fish," I said.

She laughed and it was like a little bell tinkling in a pasture on a frosty night.

"You're a darling," she said. She looked at her wristwatch. "I must go now." She was sort of all sad again. "And our bargain—we mustn't forget that. It's just a simple thing really." She seemed to take a deep breath. "I want you to kiss me on the forehead and . . . and say, 'Good night, my daughter.'"

I bent and I could smell her soft skin and hair and I felt a little foolish because a tear dropped down on her nose as I drew away; but I managed to say:

"Good night, my daughter."

And she turned quickly and left the room.

2

It was getting later and I was beginning to think it was taking Mr. Arliss a long time to get My Agent settled; so I said to myself how about going in and see what's keeping them. As I started over four men of varying sizes stopped me and said:

"You ask him, Ricardo."

"No, you ask him, Philippo."

"No, you, Steveno."

"No, you, Edwino."

"Ask me what?" I asked. They had their arms over each other's shoulders and me in the middle of it.

Finally Steveno, who had a smell of licorice on his breath, said: "Are you R. H. Saybrooke?"

"No. Budd," I answered.

This seemed to disconcert them momentarily; but soon they were saying in great excitement:

"You see, Ricardo!"

"Now will you believe us?"

"This is the sixteenth mistake for you tonight, Ricky."

Then Philippo, drawing back his face from mine so our noses just touched, explained:

"You see, darling, Ricardo is really R. H. Saybrooke him own self. He is, what shall you say, a projectionist."

"His psyche," Edwino said.

"He projects his Id into other people," Steveno said.

"Sometimes these peasants are stubborn," Philippo said. "They do not wish to return it to heem. Why, once ago, in the I.R.T. underground—"

"Where lurks the minotaur," Mr. Saybrooke interjected.

"Haunt of the coot on his way to Hearn's," Edwino also interjected.

"Ricardo transverberated his Ordus into a pallid citizen whom we named The Unfathomable Cavern," Philippo went on. "Because, darling, though we had to follow him all the way to Palouse, Idaho, before he would release our friend's starkest Biramego—"

"Not once did he fail to dig out a beaut," Steveno continued.

"And his nose was little more than average size," Edwino said reminiscently.

"The phallus on the tomb of the Dire and the Uffalo," Mr. Saybrooke remarked.

"Oh, you phallus are all alike," Steveno said.

Then they suddenly dropped their arms and moved away.

I started to resume my interrupted trip but quickly became conscious that my suspenders were slipping about more than they should. I nearly went sprawling as my pants fell down around my shoes, and as I hurriedly pulled them up was surprised that they were now on me with the front where the back ought to be.

A little old lady who had been an interested observer of this occurrence, said:

"Our clothes do seem to have the strangest taste in people."

I'd have to go to the bedroom to fix my pants around if nothing else, so I resumed my trip again. This time my attention was strayed by a small man in a red bowler who was staring intently at one of his feet.

"Anything the trouble?" I asked him.

"It's asleep," he said hoarsely—"for two years now." He took hold of my arm and pulled me down. "Listen." Nearer and nearer I bent to the member in question.

Then I heard it . . . a gentle snoring.

"You see!" he said. "And you ask me if there's any trouble!"

He snorted, and went back to looking at his foot.

Mr. McGranehan tapped me on the shoulder. "Give me a hand, hunh?"

George Arliss, his eyes like pieces of blue toast floating in gray milk, was slumped up against My Agent.

I wondered why such a tiny person would be that heavy but when I took hold of his other side it was all the two of us could do to drag him over to the window.

"He won't let anyone take the lead out," Skujellifeddy explained, lifting out what looked like a little loaf of bread from his associate's coat. "Heft." And he handed it to me. I almost dropped it. "Twenty pounds apiece, and he's got six of them in his pocket." He put it back. "That's so when he sobers up he'll have a load on, and the kite won't pull him out of the window."

"The kite?" I said.

"Sure," Mr. McGranehan said. He pulled a big box-kite out from under the couch. "He'd go nuts if he didn't have it when he unlushes."

"An odd habit," I said.

"Not at all," My Agent said. "He just don't want to hurt its feelings."

I must have looked my perplexity, for he went on:

"Take you're a kite, see. How would you like it if somebody went higher than you could?"

"Not very much," I said.

It was then I noticed that Skujellifeddy's appearance had suffered a change. Both of his eyes were swollen and black. There was a deep gash in his cheek. His shirt had been torn to shreds and his suit was sopping wet. Even his hair was in bad disarray. About an inch of flesh was missing from the left side of his nose.

"That's the way George brings me round," he explained. "And every time he musses me up a bit, he has to have a drink. It's the old inverse ratio, see. I come out—and he goes in. Once he got so potted I couldn't walk for two weeks."

"You're wanted on the phone," a voice told me. It was the same man who had asked me to pretend we knew one another; so I was suspicious and hung back.

"Budd, aren't you?" he asked. And when I nodded, he said: "Well, get a move on. I think it may be important."

I said hello into the phone and before I could say anything else, I heard this woman crying-like; and she said:

"Darling . . . O Jim darling . . . It's Tommy—He was playing on the stairs—I was up in my room—and . . . O Jim he fell and . . . and the scissors went—" She suddenly stopped; then, her voice all different and cold, she said: "Tommy is dead, Jim."

In that half minute my hands had got so sweaty I could hardly hold onto the receiver. I kept thinking: This must be some kind of joke, but—I didn't know.

"Who . . . whom do you want, please?" I said.

A hand closed over mine, putting the receiver back.

"Nice party, isn't it?" asked the man who had called me Charlie.

3

"Puft, puft."

I said good evening, you seem troubled by something.

"Fairies," he said.

"Do you see them, you mean?"

"All around. Everywhere I go."

I leaned over to see if perhaps his breath wouldn't tell me something.

"Oh," he said. "You too, hunh?"

"Me too what?" I asked.

"Fairy."

"Well, maybe in a way. . . ."

He started to back off, looking about him nervously.

"Maybe in what way?" he asked.

"A little the same way you are. . . ."

"What the h—l are you talking about?"

"I have a theory," I explained. "There's a good deal of us in what we imagine. With you it's fairies, with me it's—"

"Imagine . . . . !"

"How do they come to you?" I asked, trying to remember the picture books I'd had as a child. "Do they have pretty little dresses? Do they come tripping up to you on tip-toe . . . . ?"

He was breathing rather heavily now, and still no odor that would tell me he was not bona fide.

"You must not fight against them," I went on confidently. "Perhaps as you get older you will be grateful for the company of your little playmates."

"Well I'll be d—ed," he said. Then I saw the rest of the color leave his face and he scuttled off like a frightened bunny.

There was a thick smell of onions and the two heavy-set young men hurried past me. As the bunny turned to give a startled look back at them, I observed that he'd be feeling cool in front before long too. As protection against misadventure, buttons can never supplant the zipper.

Something rubbed against my chest and I almost swallowed the tongue out of my mouth. It was a dog, or rather about ten dogs using the same four legs to walk on.

"Windy likes you," a woman said. "Don't you, Windy dear?"

Windy reared up and the only thing I could think of was Tom Mix's horse—only Windy didn't have hoofs, though he was probably bigger. He rested his paws on my shoulders and I just sat down with him on top of me.

"Don't do anything to startle him," she said. "He's a very nervous disposition."

Windy was lapping my face by now and twice I felt my chin touch my nose like the whole thing was rubber. I could smell raw meat on his breath.

Somehow I managed to get out from under and crawled across to an enormous hassock. I climbed up on it and sat down. The woman and her owner followed me over.

"If you are wondering about his name, we got him in Chicago," she explained. Then she looked up into his face and said: "Now don't let anything frighten you until mamma gets back, precious."

As soon as she had gone a boy in a blue sweater came over

and sat down on the hassock beside me. Windy gave him a very unmannerly look from his eyes which had the appearance of yellow baseballs peering out of a bush made of dirty hair.

"I loved her," the youth said.

"That's nice," I answered, not taking my gaze from the baseballs.

"She had everything," he continued.

"That's nice," I answered again.

Windy slowly turned around so his back faced me—only in a dog you can't call it that.

"Class," went on the youth.

What I could see of Windy was starting to sway gently. And it kept edging in on me until I got the funny feeling I was standing in front of a pawnshop.

"Breeding," he elaborated.

"That's important," I said.

I moved a few inches around the hassock, but all I got out of that was that that part of Windy was just a little closer when he finally got back in position.

"Looks. God! she was beautiful . . . . !"

He stopped short and sprang up and saluted three Corporals or Generals who were passing. Two of them seemed a little surprised but saluted him too; the third one had his eyes closed and his tongue swung back and forth as they carried him.

"They're rank," he explained.

By now we were moving around on the hassock pretty fast and Windy had perfected a little side-step that made him grin with pride. I forgot to say that the room was nothing but mirrors covering the walls and everytime I could manage to see around him I saw about four hundred dogs grinning at me as they reflected. We looked a little like a merry-go-round but I didn't feel like one.

"What was her name?" I asked. We were both getting out

of breath and I thought he must think it was a funny way to conduct a conversation.

Sometimes when he got up to salute I'd be around twice before he could sit down again.

"Evangeline," he said, or rather I should say panted.

"That's a nice name," I said.

This jarring him up only makes it worse, I thought finally; so I stopped moving around and resigned myself. Windy moved in a little closer.

"But not nice enough for Evangeline," he said, jumping up to salute again.

"What the h—l's the matter with you?" this particular Leftenant or Rear-Admiral said.

"As you wish, sir," the youth said.

"As I h—l," the other returned. "Maybe you're just a little too big for your pants."

Not as far as I could see, and they were buttoned too.

"It's because I got the hello," the boy volunteered.

"You got the what?"

"From the big white man . . . ."

"Please consider this another question," the maybe Major said. His face looked like a field of tomatoes in the mirror.

"In the same colored house. . . ."

"I think we have just room in here for another one."

"Greetings."

"Now I'm Gates I might maybe just take a little swing. . . ."

I guess the boy thought so because he took out a paper and showed it to him.

"All the way from the Corn Belt, eh?" the officer remarked.

"Yes, sir. Iowa. You see I wanta be all practiced-up so's when I get in I'll—"

"Look, Johnnie, at a place like this you don't salute officers—" He started off. "You roll them," he said over his shoulder.

The boy seemed very unhappy for a little while, and in this it wasn't any effort for me to join him. Windy was swaying in a very satisfied manner indeed. My chest felt rubbed raw from the backs of his knees.

"Evangeline understood me," he said at last.

"Will you marry her When It's All Over?" I asked.

"—All six hundred and fifty pounds of her," he evaded.

I had heard of such things— Even a midget married to one of them.

"Does she find the life interesting?" I ventured.

"Find what life?"

"In the circus."

"What would Evangeline be doing in a circus?" he inquired.

"Isn't it sort of hard otherwise? Special beds, getting moved about— And there must be a lot of people who'd like to see her."

"They cut her throat," he said. "Right in front of my eyes— And her looking up at me so sort of trusting and perty. . . ."

He started to cry but just then the lady came back for Windy. She made a cooing noise at him and he opened his mouth and yawned so it looked like everybody had about two seconds to live as all the mirrors filled up with teeth as long as white paring knives.

As he shambled off with her I wanted to say you're a liar which wouldn't be nice to say to a lady even with such a companion— But she hadn't told me the real reason they gave him the name they did.

"The Diver sent me to tell you it's time you came home," a little man said.

He smiled at me in such a beautiful way that I thought: This is a very good little man.

Skujellifeddy was nowhere in sight and George Arliss was just getting the kite out of the window so I knew he'd be tied up with that for a while.

"I am kind of tired," I said.

"I'm Donald Wan, the inventor," he said.

As we started across the room to the hall I asked:

"What do you invent, Mr. Wan?"

"Oh, wonderful things," he said.

He took what looked like a hypodermic needle out of his pocket.

"This will be the best," he went on.

"Haven't you perfected it yet?"

"In a way, yes. . . . But, you see, it needs faith."

"I'm sure you can work it out, Mr. Wan."

"Oh, it isn't that," he said. "There isn't much more I can do to it. You see, it's the other one who has to have the faith. . . ."

"Faith in what, Mr. Wan?" I asked.

"In God," he said—"for lack of a better word."

"What will your invention do?" I said, not knowing what he meant by the other one having faith.

"Anything," he said.

"Anything at all?" (This was a very remarkable invention.)

"For the one who has faith," Mr. Wan answered.

"Just believe in God?"

"Just believe in God."

"Why, I probably do myself, Mr. Wan."

"I've been thinking that," he said slowly.

"But what kind of anything?" I asked.

He moved the needle up so the point just touched my wrist.

"Albert Budd," he said very solemn-like, "what would you like to be?"

"Be?" I asked, not knowing what he meant again.

"For instance, what animal do you like best?"

I had to think a little about that.

"The horse, I guess, Mr. Wan."

He pressed the needle gently into my arm, and pushed a plunger.

I cantered down the hall. I had a little trouble with the first flight of stairs, but by the time I got down to the lobby it was like I'd been using them all my life.

People were somewhat surprised to see me frisking down the sidewalk. I guess they thought it funny a horse around that late at night.

"What a beautiful little colt," I heard someone say.

Mr. Wan didn't put enough in, I thought.

When dawn came I felt sort of hungry and thirsty, so I went into a little lunch room. I had a hard time finding out I couldn't sit on a stool at the counter; but the worst was I couldn't say I want two eggs, toast, marmalade and a large glass of Hemo.

THE FIRST REAL HOME I EVER HAD

A steady rain beat at the windows of the room. Bocardi was over working around the oven. The smallest of the Veritas Boys said:

"Eight to five three don't make it in the next two."

"I'll take that," the middle-sized one answered.

They watched a little circle outside the pane where grease had been rubbed. The falling drops hit the top of it and slithered down around. Finally one cut through, sort of shuddering-up as the grease fought it off.

"Thirty-nine seconds," announced small Veritas. "Forty-two on the next lap and he's got it."

"Sixty-four," said middle Veritas.

"He never was much good on the turns," big Veritas said.

"One minute, eighteen," l.V. said, very excited.

At that moment two drops went in.

"Here's your take," m.V. said to l.V., handing him five glasses of wine.

"Always slow in there on the second turn," b.V. said, "but he always romps in."

"Doesn't he like wine?" I asked.

"Loves it," they said together, smiling at me as though I might be very young.

Then l.V. said:

"Seven to four three don't make it in two."

But then Bocardi put a turkey that must have weighed thirty pounds on the table and a lot of people came in and started to eat the stuffing out of it.

"My own special parturient," the Chef said to me, as he piled my plate high.

"May I have some of the dark meat, please?" I asked.

Bocardi's face showed great surprise, and unmistakable hurt.

"My friends parturient here eat only the stuffing," he said, putting more on so it spilled over onto the table.

"What do you make it with?" I asked, hoping to take the taste of my faux pas out of his mouth.

"The grapefruits soaked parturient in the blood of field parturient mice," he said proudly.

I took as little as I could and be polite.

It was delicious.

The Diver came in with Donald Wan. They still had their hats and coats on so I figured just in from outside.

"I'd expect your hats to have little pearls on them," I said to Mr. Wan.

"Little pearls on our hats . . . ? Oh, you mean the rain?"

"We have a sprinkler system for that," The Diver explained. "Donald fixed it so they could play their game anytime they want."

A man came in and all the others started to watch him. He grinned in a sort of sly, quick-faced way, looking about him very alert and eager.

"That's Harry the Habit," Mr. Wan told me.

"Why does everyone watch him?" I asked.

"You'll see," the Diver said. "Though it never does any good."

"I'm Lorenna," a girl with long golden hair whispered to me. "I used to know Dillinger."

She moved a little closer and suddenly shouted:

"He kissed me!"

Nobody seemed surprised and after a while the ringing went down enough in my ears to hear the rest of her story:

"—out of the Second National. 'Did they nick you, John?' a buddy asked. 'Stow the lip,' John replied. Twenty citizens sprawled dead in that narrow street. For these were desperate men who loved their freedom e'en as the sedgehen on the wing. For these were indeed those unregenerate, ungentle, unput-upon, un-come-right-here-to-me,-you-jackal, unCongressated, unSenatitized, unPresidentimentilated, UnGodinheavenasated, unremiserated, undefeganilemooted, unmepeoplepopuloused, undarktownstrutekadised hombres mentioned to us by the Prophets. As though their mothers weren't women too. So John said, 'Lorenna, we're out beyond the last outpost of civilization, far from the shorelights of our fellows, lost in a no man's land of suspicion, doubt, misundertakings and thickening dread. Where we are going, by whose agency, will, or unspoken command, we know not—following what star upon this terrible and speechless journey into a netherworld of our own pain, dismay and heartbreak. . . . Ah, darling, were we to stand at the feet of Horror itself, we could not joy less than in these wilds; companioned by the slavering dog; our only neighbor, the blood-flecked moon; our only guide—and destiny—the eye which has only itself to see. . . .' "

At this point a little cry went up from the others and all attention was centered on The Diver as he searched rapidly about the room.

"Ah!" he cried.

I went over to look too. On the linen cover of a highboy in the corner was what appeared to be an ink drawing of the two halves of a giant pear.

"Did Harry the Habit do that?" I asked, because I had noticed that he was nowhere around.

"He sure did," one of the Veritas Boys said, stealing a worried glance at the grease spot on the windowpane.

"He draws very well," I said.

"Draws h—l," The Diver said. "Them's his prints— What he does is ink up his bare bottom and go around everywhere leaving his prints."

"But how could he . . . ?" I began.

"He slips them down all right," went on The Diver.

"And nobody has parturient ever caught him at it," the Chef advised. "And he never parturient meets with failure parturient."

Donald Wan took my arm, pulling me aside.

"We have two rather unusual people here I'd like you to meet," he said. "We call them Bogard and Humphrey," he continued, as we walked down one flight of carpeted stairs and then up three—"because of the way they act and talk all the time." He rapped sharply at a room with a little grilled window. "However, their real names are Alan Bogard and Humphrey Ladd."

"Hello, Inspector," one of the men said.

He had a cigarette right in the middle of his mouth and I couldn't see his face for smoke.

"This is a new friend of ours," Mr. Wan said.

Nobody took any notice of me at all.

"Why don't you call a spade a spade?" the young woman demanded.

Cigarette glanced over at another man.

"You're archer than I thought," he said.

His mouth was twisted in a wolfish grin and I knew that there must be a lot of pressure behind his eyeballs.

"Bringing the skirt here, you mean?" the other man said. He had an open watermelon on his lap and was engaged in putting the ripe seeds in one bottle and the unripe seeds in yet another.

The fat man spoke for the first time:

"We shall accomplish little by this, shall I say . . . uh—" He looked very significantly at a young youth who was twirling two heavy revolvers in his skinny fists—"effete balderdash."

"Where is it?" Cigarette asked, almost dreamily.

Fat Man spread his hands. There were only six fingers on one of them.

"Why don't you ask Wilberforce?" he asked.

Wilberforce's face broke into a snarl.

But Cigarette was getting up a good deal of pressure behind his eyeballs by now.

"You and your cheap gunsel," he sneered. The wolf on his lip howled once, softly.

Then he walked across and hit the Skirt deftly on the cheek with a small Police Positive.

The bottle with the unripe seeds was about half full; the other had only a quarter as many, but they looked better.

Skirt stirred and Cigarette kicked her twelve times in the temple.

Gunsel's snarl spread, almost upsetting the bottle with the ripe seeds.

Cigarette backed away until his hand found the knob of a little cabinet.

Quickly he poured two straight ryes. One for himself—and the other for the wolf.

Fat Man was still in his chair.

And Gunsel had his 22:20-on-a-45.-frame levelled right *at* him.

But just then Cigarette's eyeballs splugged out and nailed him to the wall.

As we rounded the turn in the hall I thought I heard a muffled sound behind us.

"That wolf's much too young for all that hard liquor," Mr. Wan said reproachfully.

Somebody in a diving suit passed us.

"That's Edgar, the man who drove the last spike in the Atlantic Cable."

On the next floor down there were hundreds of little Negro children playing and singing in what looked like a huge nursery. Lambs and tiny goats with red and green markings frisked about amongst them. I noticed several pretty lion and bear cubs too.

"Who looks after them?" I asked.

"The angels," he said. "Would you like to see my laboratory?"

"I'd like to very much," I said.

He led me into a room which I'd like you to look up a description of in some treatise on the scientific.

"This is a machine that writes books," the Inventor said. "See these buttons—*Description, Characters, Setting, Plot, Type*— Well, first you press the *Type* key—that's type of book— All right, you want a Light Novel. Set where? New England. O.K. 'Light Novel' under *Type*. 'New England' under *Setting*. You like nice characters or meanies? Meanies, eh? We push down *Characters* . . . 'Sophisticated.' *Description*

—let's make it, 'Not Too Well Done.' O.K. *Plot*—'Mama Don't Love Papa No More.' We're all set now. Every key goes back to a number of choices. . . . Take *Setting* as an example. We got New England on the second tier of buttons. What's in New England? Cities, towns, hamlets. But since you want your book sophisticated, the interlocking control will probably give you a city or hamlet. The meanies don't like Arlington. The machine, of course, has keys for them all—and it doesn't matter in the least which gets tapped. It's really a simple matter of ascending progressions; until we get back to one set of people out of the millions of possibles, one house, one chair, one particular incest, adultery, rape, or talk around a cocktail table about them. . . ."

"And what do you do with it?" I asked him.

"Why, write books, of course," Mr. Wan answered. "Would you be surprised to know that about ninety percent of the stuff you see reviewed was written by this machine?"

"Even in *The Times!*"

"Over there I've got a machine that writes the reviews for *The Times*—"

"For *The Times*' 'Book Section'!"

"Sure. Why, before long I'll invent something that will even read them."

"What about the Liberal Weeklies?" (As I'd heard Mr. McGranehan refer to them.)

"That's beyond anything not human— You see, the basic principle back of all conceptions is logic. Suppose you rigged up a machine to present The Party Line—say, I'd have pieces of machinery flying around here for the next two months." He wiped his brow at the thought. "No, you can't expect a gadget to think with its switch-bone."

"What about books about people?" I asked him.

"Biographies are very simple. If somebody comes in and wants a job done on so and so who perhaps was a great admirer of Randolph Bourne, I don't say, 'That's fine, category 31C'; not at all—I ask, 'What does this so and so think of Randolph Bourne now?' Or maybe, say, somebody else will— Ah, it's no use, Mr. Budd . . . I'd rather not work myself up going into it. But right off the bat I would want to know: What is he doing now? Who are his friends? What is he known to believe in? How does he make his money? You see, once somebody tells me, 'Well, he doesn't exactly think that's right, but conditions seem to call for some such course'; I push down hard on 'Hypocrite and Fraud, Capable of Any Crime Under Heaven'—for it seems to me that any man who expects to put Truth in the same pocket with the bloody plunder of its betrayal, is not only a fool but a maggoty fool—and God help us! Mr. Budd, the earth is alive with these slimy creatures now— You can't weep dollar bills listening to Beethoven's 'Victory' symphony and at the same time froth like mad dogs about exterminating the German people without convincing me of one thing, and that is a very simple thing: The victory symbolized in Beethoven will be a victory over just such as you."

He stared off into the distance for a long moment.

"These are dangerous men," he said slowly. "If I had a little son I would know that their hate was preparing his grave —and the graves of his sons. Because these men do well to hate and fear those in other nations whom they call Enemy; for they are the same man everywhere . . . and they shall be perpetuated until those like my unborn son can look upon their brothers and say:

" 'It were better for us to live in peace together; it is their greed and hate which have made us kill one another.' "

Mr. Wan began to cough and when he put his handkerchief away I noticed a bright stain on it.

"I think I'll take a nap," he said. "Up pretty late last night working on my newest invention."

"What's it like, Mr. Wan?" I asked.

"I call it the 'Everything for Everybody.' Show it to you tomorrow."

We parted and I walked down to my room. There were a lot of packages and letters on my desk. Just as I settled back to open them a very tall young man came in and said:

"When you get a minute I'd like to tell you something about my records."

"Are you an athlete Mr. . . . er . . . ?" He was about 6'8".

"Milen Berg," he answered. "They call me 'The Joys Hot.' I'm right down the hall."

He bent his head and went out.

"When you get a minute I'd like to show you my books." This time it was a little man with a beard growing on half his chin.

"When thou hast a moment, Albert the Good. . . ." A gentle, beautiful old man in sandals and a long robe.

I locked the door and turned again to my mail. The first letter seemed to me a little out of the ordinary:

Dear Mr. Budd,

If they think they are going to turn you from me like all the rest they have another think coming God has given me His Hand and in His mercy sleeping where I wont be harmed like my husband pretending to get a drink of water at night but sharpening the knife and standing above me like saying dont laugh Carrie (my own name) you will get tired as though I could ever get tired with His Grace shining about me even in the street slipping in and out of stores so I will not know they are following me and my two babies shall not be maimed and hurt by them playing Bridge and everything just the same as always but I am not fooled how they watch me and talk about me when I go in to fix sandwiches or making tea oh Carrie you look so charming this evening

Babies Babies oh my pretty little babies
where is the ending turning to return and then return return
Mr. Budd for in the answer is the thing I can understand and
take my love to my mother and the mother I am for inside I
can hear what James (my husband's own name) is trying to
tell me Don't cry Carrie oh Don't cry my little girl
so that is why the butcher sends chops instead of the round
steak I ordered before I can really get wide awake in the
morning they want me to move out of this house and leave my
babies for the care of another woman because even in the
magazines they talk about me without ever using my own name
so in the drawings they disguise me as a man in a smart suit
and gloves or a child waving after a boat and then people smile
and say did you read that clever story in *Housekeeping* or
McCalls it was just too amusing oh Mr. Budd come and take
me away from here
and take me away so I will not want to look behind me to
return or returning end what I can not understand since God
has asked me to use the white and silver door
It is safe now
they are opening so soft and the smell of soap but I will not
cry anymore
my husband's own name saying
What have you done to them Carrie
and he will cry forever now and not return or give me
fear
oh you will understand and love them too Mr. Budd for I
have wrapped them so tenderly and their blood is clean
for in the blood that brought them do I send them forth to
sleep at His Hand
please tell them I have no more pain now and what the
others say is just a spiteful lie to hurt you
Yours truly,
Carrie Otis Steel

I decided not to open her package just then.

The rest of the letters were pretty much the same as I got every day now. Two hundred and forty-six proposals, a number of them for marriage. Almost five hundred photographs taken in various stages of undress, the majority in the last. Several invitations to strange places where they wring the necks of chickens and take turns beating each other with whips, etc. (In case any of these correspondents may chance to read my book, I'd like to just say this to them: Doubtless you are sincere in what you do, but it does strike me that more useful pursuits could be found for grown people to spend their time at.)

When I unlocked the door a man, who must have been waiting outside it for just such an opportunity, walked in and said:

"Now I'll do some mindreading." He put a pair of opera glasses to his eyes and moved up so close I could see him like he was two inches high through them. "I get a thought here—" he said. "What's this Budd's racket? Is he maybe a Japanese spy he gets so much mail? Two-bits these packages contain infernal machines."

"I thought maybe you'd like to see the paper," another voice said. "Lay off him, Delbert." He smiled at me. "Delbert's got the wrong slant on mindreading. It's true he can do it, only the mind he reads is his own."

"What's the matter with that, Bluggle?" Delbert demanded, training his glasses at a window across the way. Even without them I could see that she should have pulled the shade first.

I looked at the paper. It was the '*Lame Deer Gazette and Chronicle*,' Lame Deer, Montana.

"I go up to Times Square for it every morning," Mr. Bluggle explained. "That one's only five days old."

"Are you from Lame Deer?" I asked.

"Never been west of Newark in my life," he said. "I don't

know, somehow I just like to read about what's going on out there . . . sort of touches a chord. Look—" And he opened to page four. "Mrs. Stearhyde had a twenty-six lb. boy last Tuesday. Doesn't that make you feel good, Mr. Budd? For me, it's the little mundane things like that that make life worthwhile."

"This looks like an interesting dish," a newcomer declared, as he held up one of the photographs.

"What's the extra one for?" Delbert asked, studying it through his glasses.

"Case she has triplets, they can all eat at once," Mr. Bluggle ventured.

I noticed that a red stain was spreading on the table under Mrs. Steel's package.

A brief word concerning the newcomer might not be out of place here: His head was shaped like the used eraser on a pencil and came right down to his shoulders. Little sort of dark blue whiskers shot out around his mouth which had a vacuum look. His arms and legs were exactly like a gingerbread man's in shape, differing only in number, as he had three of each.

"Does he work in a fish store?" I asked, after he had slithered out.

"Who him?" Mr. Bluggle said absent-mindedly, reading his paper. "The Crazy-Bar-O's round-up is set for the 15th—let's see, that's on a Wednesday. . . . Nah, that's just his own natural smell."

"What's his name?" I asked.

"William Calamaris, but we sorta nicknamed him Billy the Squid."

Then I walked down the hall and knocked on Milen Berg's door.

"Come in," he said, taking a record off the phonograph.

"These are the disks you'll have to get if you want a basic jazz library. Just sit at the table over there and take them down. All set? O.K., here they are:

"*Snake Rag*, by King Oliver and his Creole Band.

Dixie Jass Band One-Step, by the Original Dixieland Jazz Band.

Maple Leaf Rag, by the New Orleans Rhythm Kings.

Evil Turkey Blues, by Lake Edward's Second Detroit Boys.

Shuffle For a Lousy Ten Spot, by Midge St. Elglade's Happy Brass Deceivers.

Mahogany Hall Stomp, by Louis Armstrong and his Orchestra.

The Chant, by Jelly-Roll Morton and his Red Hot Peppers.

See-See Rider, by Ma Rainey.

That Old Mr. Death Blues, by the New Orleans Mad Men and Carter.

Courtin O' The Angels, by the same outfit.

Long Heaven Scramble, by the same.

I Don't Want Nobody Else To Die Nomore, by the same.

Tiger Rag, by Bix Beiderbecke and his Wolverines.

Heebie Jeebies, by Armstrong and his Hot Five.

Just A Closer Walk With Thee, by George Lewis and His New Orleans Stompers.

Careless Love Blues, by the same gang.

When You Feel Like God Done Close' His Big Shop, by Lake Edward's Original Hoppers.

They Put My Baby On That Little Dark Sad Train, by the same.

Well, It Was So Lonesome I Cried, by H. Jones Chelmin and His Eagle-High Five.

Storyville Blues, by Bunk Johnson's Original Superior Band.

Panama, by Kid Rena's Jazz Band.

Potato Head Blues, by Armstrong and his Hot Seven.

Blue Washboard Stomp, by Johnny Dodd's Washboard Band.

Pad House On Gravier Street, by Kid Light and his Friars' Inn Doublers.

Headless Body Hop, by the same boys.

Love and Charity Hall Blues, by the Royalle Weekenders.

Bull Club Stomp, by the same crowd.

Irish Channel Walk So Fine, by the Hi-C-Penny-Low Gang.

Original Rags, by Jelly-Roll Morton and his Orchestra.

Stonytown Gut-Scatter, by Abe Wesley's Climax Five.

Them Moanin' Slides Done Killed My Honey, by Wesley's Original Dauphine Street Terrors.

I Got De Kansas Wobble Blues, by The Ponchartrain Pick-ups.

Gin Done Made the Worl' All Mellow, by Eddie Owl's Bottomland Syncopators.

Jazzin Babies' Blues, by King Oliver's Jazz Band.

Lazy Daddy, Dat Street Car's Comin' 'Long, by Big Rabbit Gary's Plantation Boys."

He put another record on. "That ought to get you started, Mr. Budd," he said, a far-off look coming into his eyes.

"Thank you very much, Mr. Berg," I said, stepping into the hall.

The little man with half a beard took my arm and led me into a room which had books up to the ceiling on all the walls.

"My library," he said proudly. "If you're wondering why I grow a beard only on one side it's to accommodate my two personalities—I'm a true schizo—Rudolph likes to be clean-shaven, Timothy prefers a beard. Simple, isn't it? But tell me, what do you think of them?"

I reached out and took down a book. It was *The Girl of the Limberlost* by Gene Stratton Porter. I took down another. It was a book by Gene Stratton Porter called *The Girl of the Limberlost.* The third one I took out was *The Girl of the Lim-*

berlost by Gene Stratton Porter. So was the fourth, and the fifth. . . .

"You see," Timothy and Rudolph said, "I thought it would be much more sensible to have one book we really liked than a lot of books we just felt luke-warm about."

As I left them a very large woman grabbed hold of me and took me into her room and threw me on a bed. Working with feverish haste she managed (despite anything I could do) to get my pants off. Then she sprinkled talcum powder on and rubbed it in. Next she folded a big square of cloth to make a triangle, wrapped it around me, and fastened it in place with a safety pin. Now for the first time she spoke:

"Be still, Rosie—Mama's got your supper all ready."

She ran to the stove and came back with a bottle. She bent the nipple on her wrist so a few drops of milk came out, then she rammed it into my mouth.

As I started to fight her off again, a voice from the doorway said:

"Better be a nice little Rosie, Mr. Budd. Mama can get tough when she wants to."

Three hours later, after I'd had my nap and had been changed and fed once more, the woman's attention was diverted by a man I got to know later as Henry Van Dyke, who was just passing. She flew out after him and I tore off into the first room I came to.

"God hast brought thee to me," said the old man in the long robe. "Let us pray together. O merciful Father, Who hast fixed the stars in their majestic courses, Who hast freed the rain that it may fall upon the earth, Who hast fashioned the snow that the eyes of heaven might be made clean, Who hast given to the trees in the forest Thy wondrous token of growth, and to the birds of the air feathery havens in their flight, and to the animals of the field strength and humility to venture unto pleasant realms—unto these realms then, and my good Father, these realms and the shadows thereof art Thine, where tree and bird and beast have their homes and furthering. . . . Forgive me if I get mixed up, if the words of my heart outdistance those of my tongue. . . . O all I say shout my great God—" (He spoke so rapidly now I could hardly follow.) "as I bring Thee the fruit and the bread of the whole world— As I raise Thee an altar above the waters and the blackness. . . . God! God! O my Father, still the sorrow of this, Your least son— Because it is all going too high. . . . I can taste the stars as I pass, I can hear the child in the womb, I can see the face of Mary. . . . Jesus is sitting here with me, God. . . . Down, dog! Down! Wouldst mock the citadels of eternity itself! Old man old man old man thou art too full of glory— Bow low thy stupid head— O God, my sorrow is I am too full of peace. . . . The screams of the dying are as the murmuring of bees in sunny fields. Cast down my spirit, Lord, that I may serve the ends of Your bitter and angry Word. . . ."

2

"And that's how I first got a taste for long pig," Mr. S. B. Twiddleford-Smellers, the XXIV said pensively.

"I am quite fond of chops fried with caraway seed myself," I said, realizing I hadn't eaten for three days in the excitement of meeting my new friends.

"There was a lovely, plump young lady who came to live with us," he went on. "The most succulent, full-flavored, appetizing—" He broke off, sighing deeply.

"It must be very upsetting to like someone that much," I said, remembering the hurt of my own loss.

"Always eat too fast," he said in self-criticism.

"I always heard that love made you lose your appetite—"

"Oh, Mr. Budd," a voice called, "when you have a minute I'd like to show you some clippings."

"Will you excuse me, Mr. Twiddleford-Smellers, the XXIII?" I asked.

"Fourth," he said.

"I'm sorry," I said.

"This will only take a second," he declared. Then he sort of pinched me all over, pressing his fingers into my arms and legs, and examining the palms of my hands very carefully. "The best part," he murmured dreamily.

I could have sworn there was a little trickle of saliva running out of the corners of his mouth. And he belched softly once.

"Well, that was our schedule, Mr. Budd— My name's Kelvin, good old Ed 'Take-the-Penalty' Kelvin— And a man-killer it was. We started the season with Oconomowoc— Me in there at left guard— Here, look these over while I tell you about it— Wibbenfield Poly. Inst., that's us. . . . Wiff! Wiff! Wibben! Fipp! Fipp! Wibb! Wibb! Fiff! Fiff! Wibbenfield!" He had a huge blue "W" on the yellow shirt he was slipping on. His shoulders looked about six feet wide with the pads in, and the cleats on his shoes dug in the floor as he shifted about. I tried to keep my eyes on the clipping, but the paper was so old it kept falling to pieces in my hands, and the ink was just a faded brown blur. "Next came Enumak, and boy! did they ever have a team that year! Big Steve Johnson at right end, Crusher Smythe at left end—" He named off about forty names. "So that was them, subs and all. But I'll give you the rest of the schedule now—Pulaski, Goose Creek, Jaspar, Sugar Notch, Punxsutawney, Wapakoneta, South Amboy, Bemidji— Don't you just love American names, Mr. Budd?—and last . . . leaping leopard-fish, what an outfit . . . ! the Half-Minute Men from Mishawaka School of Mines, Mills, Perambulator-Factories, Swiss Cheese-and-Clock Works, Nine-And-Tanneries, Hatchet-Honing Foundries, Steel-Wool-and-Other Porteries, Wire-Brush and Missing-Link Losteries—" He seemed to be bracing his feet and I couldn't even tell where the door was for his shoulders. "So we have them all bottled up down on our own two-inch line. I'm playing wide. . . . The ball is snapped—" Suddenly he ran all his weight at me and as I hit the wall he brought his knee up— As I came to he was saying: "Certainly we'll take the penalty. Nobody's going to beat us out of a penalty." Then suddenly he jumped on me with both feet and started to yell: "Wiff! Wiff! Fipp! Fipp! Wippi! We want a penalty! We want a penalty!"

One of his cleats was stuck in my side and he had a hard time pulling it out.

"Thanks for letting me see your clippings, Mr. Kelvin," I said, when I could talk again.

"I averaged fifteen yards on every play," he said proudly.

A swim might not be out of place now, I thought. But first I went down to the kitchen and asked Chef Bocardi if there was anything left over from lunch.

"You are parturient in luck parturient," he said, giving me a generous portion of veal and lima beans. Seldom had food tasted so good. I ate another helping, and another.

"You will please thank the parturient lady for us," the Chef said.

"What lady parturient?" I asked.

"Theese one who has parturient been so kindly to send parturient the package to you. With this rationing it is sometime parturient difficult to get so much to going around." Then he wheeled about and shouted: "Mistofer Twiddle-Smells, twenty-five times I don't care, keep your hands parturient out of that pot! On the plate I'll put so as everybody parturient else."

While I was changing into my Jantzens back in my room,

I had a moment to wonder how *The Spill* was selling; so I went to the phone and called Mr. McGranehan. This I accomplished with a little difficulty because I didn't realize you had to turn the crank before the operator would come on.

My Agent seemed to be in a good mood. After I said hello he said:

"This is Philip Morris speaking."

"Mr. McGranehan, please," I said.

"Do you mean to say this isn't a call for Phil-ip Mor-r-r-r-ris!" he demanded.

I heard a bottle break in the background, then two shots fired so closely together they could have been three or even five.

"Skujellifeddy, this is Mr. Budd," I said.

There were sounds like somebody taking a chair and breaking out the windows and a woman's voice pleading: "Stop! Stop! You're choking me!"

"George got weary of his mole," My Agent said. "Now he's doing his Black-face Act with Miss Chalmers. But there's nothing to worry about. . . . Her face isn't even a good gray yet."

"I was just curious about sales—" I began.

"There won't be a tree standing in all of South America in another fortnight," he interrupted. "And I wish you'd give me an accounting on royalties. If you think you can get out of paying me that 75% called for in the contract, you're crazy, Mr. Judas Iscariot Budd!"

And he banged the receiver down so hard the Budd sounded very much like Burr.

On my way to the pool I met the man they called Henry Van Dyke. I noticed that he still had the diapers on, and that the pin was working loose.

"Isn't that an affecting little tableau?" he asked, as we passed the open door of a room in which sat an old man painting and a younger man handing him brushes and exclaiming over the beautiful color he was getting. "For fifteen years now—Dennis, that's the young one, has been telling him that his paintings have been bought by the Metropolitan, Whitney, the Modern, Downtown, and so on. . . ."

"And haven't they really bought them?"

"See for yourself."

When I did walk around so I could see what he was painting at, all there was were a lot of splotchy lines in muddy greens and tans.

"This one is called 'The Queen of the Sky,' " Dennis said. "Do you notice how beautifully her pale silver gown models her lovely, pure shoulders. . . . How the light in her eyes seems to come from within the canvas. . . . Ah, Master Paul, she is even more breathtakingly noble than your 'Girl Who Dreamed She Could Speak to the Stars.' "

"I am happy to have such a flattering estimate of my lowly effort, Dennis," the old man said.

"Who has contracted for this one?" Mr. Van Dyke asked.

"An important private buyer from San Francisco," Dennis answered. "When he was here yesterday he said he planned to present it to the Mount of Perfection hermitage in Arevalo."

After we got settled comfortably in wonderfully soft chairs of tiger skin in Mr. Van Dyke's study, I asked:

"Has he always been blind?"

"Oh, no. . . . He had a brilliant reputation with the critics as a youngster. Then, one morning many years ago, he opened his eyes and . . . Well, that's the way it was. There's a story that he saw something, perhaps a vision, during the night before. . . . Something that no man could look upon without paying with his sight—if not his reason—or so the story goes. But Master Paul himself, as far as I know, never said a word of what took place—if anything really did."

I thought maybe glasses might not be such a bad idea after

all, though I hadn't had much opportunity to imagine anything unusual since coming to live there.

"But now let us concern ourselves with you, Mr. Budd," Henry Van Dyke said. "You are, of course, familiar with his work?"

"Whose work?" I asked, because I wanted to know.

"Henry Van Dyke's, of course. What other possible work could we talk about?"

"Have you done much work?" I asked, for the same reason.

"I've done no work at all. Do you think I'm an idiot?" he demanded fiercely, dipping a lady-finger into his tea. "That's what I can't understand—why should anyone feel called upon to write anything when he has said it all . . . and so much better?"

"You mean Mr. Van Dyke?" I inquired.

"Can you scan?" he demanded, reaching for a book.

I thought I would look thoughtful for a bit.

"Well, if you scan, tell me, Mr. Budd."

"I'm afraid I scan't," I said.

"All you have to do is pronounce the accents at isochronous intervals. Thusly:

'The splen—dor falls—on cas—tle walls

And snow—y sum—mits old—in sto—ry' Do you understand now?"

"It's wintertime," I said.

"What are you talking about?"

"Snow on the upper stories of the castle."

"Well, then, listen to this": He read from the book. "Do you see how suavely Van Dyke handles his amphibrachs? How his dactyls nose ever so gently into his trochees; and the almost wild grace of his anapests— Are you really interested in this, Mr. Budd?"

"I don't remember of hearing about some of those," I ad-

mitted, "but I did read a little about the Chickasaws, Kicka-
poos and Pawnees when I was a boy."

"Very well. Even in Coventry Patmore you don't get it,
that sense of a man baring his breast to a hostile, unthinking
universe, and declaring—nay, affirming: 'Let Loveliness
wound me, whittle me down to a little, lonely, lorn lump; but
I shall fight back!' Not even in the best of Austin Dobson—or
even in J. Crowe Ransom— Do you see now that you don't
get it, Mr. Budd?"

"I see that all right," I said.

Mr. Wan beckoned to me from the doorway and with little
reluctance, I joined him.

"Like to see 'Everything for Everybody' now?"

"I was thinking of having a swim," I said. My suit had got
me itching very badly during the last hour, and I felt a bit
self-conscious going around the house in it.

"This'll only take a minute," he replied.

A man came up then and extended his hand to me. I could
see it all right but when I tried to shake it there wasn't anything there.

"Finegan's awake," he said to Mr. Wan.

Then he turned and sort of half floated a little way, finally
just disappearing through the wall.

"Little Cudahy's father was a ghost," the Inventor explained. "But let's look in on Finegan before he's gone again."

A giant lay sprawled out on a long plank, his legs stretching
about twenty feet out of the window. Attached to one of his big
toes was a clothes line on which a big washing hung.

He rolled his huge head in our direction and remarked:

"Ho! broder Bu-dde, dost h'ear mä Decree!
:

Meen speken Lilli burlero bullen a-la : lero Lero lelly
wi' gutts dulleo layi dyen-a la-'s. Aan d hee

SIT   Will cutte aLl dis sthupid troate . . : fourloin!
snug-ge   buy mi shoul! law's on dare sighed aaAnn
onne thi   Chreish nos wHAT ooa wass in' eld frofesy
rot TING fo Un:d en A bOg. teahe WHiRLEd shal
bu t'teS   B ruulid bye ane asSS und eine Dodg"

The only thing I could think to answer was nov shmoz ka pop
but since one of his two-hundred lb. arms was reaching out
for me I didn't say anything.

"He's getting wilder by the minute," Mr. Wan said, as we
walked down the hall. "You were lucky to get out by the skin
of your teeth."

"Death to the *Cientificos!*" a young man shouted at us as
we started past a room with a lot of rifles stacked up in the
doorway. With him was an old man in a huge white hat and a
big silver belt who mumbled a few words as Mr. Wan led
the way in.

"What's he have to say today, Manuel?" the Inventor asked.

Manuel said something to the old man and the old man
said three words back to Manuel.

"He say—and I quote—Huerta told him not to move his
men. So what thees snake do?" He spread his hands and the
old one's eyes flashed like fire. "He's lynching Madero's biggest brother." He demonstrated how someone has a rope
around his neck. "Viva Madero! *Viva la Revolucion!* Where
is the land for my people? he say. Where is the rich, verdant
land that they promised?" The old man was busy now putting
some frying pans and blankets on the two little burros. His
hands shook with excitement and his hat looked like a big
white flower getting ready to ride off somewhere. "His men
are waiting— One word from him and the ringing of horses'
hooves will drown out even the sound of blood crying up from
the warm, beautiful soil of Mexico. . . ."

"Walk on tip toe," Mr. Wan cautioned as we slipped out; but since I was in my barefeet anyway it seemed an unnecessary precaution to take. "We'll drop back later," he went on. ("They won't even know we've been away.")

I guess he noticed me scratching because he advised:

"Let's get that wet and it won't itch so much."

So we went into a room that had a shower and I stood under it for a while. As I came out the occupant said:

"I don't know what further proof anybody needs . . . Irwin Trockett was born in Attleboro, Mass.; he went to Schuyler Kerrt's Day School for Boys—"

"We're in a hurry just now," the Inventor said.

The water had dripped a big puddle on the rug; but the itching was almost gone.

"I see. Well, I'd like to ask Mr. Budd just one little question. . . . If Irwin Trockett didn't write Longfellow, then who did?"

"He'll have an answer for you in a few days," Mr. Wan said.

"I hope he's enjoyed his drip anyway," the occupant answered.

In the hall again, a man in a huge black cape and his hat pulled down over his eyes hurried along ahead of us and swirled into his room. As we passed I heard a bolt being shoved quickly into place.

"What does he do?" I inquired.

"He's never told us and we've never asked—" There was a blood-curdling scream from behind us and a moment later the hall filled with the smell of burning leather. "Lots of young ladies visit him . . . I guess he has a secret passageway or something to let them out, because nobody ever sees them leave again."

"Will you show me your invention now, Mr. Wan?" The suit was drying out pretty fast.

"Here we are. I press this switch. As you can see, it has an external resemblance to television." (I was rubbing my nose from where the little man on the screen had hit it.) "That's one of The Diver's best welters—kid with a real future." (He was only about a foot high as the machine brought him in and I thought if he can hit that hard small-size, real-size I'd not want to say anything unkind in his presence.)

"The current brings him in all right—so far pretty usual—Now watch. 'Fabbicio, come over and say hello.'" (The little fellow stepped out of the screen and advanced along the table, his tiny boxing-glove held out in front of him.) "'How you feel, boy?' 'I'm gettin' my share, I guess.' 'That's fine, Fabbicio.'" (Now Mr. Wan pressed the button again, and in the middle of saying something else, Fabbicio just disappeared as the screen went dead again.) "Before long I'll bring him in full-size. But you see the possibilities. . . . We'll be able to send washing-machines or automobiles or Clark Gables or anything you want to eat or drink or wear or make love to. . . . Anything under the sun to any place under the sun. All you need is a Sender powerful enough, and everybody in the world can have anything they want. Take any one article . . . a roast beef, say, or a ton of coal. . . . One roast beef and one ton of coal are all you need to supply everyone on earth who wants them. Or suppose Joe Jigis out in Cedar Rapids or in Johannesburg wants to have the company of a movie actress or an extra hand at Red Dog—he just pushes the button. But don't get the idea, Mr. Budd, that Miss Moviestar or Mr. Extrahand have to sit around in front of the Sender all their lives . . . by no means, once their images have been recorded, they last forever. You will see that this opens up another vista— *Nobody need ever die.*"

Mr. Wan had a fit of coughing and I saw again that his handkerchief was red when he finished.

"And can you eat the roast beef?" I asked.

"Of course you can eat it."

"And you mean Mr. Gardner would talk to you all you want?"

"I don't know what Mr. Gardner you have in mind; but if his image were put on the Sender, you could bring him in to talk all right. You see, Mr. Budd—perhaps I didn't explain it very well—if you happened to want a house, the one you tuned-in on would come off the screen exactly as the original house. The motor-boats would run, the dogs would bark, the desired woman would be quite capable of brushing your hair. . . ."

"And if something came and you didn't want it. . . ?"

"Just press the button."

"You mean you could have firemen come to put out a fire?"

"Firemen, policemen, the plumber, the baker—"

"What about armies?"

"We'll just take it for granted, shall we, that no madmen will ever get the say here. And if by some chance they did, who would be fool enough to want to fight when everything in the world was his for the mere asking?"

"I'm glad it has that feature," I said.

Then stealthily we made our way back to the room which had the rifles and machetes in the doorway.

"—so they pretend that he has been shot, but his people are not fooled by this . . . not one man came to walk in their funeral procession! Ah, yes, he say, his people know that Zapata does not die; that somewhere he waits like the avenging eagle to strike terror once again to the hearts of those who would steal Mexico from her children!—and I unquote."

The old man with the big white hat was sitting up on one of the burros by now, but a sort of hopeless look had come on his face and tears were streaming down his wrinkled cheeks.

At that moment The Diver tore past and we ran out after him. "Trouble downstairs," he called over his shoulder.

When we got down we saw a policeman talking to Chef Bocardi and the kitchen full of worried-looking people.

"What's the trouble, Mr. Blue?" the Inventor asked.

"Somebody parturient—" Mr. Blue began. "D—nit! Somebody from this house has been going around cutting the seats out of people's pants. In all walks of endeavor, the rich and the poor, the good and the wicked, the just and the unjust, the scoffers and—"

"But why does he have to suspect my little brother?" Billy the Squid protested. "He's never carried scissors around in his whole life."

His brother, whose face was a bright, polished red, grinned in comfortable fashion at Harry the Habit who had a pleased-with-the-world look too.

The Veritas Boys were standing with their arms around each other's necks singing a song about a poor, unfortunate girl called Barbara Allen. Sixteen five-gal. wine-jugs stood empty on the floor around them, and each had a half-full one to his lips as he sang. The sprinkler-system had been turned off for the first time since I had come there.

"We'll let you know if anything turns up, Mr. Blue," The Diver said.

And as Mr. Blue turned to go I saw that his red flannel drawers showed where the seat of his pants ought to be, and nicely placed on the flannels was the print of a big half-pear. I also noticed that when Billy the Squid's little brother took his hands out of his pockets, they were hands like a lobster's, one about three times as big as the other. The Veritas Boys were singing *The Children in the Wood* as I walked out. It was like somebody being too happy to cry, but crying.

I found the water in the swimming pool very cold at one end and very warm at the other, so I splashed about in the middle. After I'd been in a little while I was surprised to feel something very slippery slide across my leg, and even more surprised to have a shark with his mouth open come up about three feet away.

"Don't be afraid of Freddy," a young girl with long golden hair and in a bathing suit like shimmering silver said. "He wouldn't hurt a fly."

I didn't tell her that I was sure he wouldn't hurt a fly; but I did crawl up on the cement edge and pulled my legs up after me.

"It's just that I've always been sort of shy of fish," I said.

"Something in your childhood, I suppose," she said.

"That's possible," I answered, watching some little Eskimo children chasing Freddie down at the cold end.

"Are you sure I don't frighten you?" she asked.

"Oh, not at all. Have you used Marchand's very long?" I replied.

"Never," she said, and I couldn't help thinking that I'd yet to see a bald woman. "My story is not a very romantic one. Father was forever carping about something. I just floundered around until I got in the school, and even there we were packed in like sardines. My teacher was an old crab and we never had a minnow to ourselves. It was just one long haddock."

"Who was your father?" I asked.

"That's the halibut," she said, pulling the rest of her up out of the water beside me. "He ran a little spawn-shop, but like all simple salmons he was always starting roes."

She wiggled her tail and I couldn't help thinking that even half a woman could have such beautiful hair without shampoo or anything.

"When you have a minute, Mr. Budd, I have something I'd like to show you," a voice said.

"As soon as I've changed into my clothes," I answered.

"It won't wait that long," the owner of the voice said, starting to hurry off.

So I followed him—or perhaps I should say 'it'.

MY LIFE AS A PRIVATE INVESTIGATOR

I took the pint of rye whiskey out of the drawer of my bat-tered desk, uncapped it and poured about three fingers into a water glass. It had a terrible smell—so I thought I'll just pour this one out in the sink, then if anybody comes in I'll give them a fresh one out of the bottle. But as I started to pick it up my hand slipped and it went all over the front of the yellow suit I had just bought that morning. Naturally I sponged it off as well as I could, but the smell only seemed to get worse and the color began to run pretty badly in my suit.

This is as good a time as any to clean my gun, I thought. It wasn't exactly the type I wanted but you didn't have to have a license to carry it—and I've never liked to fill out forms and answer a lot of questions, particularly if they should ask me what I wanted it for since I didn't have the other license either.

I thought it wouldn't be bothering anybody when I got the janitor to paint

A. BUDD
PRIVATE EYE

on the panel of the door, and also hang a little sign with the same on it from the window. If anybody really became nasty and maybe reported me to the Detectives' Union or anything like that I could always say it was just eccentric on my part, or perhaps starting a new religion.

The revolver, though it was more like a little rifle in length, had certainly not received proper care. By the time I scraped down to the date on the handle (1861), my desk was covered with rust and a lot of it had worked into the wet on my yellow suit.

Just then the door opened and a man walked in. His nose started to work like a rabbit's and as he stared at me I had an opportunity to appraise him. He had on a leather coat, light brown corduroys with frayed cuffs, a dirty blue shirt, and shoes whose toes were badly scuffed. His hair was hidden by a sort of bandana but from his eyebrows and a huge black mustache I judged it to be healthy and quite adequate.

"Wash," he said, eyeing me almost suspiciously.

I thought if he was a cleaner's representative they certainly worked fast.

"Da windah," he went on.

"Oh, you want to wash the window?" I said.

He didn't wait for my reaction to this but went out and came back with a pail and some cloths. As he went over and raised it he made a big circle around me.

"I haven't been drinking and this gun hasn't been loaded

for many years," I reassured him, getting up to help him put his equipment out on the fire-escape. My foot caught in the wastebasket and the gun went off with such a roar I thought the walls would cave in. I looked up from a hole about a foot wide in the floor and tried to smile at the window-washer. He gave me a very terrified look and scampered down out of sight. I thought I better tell him that he'd forgotten his stuff, but as I leaned out the barrel of the gun struck the bucket and he yelled like something crazy when the soapy water hit him.

I could see into the office below now. There were five men sitting around a table. Their huge hands were playing with the pieces of lath and fallen plaster as though nothing unusual had happened.

"When's he get in, Thomas C.?" one of them asked.

"Tonight, Myles L."

"Will you be there, Hessian A.?"

"We'll all be there, Joseph E. N."

"Including yours truly, Thomas J."

Then they all laughed very hard, and although I could only see the tops of their heads I judged them to be sort of banker type men.

"Yuh, Tony'll get in tonight— And then watch the fur fly."

They all squeezed lumps of plaster so the dust dribbled down on the polished table; then they pushed the little mounds into the shape of seven-pointed stars, laughing uproariously as they did this.

I wondered who the two extra points were for.

The phone rang and I said hello into it.

There was just a sort of heavy breathing for a little while and I kept saying hello over and over . . . then I heard the click as the connection was broken.

The door opened and a very fat woman walked into my office. She was the fattest woman I'd ever seen—or man either.

"I want you to watch my husband," she wheezed.

Before I could tell her that I was kind of a make-believe operative and even if I hadn't been I didn't want any divorce-case business, she went on:

"I've come to you, Mr. Budd, because you're not a licensed shamus. I know that it would give you great pleasure to have an excuse to tail somebody." She waved an enormous hand at me. "I also know that you have a deep sympathy and love for people. You will help me."

She had started to cry and I thought maybe she wouldn't be offended if—

"Thank you. I need one." And she tilted the bottle up and drained it without hardly stopping talking. "I don't want to hurt Luther—that's my husband, Luther Davis McCoy—my name is Madge, Madge McCoy—I want to help him. I just want you to tell me who he sees every Friday evening, and where. And I may say, Mr. Budd, that the where is much more important than the who."

"But—" I said.

"Luther will be sitting on a bench in Inwood Park at 3:15. It's ten after one now. Take the IRT local to 207th Street and walk west down the lane, in the direction of Dyckman. Got that?"

"But, Mrs. McCoy—"

"You'll have no trouble at all recognizing him. He's been having some scalp trouble, and his hair's turned a bright green from the salve he's been using."

"I can tell him several excellent remedies."

"What ever you do, don't let him discover that you are following him. Give me a description of the woman he sees, and tell me precisely where they meet and the route Luther takes to get there," she said, getting on her feet. "Are there any questions, Mr. Budd?"

"Did it come in a rash or did he just feel it a little tight?" I asked.

"I may have been a trifle of the former coming here," she answered, "but I'm certainly more than a trifle of the latter as I leave. All you have to worry about Luther's hair right now is that it's green like the proverbial grass."

And she waddled out like an elephant with rubber legs.

The five laughing men were gone when I looked down the hole again.

2

Just as I left the building I saw Leroy Shelby, who had walked out on Mabelle Frances and his little family in 1936.

"Leroy!" I called, starting to run over.

At once a group of very tall men in fur coats and high hats of the same material drew in close around him.

"Who iss thees peasant, Baron?" one of them with a luxuriant red beard demanded.

Leroy said something in a deep, foreign language.

"It's Albert, your brother-in-law!" I said as loudly as I could.

But Leroy only frowned very hard and spoke again very deeply to one of the men who quickly opened the door of a big shining car with three extra tires and they all drove off singing like church music. There was the design of a dragon swallowing a duck painted on the door and Leroy had a gold sword with diamonds in it strapped around him in a purple sash.

That's funny, I thought to myself, but I better be getting out to Inwood Park because it's already fifteen of two.

When I found Mr. McCoy I couldn't help thinking that if he spent much time in parks he couldn't have used a more appropriate salve, for he looked like a little bush with a man sitting under it. As soon as I got there he went to the subway and rode to Broadway and Bleecker. All the way there people

sort of edged away from me like they didn't like the smell of
my suit any more than I did, and one old lady muttered,
"Keeley'd soon get you out of yellow suits and sombreros."
Mine was only a five-galloner but I guess the yellow was unusual in a hat. On Houston Street Mr. McCoy went into a store
that had a lot of baby chicks in the window. I was surprised
when he lifted the cover of his basket and took out a baby chick
which he handed to a clerk who did a little dance, whirled
around a few times and then slapped Mr. McCoy across the
cheek so hard I could hear it from where I was pretending great
interest in a double-malted on the other side of the street. It
said *Thomas C. Helgering* up above the chick store.

Then we rode down to Boro Hall and he got off and I followed him down Schermerhorn Street to St. Marks where he
went into a newsstand and bought two O'Henrys. He took the
wrapper off one of them and threw it away. Being careful not
to be observed, I bent quickly and picked it up. There was a
little note crushed up in it which said: 'Your hat's on backwards.' And when I took it off, it was.

When I caught sight of Mr. McCoy again a bus was just
pulling in to the corner at Dean and Franklin where he was
standing. Just a trick to lose me, I thought; I'll never make
it now.

I started to run—but the bus pulled out while I was still
half a block away.

And there stood Mr. McCoy, quietly peeling his second
O'Henry. Once again he threw the wrapper away, and once
again I picked it up. The note said: 'It's still on backwards.' No
you don't, I thought; I just finished turning it around. But it
was.

This time he walked all the way out to Ralph Avenue on
Fulton before he stopped in front of a pet shop that had dozens
of little water spaniel puppies in the window. A sign said
Myles L. Raaney & Co. I was simulating great preoccupation

with a Chocolate Delight across the street when Mr. McCoy went in and, lifting a little water spaniel out of his basket, gave it to the clerk. Once more the little dance, the speedy whirling around, and a slap harder if possible than before.

Next he walked to E. 98th Street and Eastern Parkway where we got on the Brighton Line and rode out to King's Highway. Mr. McCoy's face was beginning to look sort of puffy and I wished I could soak my feet somewhere. He went into a store which said *Jos. E. N. Praetz Fancy Florist.* The window was full of very strange blue roses. Mr. McCoy gave the clerk a blue rose and the clerk went through the same thing again. For something to do I counted the number of whirls— seven.

This time I pretended interest in a Bobby-sock Special— and I really did pretend interest in it.

How we got to Willets Pt. Blvd. I don't want to go into. He ate O'Henrys all the way there and the notes always said your hat's on backwards; and every time I looked, it was—so I finally gave it up.

Hessian A. Basil, Tropical Fish, the sign over the shop read. Mr. McCoy took a fish like in their window-tank out of his basket and gave it to the clerk. The dance, the whirl, the slap. . . .

Mr. McCoy's nose was starting to bleed a little bit and the right side of his face was all swollen-up as in mumps.

I hadn't been able to eat anything this time, and I was too tired to cross the street to watch from a safe vantage point.

Coming out of *Thomas J. Carey's Studio Portraits* where Mr. McCoy had given the clerk the same photograph of a little man with terrible wrinkles in his forehead and side whiskers like they had hundreds of in the window, I heard someone call:

"Hey! Hey, Joel! Joel Ruvinsleff!"

And Mr. McCoy, handing me his empty basket, said:

"Why hello, Norris. Haven't seen you in a dog's age."

As they shook hands, I said,

"Then . . . then you're not Luther McCoy . . . ?"

I had a hard time not having tears in my eyes.

"No. No, I'm not Luther Davis McCoy," he answered, turning back to his friend.

I started to limp away.

"Please don't take my basket, Budd," he called after me. "And you needn't be upset . . . Mr. McCoy's just across the street there."

The handle of the basket slipped out of my fingers. I turned to look—like someone walking in his sleep.

And there, a few feet away from me, stood another man with green hair.

3

I followed the real McCoy to a saloon on the corner of Barrow and 7th in The Village. He walked immediately to a phone booth on the side and tapped on the glass. After a short conversation a woman emerged and they kissed each other very tenderly. Even through all the smoke I knew that I wouldn't be seeing two women that big on one day, and as they moved nearer I saw that it really was Madge McCoy.

Since there was a stool vacant just then and I was very tired, I sat down on it. Mrs. McCoy came up and sort of gave a little bump which sent three men who sat next to me sprawling on the floor, then she motioned her husband to one of the stools and sank down on the other two herself.

"I wish you'd explain—" I started to say.

"Listen, masher," she interrupted, "another crack like that and I'll pin your ears back."

A sweaty hand took hold of my arm from the other side, and as I turned around I jumped about a foot because I thought for a minute it was a big owl.

"Didn't I meet you in *The New Masses* office?"

I tried to look around the horn rims to see her face but she moved it up so close to mine I could feel lipstick on my nose and chin and a large pin she wore was digging into my chest so hard I had trouble breathing. Hoot would have been the name of the owl.

"I suppose you know our new slogan," she persisted.

When I started to nod my head, her tongue almost put my left eye out.

"Why Hegel about it—vote for Hague today."

I heard the bartender ask Mrs. McCoy what they'd have.

"Two boiler-makers for us and give Comrade Paint-in-the-Puss a hooker of lemonade," she replied.

"Have you heard *Ballad For Americans* lately?" my new-found acquaintance went on. "Don't you just hate those carping little saboteurs who say it's only great poetry? But Shosta-kovitch . . . !" She moistened my upper lip. "I simply *chill* to The Seventh. Those wonderful drums—Ta ta te tum *tum*. . . ." She started to click her teeth and I knew that all the red on the tip of my nose wasn't make-up.

Suddenly I felt her lurch back and Mrs. McCoy's massive arm stretched across where the pin had been eating through my shirt.

"Look, sticky," Mrs. McCoy said, "how about opening up this poor guy's front some other time, hunh. There's a coal miner looking in the window—be a nice little Josephine and go over and kick his teeth out."

"Why, you—"

"And when you get that done there are some kids with rickets down the block you can put to sleep with that little song of yours called *Free Enterprise And You Make The World A Safe To Keep The Bloody Profits In*," Mrs. McCoy continued.

A man broke off the top of a glass on the edge of the bar and shoved it into another man's face.

It was awful. It was very awful.

"Drink up your lemon drink," the huge woman said above the commotion. "The joint's jumpin' too good."

You can't fool me like that, I thought, as I observed her putting some drops from a tiny vial into my glass.

"I know all about knock-out drops," I told her, trying to move away from an inebriate who was beginning to snore down my neck. I could smell gunpowder on his breath.

"Don't be silly," Mrs. McCoy said. "Here, see for yourself— It's quite harmless." She handed me the little vial. "Go ahead, Mr. Budd, take a sip or two. . . ."

I took only one.

When I came to I was lying on the floor in a strange room. One light bulb swung by a long cord from the ceiling and I could see that aside from myself there wasn't another thing in the room. No furniture, no pictures on the wall, not so much as a rug on the floor— And somewhere I could hear a terrible beating and moaning— Then, nearer . . . so I wanted to yell for someone to come . . . *and nearer* . . . a faint scraping sound.

I lay there naked in that awful room.

The room seemed to be watching me.

The bulb became a . . . a white eye.

After many minutes had passed I somehow managed to get to my feet and cross to the window. Beneath stretched an angry sea, huge waves lapping within inches of the sill, and far out, almost hidden in the dark wild, tossed a single great light.

A noise behind me . . . I spun around and a little man with a huge flashlight stood in the room. When he snapped it off I saw a wonderful and horrible thing in the reflector—

*for the face which reflected back at me was one I had never
seen before.*

"Everything is ready, Tony," he said in a language which
I didn't know at all—not even the name of; and I heard my
voice answering him.

But the strangest thing is that although my answers then and
later were completely understood by the others, I haven't the
least idea now what I said or thought—I can remember only
what they said.

"Put these clothes on and we'll be on our way," he went
on, wrinkling his forehead in a great scowl and tugging at the
dirty, gray whiskers which grew on either side of his chin.

I wasn't startled to find a jagged hole in the front of the silk
shirt, and ones which corresponded in the tweed jacket and
black camel-hair topcoat. The shirt was pretty stiff from the
dried blood but I didn't seem to notice that after I had it on
awhile.

We walked across the water and came to a great forest.

"Listen," the old man said softly.

I heard singing off somewhere among the trees.

What I said about this made him quite angry. He took hold
of my arm very roughly and led me to a little clearing. Here
there were a great number of people sitting at benches before
a very long table upon which stood a man in a yellow suit
making a speech. From time to time he would pause, stare
intently at first one face then another, his lips moving without
sound, and then he would point at five men who were dangling
from ropes which came down out of the sky—as much as to
say: Do you see now what I am trying to tell you?

And suddenly it was snowing, the flakes coming down like
the short feathers of very lazy and sleepy geese. As I stumbled
into the cave, drawn by the warmth and light of a small fire, I
sensed rather than saw that the young woman was crying. I
said something to her and she put her arms around me.

"You have been gone so long," she whispered. "Many of us had given up hope of ever seeing you again. It has been so cold, so dark—not even the star we loved as children could penetrate here."

Then I became conscious that from the shadows in back of the fire a pair of eyes was watching us—watching with such hate that the taste of it filled my mouth.

"Isn't it beautiful!"

The pony lifted its feet in a proud dance, its back arched as though to the touch of an unseen rider.

"In a moment they will sing," a voice said.

Stretching for miles across the desert, motionless in the pale greenish light of the moon, stood the shaggy little animals in hushed attention for a sign from their leader . . . and the leader, beautiful in a strength and grace which beggared the waiting heavens, slowly raised his muzzle—

The air filled with their singing.

The five sank to their knees beside me.

"They are speaking to the angels," Mr. Helgering said.

"They are asking their dead to be comforted," Mr. Carey said.

Mr. Basil and Mr. Praetz tried to say something but a sudden wind filled their mouths with sand.

Coughing, Mr. Raaney said:

"There are only three songs more beautiful in the world . . . the song of the weather-vane on the spire of Our Lady of Sorrows in Regensburg, the song which the shepherds of Norway sing at the Easter, and the song of the bull crocodile in the rites of his darkling love."

When we got about fifty miles in from the coast I saw that the young lady I'd met in the cave was just tearing a little black puppy out of the mouth of a snake which had the size of a tree. Two wonderfully marked lions were slowly circling a blazing bush—but I couldn't quite recognize the man who was standing in the heart of the flames. A small herd of antelope were drinking thirstily at a brook, lifting their gentle faces now and then to stare at a tiny naked child which was sleeping peacefully on the bank. Slowly a wrinkled old man slit the throat of the puppy and after a little while its innocent surprise was stilled.

When we got to the White House the President was on the point of signing a very important document. Then without warning a hole appeared in the ceiling and the face of the man in the yellow suit looked down. Very solemnly, his attention seemingly distracted by the voice of someone leaning over him, he tossed an enormous hat upon the President's table.

"That should give Kansas something to think about," Hessy said, taking out an address book and writing 'Matilda Plunkett—WA-9-2417' into it.

"They just hadn't counted on Rhode Island's Favorite Son, had they now?" Tom C. chuckled.

Tommy J. took the lighted end of his cigarette out of his mouth before saying:

"Well, Cyrus X. Twitchbutt's my boy in '48."

Joey and Myles Low walked over to the short-wave and told somebody in Japanese that they'd just have to stretch out the scrap iron the best way they could for the time being.

When we got on the Twentieth Century, the huge fat woman became stuck in the chromium lane leading to the dining car, and they had to stop the train each time so the passengers could get out and up around to eat. But I noticed that every member of the wrecking crew had a tropical fish tattooed on his forehead. As we pulled into Aliquippa it was learned that starting with and including the engine, every second car had its wheels suspended about three feet above the tracks. And as the engineer climbed down out of his cab, I noticed a yellow suit carelessly draped over the steam-gauge, and pressed into the grimy skin of his chest—possibly from the pressure of a brooch or ornamental pin—was the imprint of—

This is Thomas Dreelson writing from the spirit world. Here are a couple things I'd like to put in this book:

What hate hath a man!
O see the deer have reached the forest
And the heavens ache with love of them . . .
Ah God! I have seen the deer
Entering this beautiful forest!
What man dare hate his brother!

The days of wonder shall increase
And the temples stand above the water . . .
For whosoever hath knowledge of love
Shall be loved; and whosoever of hate,
Him shall we love before all men.

☆ ☆ ☆ ☆ ☆

When at last the heart of the world is made pure
And the things of God are rendered unto Caesar—
For until then shall Caesars be

☆ ☆ ☆ ☆ ☆

Everything in heaven is an eye . . .
And the eye sees itself.

(As I was saying)—was the imprint of a little halfmoon with a hammer thrown through it.

When we got to the lonely house on the moors it appeared at first as though nobody was home; but after a little three tiny girls in crinolines with long golden braids coming down over their shoulders unbolted the great bronze door and we were conducted into the presence of an ancient old man who was eating pig-jowls and sauerkraut out of a silver tureen and drinking gin out of a rubber boot.

"It be a weerd wil' nicht tahnicht, Tony ladde," he said with an accent.

A little orange worm crawled out of his whiskers and looked about with a peculiarly intent stare. It was not until much later that I realized its handicap to be a glass eye—and someone had been pretty careless because it wasn't the same color as the real one.

Then Mr. Raaney handed Madge, the youngest of the wee girls, a really lovely blue rose.

The ancient immediately held his left hand up—his middle finger was missing.

I held my left hand up too—both the middle *and* the index finger were missing on mine.

Sadly he selected a particularly mouldy piece of jowl and popped it into his wrinkled mouth. As he raised the boot I saw that his eyes were like peachstones, and that growing from each was a little tree.

When we got to the courtroom Judge Nespich O'Renahoula-monihan-Levy was just remarking:

". . . . . say before sentence is passed?"

The prisoner at the bar's yellow suit looked badly rumpled and the bristles were coming out of the hairbrush which he dangled in his hand.

"Your honor," he began timidly, "is my life worth five thousand to you?"

"Ten."

"Seven."

"Eight."

"I'll see eight."

"You'll see h—l. I sentence you to be hanged until that bald spot on the top of your head fries to a crisp and the last whiff of the cyanide rots your stinking lungs out."

The defense attorney took a baby chick out of his briefcase and held it up so all could see.

"Why didn't you present this in evidence before, Mr. Carey?" the judge said, quitting his bench and coming around to embrace the man in the yellow suit to whom a delighted spectator had already handed a perfectly brand-new brush.

"An Ogilvie de-Luxe!" breathed the embraced recipient, in his excitement taking out a handkerchief and rubbing lipstick all over his forehead.

When we got back to the sea-coast a huge wooden platform stood at the waves' edge. Thousands of people waited motionless on the sand and more thousands blackened the ocean as they swam silently in. After a moment a man walked to the middle of the platform and said:

"There are many tragic and awesome tidings I could give you; but it is my wish now to speak simply concerning that relationship with the universe which all men desire knowledge of—that out of this knowledge may rise the cathedrals of a humanity geared to outglory the very stars. And the key to this knowledge—is there any doubt in your hearts? does not the word form itself on your tongues as naturally as morning's dew on the mountainside?—need I indeed remind you that this key, this altar and untarnishing sword, is a love of all things?

"To love all things is to understand all things; and that which is understood by any of us becomes a knowledge embedded in all of us; for when the single tree in the forest has reached a height greater than its fellows, then may we say that the height of the forest is not less than the most-distant leaf on that tree.

"To recognize truth it is only necessary to recognize each other; for no man was ever born into the world with the necessity to lie about anything whatever—and it is exactly as the world demands a complete cessation of all truth that a few men turn against every manifestation of the lie.

"Perhaps, since we are speaking of serious things, it would

be helpful to examine some of the tenets by which we are thought to live.

"That all men are created equal is one of these.

"Some of you may say: Here certainly, is a great truth.

"Yet it is a hideous and obvious lie.

"Because it is used to support a lie.

"The noblest utterances of brotherhood and compassion and fervencies to God which have been used to degrade, maim, and blind the nations of the earth, appear as blood-flecks on the mouth of a monster engaged in gobbling its own kind.

"Who are these who speak of brotherhood? Will the Jew on the butcher's block called Europe or in the slums and sweat-shops called the Lands of the Free—will this brother tell us? Will the Negro who cleans out the slop-buckets of Democracy at home, and slops out buckets of his blood in defense of this 'Liberation' abroad—will this brother tell us? Will the slaughtered youth of England, Spain, Japan, Russia, Poland, China, Italy, Norway, Greece, America, Germany—will these stricken brothers tell us?

"How beautifully have the careful voices hymned their well-bred compassion for those under the heel of these sub-human madmen, these 'little yellow bastards'—while the power and the gold eased in on chutes greased with the blasted hopes and broken bodies of men who had been sucked into a rat race—a rat race which was called 'saving the world.'

"Yes, but saving it for what? That the sons of our sons may be taught the use of machine-guns while still in their cribs? That we may engage the souls and bodies of every man and every woman on earth in preparation for wars to end all wars? now and forever wars without end—

"Who of these dares to speak of God!

"Where is he who tells me to kill my brother in His name!

"Where is that one who says: 'We have declared war on the enemy.'

"For he is a liar and a murderer.

"The enemy is war.

"It exists in their peace.

"It is a war to allow the few to starve the many.

"It is a war to allow the few to blind the many.

"But the power of this enemy is not in the few.

"Its power is in the many who fear, distrust and hate one another.

"Love is the kingdom.

"Love is a blinding light in this darkness.

"My brothers, many are saying now:

" 'Yes, what you say is surely the truth—but what are we to do? How is it in the least worthwhile that we, a handful lost in these stupefied millions, should try to live by what we consider to be right? Of what use would this be?'

"And I can only answer this:

"One who speaks the truth shall eventually and inevitably out-sound the world; and one who lives the truth shall have a life in every man forever.

"I ask you to love, not to hate; to live, not to die; to be filled with a great joy—because no power on earth can defeat us!"

Then when we got to the village it was wonderful to see that lights were on in all the houses. The sound of a great singing floated across the square with its hideous monuments and statues, until, growing in beauty and majesty, it finally spent itself on the moon-drenched hillsides where untroubled shepherds tended their peacefully grazing flocks. A seven-pointed star shone brightly in the heavens.

Doors suddenly opened everywhere and the streets filled with people talking together in excited, merry voices. It seemed that they had joy in being there. Even the five who had been with me did not stand apart—instead they were accepted as men who had at last come home after many weary and hazardous journeyings. I saw the young lady of the terrifying cave throw her arms around a stern-faced man and I saw him kiss her and say: "You must not ever be afraid again, my daughter."

And when the morning came a great shout of exultation and thanksgiving arose from every throat. A shy little man in a soiled, lemon-colored suit lifted a photograph high above his head that all might see.

At once a voice from the highest and farthest hills was heard, and the voice said:

"Look well upon the face which is before you, my children; for against its gentle wisdom the bondsmen of darkness and evil are as thieves and assassins who would scheme to rob the very wind of its blowing—or who would murder the sun for the heat and the light of the sun!"

The face was the most beautiful I had ever seen.

And every face before me there was that face.

THE LAST PARTY I EVER WENT TO

"We don't usually come to places like this," June said.
"But we heard that you would be here tonight," Jane said.
"And we simply had to meet you," Joan said.
"I don't either," I said; "and I'm glad to meet you too."
"Your book is very exciting," Jane said.
"Thank you very much," I said.
"It is so wonderfully innocent," Joan said.
"I'm glad you think so," I said.
"So delightfully pure and unspoiled," June said.
"I'm glad you think so," I said.

"Pardon me, Mr. Budd, when you're not so busy, may I see you for a moment?"

"Certainly."

And the woman in the red dress walked away again.

"That's Eve Pippin," Joan said.

"Oh," Jane said.

"Oh, Mr. Budd," June said.

"Eve Pippin is the most dangerous woman in New York," Jane said.

"You must be terribly careful, Mr. Budd," June said.

"Whatever you do, make sure you don't see her alone," Joan said.

"Why?" I asked.

"She's a man-killer."

"There are awful stories about her."

"She has the reputation of stopping at nothing, Mr. Budd."

"Oh," I said.

"Oh, Mr. Budd. . . . You are Mr. Budd, aren't you?"

"Yes," I said. The newcomer was a young lady of junior high school age.

"You'll excuse us."

And the three sisters moved off to talk to somebody else.

"My name is Michael. . . ." I guess she noticed that I jumped about two feet. "Why, what's the matter, Mr. Budd?"

"Oh, nothing, I just thought of something."

"Oh," she said. "Well, I'm a senior at Hunter and I'm just so thrilled meeting real, live authors! Not that my brother would let me read his copy of your book, but I'm only two hundred and seventeen on the waiting list at school—one of the girls managed to get a copy."

"That's nice," I said.

"Is it really so wicked, Mr. Budd?"

"I don't think it's wicked at all," I said.

"Just outspoken?"

"I suppose it—"

"I don't mind dirty words, Mr. Budd. If it's life, I can't see why you shouldn't use them . . . I really don't, Mr. Budd."

"Do you like your school work, Miss . . . ?"

"Just call me Michael. It stinks. I want to get married and have ten kids."

"Oh."

"It must be nice to sleep with someone you really like whenever you want to. This way it's fun, of course, but, well, it's just sorta hiding off in corners, don't you think?"

"Ah."

"And then there are always slips—I've had three."

"Puft. Puft," a voice said near me.

"They're messy, besides costing money— Oh, there's Jack! Jack! Hey, Ripper!"

And she ran over and threw her arms around a young man with a strange hair-cut.

"Are they leaving you alone tonight, Mr. Weed?" I heard the man who had called me Charlie ask the little man who was troubled by fairies.

"Everywhere," Mr. Weed said despairingly. "Every time I turn around. . . ." He looked around like he expected to see one.

"Why do you stand for it? Why don't you do something about it, Mr. Weed?"

"Do something? What can you do about it?"

The man who had called me Charlie leaned over and spoke very earnestly.

"Look, Mr. Weed— Just coming in the door. . . ."

"Is that one?"

"What do you think? Look how all padded-out he is— Isn't that disgusting?"

"Are you positive that's one?" Mr. Weed was beginning to

get a very wild look in his eye. As far as I could tell, what they were talking about was a large, maternal-looking woman who was standing in the doorway.

"Am I sure? Why, he's notorious."

"All that lipstick and padding," Mr. Weed said like he was moaning. "I'll teach him something!"

And he suddenly ran over and grabbed the front of the woman with both hands and started to yank them up and down.

There was an awful commotion and several people managed to get Mr. Weed down on the floor where they got some ropes and tied up his arms and legs.

The maternal-looking woman was stretched out on a couch sniffing something and having her wrists rubbed.

The man who had called me Charlie seemed to be having convulsions off in a corner.

"May I speak to you now, Mr. Budd?" the woman in the red dress said at my elbow.

"Why, yes," I said. "Won't you sit down, Miss Pippin?"

"So—someone's been talking about me. It's Mrs."

"I'm glad," I said before I could think.

"You call me Eve, of course. Let's go where we can have a nice, uninterrupted talk," she said, starting to walk away.

"But—" I said.

"Come on, Albert."

"All right, Mrs. Pippin," I said, and I followed her.

She took my hand at the door and led me into a room. There were beds in it.

I said, "I just thought of a phone call I have to make."

"There's one," she said. "But make it snappy."

Then I noticed with horror that she was taking her dress off.

"It's a private call, Mrs. Pippin," I managed to say.

"She can wait. We've things to do— And for God's sake what are you sitting there with your eyes closed for?"

Mrs. Pippin had had nothing on under the red dress except some high, black lace stockings.

Then I felt her hand . . . . * * . . . . . . while I tried to get away . . . . . "Please, Mrs. Pippin" . . . . She took her . . . * * * * . . . panting and saying . . . . as she . . . . under the bed where I thought I'd be safe for a little while, but she reached under and . . . * * . . . . . Just then someone opened the door and I said, "Help! Help!" as loud as I could but he only smiled and said, "Well, that's one I'll have to try sometime." . . . as Mrs. Pippin . . . . * * * *

Then she . . . . pulling the hair on my head too and . . * * . . . . . so all I could see was . . . . . . my ears beginning to ring from the * * . . . . "Oh, my gosh! Oh my gosh!" I pleaded, but she only . . * . . . . . . and the upper parts of her legs . . . . ! . ! . . . . . felt her teeth on . . . .

"Mr. Budd," a voice said. "Please come-to, Mr. Budd."

I opened one of my eyes a little way.

A woman I had never seen before was leaning over me.

"Where's . . . ? Where's . . . ?" I began, drawing the bed covers up around my throat.

"Oh, Eve left about an hour ago. She told me you were in here and . . . Oh, Mr. Budd, do that to me too. She said she never had anything like it before."

And I noticed with horror again that this one was beginning to slip her dress off too.

I jumped out of bed.

"Ah . . ." she breathed heavily.

I didn't have any clothes on either.

Somehow I managed to scoop up my pants and shirt and shoes and ran into a closet and turned the key.

"Please, please, Mr. Budd," I heard her panting, as she pounded on the door. "You don't know how I've dreamed of

this moment! My husband . . . . just a droop.
He never . . . . nothing really vile . . . . .
from an old Boston family."

After a long time I heard her going away.

When I finally got back to the party I felt so shaky I found
a chair over in the shadows near a potted tree. Right away a
very drunken young man came over and handed me a drink
in a tall glass.

"That's straight scotch, take it easy," he said, going off
before I could say anything.

After a little while I poured it out in the sand which was
around the tree—because the smell made me feel even weaker,
and this way I'd not bother anybody.

I heard somebody who was talking to several people near
me say:

"Why is it that all you boys are suddenly drooling over
Koestler? It's just that you never have and you never will do
any honest thinking about anything. Somebody like Koestler
comes along with a lot of half-digested nonsense about realizing the gravity and seriousness of the predicament which faces
the Left . . . the so-called disillusioned Marxists, that is; he
tells you that the war is being fought to maintain the nationalist
status quo, in other words, that of the Right—and what does
he propose to do about it? What are you going to do about it?
Mr. Koestler, that great, pure-hearted mystic, what does he
do to combat a war he knows to be hostile to the interests of the
people he moons over?—that's an easy one, why he simply
supports it with both fists and at the top of his lungs. That's
the kind of idealism you can really understand. It's intelligent
to be cynical. It's the smart thing to shed a tear for the poor,
hamstrung Left which has to bide its time, watch its chance,
and all the rest of that weak-livered hogwash. Sail into your
rosy little cloud of watchful waiting, but for God's sake don't
do or say anything to make anybody uneasy about you or that

would cost you your respectable position or cut into your income."

"Trouble with you, Brill, is you're a sorehead."

"Of course I'm a sorehead. What the h—l you expect me to. be with lads like you editing the magazines and . . ."

"One of these days you'll throw your weight around just a bit too hard."

"Sure I will. But I'll give you little Hitlers a run first, though."

As Mr. Brill walked away from them, the girl from Hunter's came up to me and said:

"Oh, Mr. Budd, I was afraid you'd gone home. Now we can finish our nice chat—" But she got up again very quickly, saying, "Oh, here's my chance to talk to some real poets. The short one in the tweed suit almost had a poem in *Partisan Review*. Isn't that breath-taking?"

Before I could say anything to that, she walked up to one of them and said: "Excuse me, but I hope you won't mind if I ask you a few questions."

They didn't say anything while she took out a notebook and asked for a pencil, but about ten of them held out pencils.

The very drunken young man gave me a fresh glass and I held it off as far as I could until I'd get a chance to pour it out in the sand.

"Who, in your opinion, are our most vital poets?" she asked, moistening the point of her pencil.

They shifted their feet quite a bit, looking at each other pretty carefully.

"Well," one of them said finally, "Eliot."

"Thomas Stearns Eliot," she said, writing in her notebook.

Mr. Brill wandered over just then and said:

"Can you whistle them yet?"

They didn't look very pleased.

"And Kipling," another one said.

"What do you mean?" she asked Mr. Brill, instead of writing Mr. Kipling down.

"*The Four Quartets,* of course," he answered.

"Oh," she said, "aren't they wonderful!"

"Yes," Mr. Brill agreed. "They're wonderfully dull, lifeless, spineless, colorless, and, as Eliot himself says in one of them, they aren't poetry. And Eliot should know what poetry is, he's written enough of it—but good."

"It makes me like them better—to hear you say that," one of the young poets said.

"Of course it does—since you little creeps don't know a poem from a hot-water bottle anyway." And Mr. Brill suddenly fell on his face. He must have been inebriated all along, I thought.

"And who else?"

"Well, Cummings, Stevens, Jeffers—" They seemed anxious to get on to other names.

"E. E. Cummings, Wallace Stevens, Robinson Jeffers," she repeated.

"Williams."

"Oscar?" she asked.

"No, I think he's gone back to advertising."

"William Carlos," she said, entering it.

"Fearing," another said.

"Kenneth Fearing," she repeated.

"He sure writes a nice bond-selling ad," Mr. Brill mumbled, opening one eye.

"And Patchen?" she asked, pencil poised.

"Oh, Patchen—nobody takes him seriously," one of them said. "He's just a rough-neck who never grew up."

"He's just a boring child—a lot of noise about nothing," another said.

"Patchen missed the boat," Mr. Brill said. "He made the mistake of thinking a poem was a sort of garbage pail you could throw anything into and a lot of the time he certainly went beyond the pale altogether."

They got some other names out of the way, then they seemed to stiffen up. This is the part that interests them, I thought.

"Well?" she asked.

"Well—Thompson."

"Rosamund Dargan Thompson," she repeated, writing.

"I meant Dunstan."

"And," said another, "Jarrell, Rosten, Brittin, Abbe—"

"Wait," she said, repeating: "Randall, Norman, Norman A., George—"

"Russell, Keith, Lewis, Schwartz, Laing—"

"Sydney King, Joseph Joel, James Franklin, Delmore, Dilys Bennet—"

"Derleth, Shapiro, Merriam, McCarthy, Brinnin—"

"August, Sgt. Karl—I'm so glad he made it clear in *V-Letter* that he's not to be thought of as a 'war-poet' . . . so many people might have been tempted to capitalize on that very thing—let's see now . . . Eve, John Russell, John Malcolm—"

"Broomell, Henderson, Rukeyser, Pierce, Blackmur—"

"Give me another pencil—Myron H., Bert, Muriel, Edith Lovejoy, R. P.—"

"Poor li'l Ezra," Mr. Brill muttered.

"Morse, Brown, Mills, Rosenberger, Hay, Karlen—"

"Samuel French, Harry, Clark, Coleman, Sara Henderson, Stymean—"

"Now I'll give you my candidates," Mr. Brill said, sitting up. "Get these down. Dolgis Leamish, Larry Trust, Joseph Westerly, Steven Judsor, Ormand Falmore, Stephen Mittreed, Patrick Snow Wedge, Ruthanne Bloodfoot, Pamela McFrand Gleese, J. Marie Sue Ibersonne, Clarence Seadler—"

"Why, I never heard of any of these," she said, looking up from her writing.

"You will," Mr. Brill said. "They're some kids coming up . . . fine, vital lot."

The man came back with a new glass for me.

"You sure can take it, Budd," he said thickly.

Another group moved within my hearing.

"I'll tell you some things I like on records," a very pleasant-looking young man said. 'Das Lied von der Erde'—"

"Thorborg and Kulman under Walter."

"Right. Mahler's 'Ninth,' Bruckner's 'D Minor.' "

"Who does the 'Bruckner'?"

"Von Hauseggen, Munich Philharmonic. And I.like Mozart's 'Prague'; Rudolph Serkin's 'Brandenburg.' Toscanini's 'Clock'; Koussevitzky's '102 in B Flat' by Haydn—also his 'La Mer'; and Ormandy's 'No. 7 in E Flat Major'—"

"Whose '7th'?"

"Bruckner's."

I poured the glass out in the sand.

" . . . you would expect of an empiricist."

"Kafka got near it."

"Gide, too. *The Immoralist* is certainly a treatise of the *a priori* personality."

"But Mann's *Joseph* doesn't quite penetrate the—"

"I agree. Even Proust's extraordinary *honneur* left him no alternative at the last."

"But not Stendhal."

"Stendhal is a giant."

"Balzac."

"In one book at least."

"And, of course, Dostoyevsky."

"Dostoyevsky."

He brought me a fresh one.

"Miro complicates it simply because he doesn't know how to handle his material."

"But Arp does, I suppose."

"Of course he does."

"You're way out in left field."

"And you're not even in the ball park."

I poured it out. The sand looked very sticky and the leaves on the tree were getting sort of yellow around the edges.

"And what about De Niro? There *is* a serious young painter."

"All right, what about Kamrowski?—or Lee Bell?—or Jackson Pollock?—or Arthur Sturcke?"

". . . Silone, the politico-dreamer who dreams his politics and—"

"Rubbish."

"He could only end as a religionist. *The Seed Beneath The Snow* is simply the plaint of a sick will demanding pardon from the real world."

"More rubbish."

He brought me still another.

"I love you," he said very thickly. "Are you sure you're alive?"

"I'm fine," I said, wondering how he managed to walk with his foot poked through the little telephone table.

"Well, as Winters says somewhere, it's perhaps less implicit—"

"But as Tate says somewhere else, and with equal authority, it's likely more explicit too."

And Mr. Brill's voice:

"Now don't forget, folks. . . . The poetry's right now in the privy."

"May I sit here beside you all?" I heard a voice say, and I turned around to see a big colored woman standing beside me.

"Yes, please do," I said, moving a chair up.

"Ain't you all got no prejudice at all all?" she asked as she sat down and leaned towards me.

"About what?" I said.

"Heh! Heh! Heh!" she laughed very shrilly. "Ain't you all scared to be seen talkin' to me all?"

"Why should I be?" I said.

Suddenly she got an itch on her leg and I was surprised to see that it was white above her stocking.

"Oh, now you know," she said in a changed voice.

"Then you're not—" I began.

"A nigger?" she said eagerly. "Confess now. . . . Isn't that what you were going to say?"

"No," I said. I could smell the greasepaint through her cheap perfume.

"I just adore them! This is my own little way of making people understand them better," she said. "Why, they're every bit as good as we are." Then she jumped up to follow somebody, and I heard her say, "Mind if I talk all with you all all? Heh! Heh! Heh!"

Then a young man sank down at my feet. There was a strong smell of violets about him.

"Have you ever had anything in view?"

One of his eyelashes was working loose.

"Why, yes, I suppose all of us do."

He paused to use a little tube on his lips, and when he ran his tongue around them I was surprised to see that someone had painted a little picture on it.

"Isn't it charming?" he said, sticking it out so I could see better. "Some day everybody will have one there. But wait, I'll show you something really heavenly—"

He started to unbutton his pants and I walked over very quickly and said:

"Miss Michael, let's please go on with our chat."

"Oh, of course, Mr. Spill—I mean Budd."

Two men passed and I heard them say:

". . . and that's how they rate Celine."

"Well, I wish I was a rat so I could write like that."

"And as for Henry Miller—he's just a fellow who writes dirty books."

"Yeah, just a fellow who's written two of the six or seven books around worth a good g——mn."

Michael and I went back to sit by the potted tree; and right away he brought me a fresh one. The telephone stand was beginning to work off his foot but he didn't walk any better.

"I wish somebody would talk about Bill," she said sadly.

"Who Bill?" I asked.

She looked at me very surprised.

"Why, Saroyan, of course."

"Is he a writer?" (For some reason I almost said wronger.)

"Is he a— Mr. Budd, you've had quite enough of that!" she said, taking the glass out of my hand.

Just then my hostess came up and looking from me to the sand around the tree, said:

"Why, Mr. Budd—I'm so sorry. You could have asked anyone. . . . The johnnie's just down the hall to your left."

"What do you study at Hunter?" I asked after the woman had gone to tell everyone about it.

"You think I'm just a baby, don't you?" she said. "Why, I bet even some of the things you do in bed wouldn't frighten me—not very much anyway."

"Do you take algebra?"

"When I was thirteen I had to go home through a sort of little woods and a man suddenly—"

"Attention, please," a voice said very loudly. "Mr. Bainbridge, who is a welcome visitor from Chicago, has consented to favor us with one of his own compositions. I need not tell you that Mr. Bainbridge is one of our most promising young percussionist composers."

I was surprised to see the man who had called me Charlie walk over to a huge piano and take the top off it.

"I never heard of no composer Bainbridge," someone whispered.

"Ladies and gentlemen, Mr. Bainbridge in his latest composition, 'Splitting the Up-and-Attem.'"

Mr. Bainbridge took a lot of nails and nuts and bolts out of his pocket and put them somewhere inside. Then he took off his coat and unbuttoned his shirt. He turned around to smile at everyone but suddenly in the middle of it he brought both his elbows down so hard on the keys that some of them popped out and it sounded like a hardware store falling downstairs. He smiled at everybody again. Then he started to kick the front of the piano with his feet and pound inside the top with a big wrench. Now he stood on the keyboard and jumped up and down . . . all at once starting to yell very hard. After a short while the whole front of the piano caved in and he started to rip out the strings. When he was all done he turned around and smiled at everybody once more.

I saw that our hostess had a sort of a funny look on her face but she smiled too.

And one young man with very wild eyes began to clap his hands and yell even louder than Mr. Bainbridge.

As soon as my ears worked again I heard some people talking:

"Charles Ives is good."

"So is Carl Ruggles and Patrick Stiles."

"I like Hindemith about as well as anybody."

"I like Milhaud better."

"I'll take Alban Berg."

"Prokofieff has done some nice things."

"So has Schoenberg."

"Copland's 'Quiet City' is a nice, workman-like job."

"Don't forget Jean Françaix."

"And Henry Cowell—and John Cage—and Charles Mills."

"And dello Joio and David Diamond."

"Why leave Stravinsky out?"

"Or Sibelius."

Michael jumped up and ran off calling, "Peter! Peter! Hey, Bunson Breeches!"

He had a pretty ordinary haircut.

"Are you alone, Mr. Budd?"

"Yes, I guess I am," I answered.

I couldn't be really sure which one it was. They were identical triplets, very mild of face and with nice, quiet manners. It was not surprising that they didn't come often to such gatherings.

"June and Jane are waiting for me outside," Joan said, because I figured that's which it was. "I just wondered if you would help me look for a pin I dropped in the other room."

"Of course, glad to," I said.

"It won't take a minute," she said, leading me through the door.

"Where did you drop it?" I asked.

"Under the bed," she said.

I bent to look under and she . . . . I struggled but her . . . .

And then . . . . fooled again by thinking somebody's a nice girl when . . . . both her hands.

My . . . . starting to sort of growl. . . . . Then the door opened and June or Jane came in.

"Please," I said, "your sister has gone crazy. . . ." But June or Jane threw off her dress and . . . . black and blue. Beginning to sort of croon and . . . . my upper legs as they . . . . "You depraved beast!"

one of them hissed, taking hold of . . . .
all around the room. Then I felt a . . . .
something not even Mrs. Pippin had thought of. Then they
simply . . . . "Oh, my gosh!" I begged.

The door opened again and Jane or June ran in and now
every one of them started to . . . .

"Oh, you filthy man!" one of them moaned.

How can anybody even think of these things, I thought, as
they began to . . . . the flesh on
. . . . fighting each other off.

And then they . . . . the inside of their
. . . . * . . . . wetter . . . * * * * . . .
. . . . and . . . . . * * * . . . .
. . . . . but it went . . . . . * * * * . . all at once . . .
. . * * . . . . on . . . .
"Oh, you glorious swine!" . . . . June or Joan
. . . . . * * * . . . . . . trying to breathe.
. . . <u>. . . . .</u> . .

. . . .
. . . . . . hurt . . . . * * * . . . their . . . .
But I . . . .
. . . * * . . . "You revolting old angel!"

And so finally they . . . .
. . . . (. . . . . . . * * * * . . . .) . . * *
For . . !?;:!?!?!:!; . . . . !!!!
. . . . the . . . . or Jane with <u>. . . .</u> !
They . . . * * . . . . !!!!!!! And . . . * . . . .
. . . . "You divine monster!" . . . . alone
. . . . put my . . . . back in place
. . . . * * * * . . .

Their upper legs too . . . . find
it . . . . bed right to the floor
?!::!:*!?:;!;*! . . . . !!!

And all of them . . . . * * . . . . in my
. . . . * * * * . . . .
"You magnificent old fiend, you . . . !"
Behind the . . . .
. . . . oh . . . . (oh)
. . . . oh oh oh . . .
. . . . * * * * * * * * * ?
When I came to I couldn't move for a long while.
And my clothes were gone.

I finally thought, well, there's nothing else I can do—so I put on a long dress I found in the closet.

If I can just slip out without anybody seeing me . . .

The hall seemed clear.

I tiptoed along.

Then Mr. Weed suddenly came around a corner.

He looked at me and gave a terrible scream, and jumped out of a window.

I felt like jumping out after him.

THE STORY OF MY LOVE

I had not been in the country since I was a small boy. It
was wonderful just to walk along the narrow dirt lane which
wandered as it liked through the soft, green hills. Once I saw
a big, sleepy-looking fish swimming slowly in a brook under
a pretty wooden bridge. And another time a big flock of blue
birds flew up from a plowed field as I passed.

Everything is so beautiful, I thought—and I whistled, fill-
ing my lungs with the warm, clean air.

A big black and white dog ran down from a farmhouse and
sniffed at my legs. I rubbed in back of his ears and patted his
sides. Then he started to wag his tail and I knelt in the dust

and put my arms around his neck. He followed me for about a mile and I had to scold him to get him to go back.

There was a tiny cemetery in the valley and two boys were sitting on headstones fixing their fishing lines. They smiled and nodded their heads at me.

Farther along I stopped to watch some cows resting in the shade of a tree in a pasture. They looked very kind and intelligent. I wished the flies would leave them alone.

In front of a red barn which had been built right beside the road stood a farmer cutting his little daughter's hair. She was sitting on a high stool and her face was sort of squinted-up against the sun. The man's knotty hands were very gentle as he snipped carefully at the golden braids.

"Hello, stranger," he said, lowering the scissors.

"How do you do," I said. "What a lovely little girl you have."

"Say hello to the nice man, Samantha," he said, putting his hand on her shoulder.

She lowered her eyelashes and wiggled shyly.

"Would you like a penny, Samantha?" I asked.

I took one out of my pocket and extended it to her. Her dimpled little hand felt cool as a flower as she took it.

"What do you say?" her father said, bending to look in her face.

"I'm obliged," she whispered, lifting her eyes for one quick second.

I started to give her all the change I had.

"Whoa!" the farmer said, resting his hand on mine. Then he laughed. "How would you like to have dinner with Samantha and me?"

"Mama's gone far, far away," the little girl said, getting down and coming over to stand in front of me.

Tears came to the man's eyes.

"I'll fry us up some chicken," he said in a low voice.

"I'm afraid I won't be able to," I said; "but I can't tell you how grateful I am you asked me."

"Come on, Samantha," he said, reaching down for her. "Upsy-daisy now."

She was standing with her little tummy pushed way forward and as her father lifted her back to the stool she stuck her tongue out at me. But her eyes were laughing and friendly.

Toward the start of the afternoon I came to an old millwheel which turned with much creaking in the middle of a big fenced-in place where hundreds of ducks were kept. I watched them running around searching for food and swimming in the deep, greenish water.

Then I passed a little general store in front of which a number of wagons and cars were drawn up. I felt thirsty but I wasn't in the mood to go in a store for something that would fizz up my nose.

When I got to the orchard my feet were beginning to feel tired and I thought it would help to have my shoes off for a while. So I entered at a white gate and stretched out under an apple tree. After my shoes were off I felt all relaxed. . . .

I lay back and started to watch the clouds.

One was the shape of a king on a horse with a very long tail. One was the shape of a woman sitting in . . .

2

I awakened to feel something on my forehead.

"It's just an apple-blossom," a voice said. "I hope it didn't startle you."

I looked up and saw Her sitting there. . . . And I couldn't say anything.

"You could get a bad burn sleeping out in the hot sun like that," she said.

She had on an old-fashioned-looking dress and her hands were folded quietly over an open book.

"Have you come far today?" she asked, when I didn't speak.

How could I tell her that I had come from the other side of the world.

"I'm being rude . . . talking away like this when you probably—"

"I . . . I knew you would be here," I said, and my voice didn't sound like mine at all.

She laughed softly. "Well, now—" she began. Then she stopped suddenly and listened. "That's mother calling me. I must have been reading longer than I thought." And she closed the book and moved to turn the chair.

I got up and walked over and started to push it down the little path. It was as though I had always done this.

"Oh, please don't," she said. "I can manage very well." And she put her hands on the big wheels.

"No, I'll take you home," I said.

"Well . . . as you like. At any rate, we'll be able to return your kindness in some small way, I hope. Have you eaten?"

"I'm thirsty," I said. My mouth was very dry and hot and I had trouble putting my feet on the ground.

"Then I can at least promise you a glass of the finest spring water in Sanson's County," she said.

"I'm very thirsty," I said. "I think this is . . ."

A very old lady was bending over me.

"Here, drink this," she said.

It tasted brown and very bitter.

"Where is she?" I managed to say.

"My daughter you mean— Priscilla's in the kitchen watching the bread," she answered. "But you must be quiet now."

"What happened to me?"

"Mild case of sun-stroke, far as we can tell."

"And did I talk or?—"

"Oh, no, you were quite well-behaved."

"I'm terribly sorry to put you to all this trouble."

"Trouble? How was it any trouble to help somebody who needed help," she said gently.

A door opened and She wheeled into the room.

"Priscilla," I said before I could stop myself.

Neither seemed to notice and the smell of baking bread pouring in from the kitchen made me realize that I was very hungry.

"Do you think you'll be able to eat any supper?" she asked.

"Oh, I mustn't put you and your mother to any more bother," I said.

"Nonsense," the old lady said. "Supper'll be ready in half an hour. Perhaps if you feel strong enough it might be well for you to sit out on the porch until then—fresh air's a splendid medicine."

"But, Mother, why can't he just rest here on the couch by the open window?"

"Because, if you must know, I want to set this room to rights, that's why," her mother said, starting to pick up some books and papers from the table.

"What's your name?" Priscilla asked me quickly.

"Mr. Budd," I said.

"Oh, no—I mean what's your first name?"

"Albert," I told her.

"Well, now, Albert," she said, "as a guest in this house you have certain privileges. And I simply want to know whether you want mother to set this room to rights, or do you prefer to eat in the kitchen—where we always do?" And she added, "It's ever so pretty a kitchen."

"I won't eat anywhere else," I said so loudly I wondered whether I still didn't have a touch of sun in me.

"In here, you mean?" her mother said, laughing.

"No, in the kitchen!" I said even louder.

"I think Albert wants to eat in the kitchen," Priscilla said, laughing too.

3

After breakfast the next morning I said that I would have to go back to the city.

"I suppose you can't neglect your business," Mrs. Cumberland said.

"I have no business," I said.

"You have people you must see——?" Priscilla suggested.

"No, there's nobody I have to see," I said, backing towards the door.

"You'd better hurry if you're going to catch that bus," Mrs. Cumberland said.

"I don't know how to thank you," I said, my hand on the knob.

"There's nothing to thank us for," Priscilla said. "It was a pleasure having you here."

"Well . . . " I said, stepping back and almost falling down the steps. "Well, I'll say good-bye then."

"Good-bye, Mr. Budd."

"You must hurry now. . . . Good-bye."

"Good-bye, Mrs. Cumberland. . . ."

"Good-bye, Mr. Budd. Have a pleasant ride."

"Then. . . . Good-bye, Priscilla."

"Good-bye, Mr. Budd. You'll be late—hurry."

And the door was closed.

Somehow I walked down the little, flower-bordered path. I opened the white gate and—

"Oh, Mr. Budd!"

"Yes! What! What, Priscilla?"

"You've forgotten something."

I didn't have much with me and I couldn't think what it might be, but I certainly hurried back.

They were both waiting on the porch.

"What was it I forgot?" I asked.

"Don't you really know?" Mrs. Cumberland asked.

They were both smiling at me now.

"I'm afraid I don't," I said.

"Albert, you can be very silly," Priscilla said. "You've only forgotten an unimportant little thing—"

"Oh, don't let's tease him any longer," her mother interrupted. "You've just forgotten, Albert, that we want you to stay."

I don't know what I said then but after a little while I was out in the backyard splitting kindling as fast as I could. Pretty soon there wasn't any more wood to chop up so I went into the forest and cut some trees down. After I had one of them in good-size pieces and hauled them in and all stacked up in a neat pile Mrs. Cumberland came out and said:

"What in the world! Why there's enough here for twenty stoves and— Albert! let me see your hands!"

"It's really nothing."

"Let me see those hands, Albert Budd!"

Priscilla's face went all white when we got in the house and I hardly felt the soap and the iodine.

That afternoon I pushed her chair down to our place in the orchard and she read to me.

I didn't hear very much of it that first time for watching the sunny-shadows the leaves made on her cheeks and the way her eyes got all filled with wonder as something happened in the book.

Once she stopped suddenly and said:

"I think Dickens understands more about how people really are than any other writer."

"I'm glad he makes you happy," I said.

"Oh, but that has little to do with it, Albert. As a matter of fact, more often he makes me unhappy. . . . You're getting me all mixed up. . . ." And she laughed. "What I'm trying to say is that happiness comes too in understanding what real unhappiness is."

"Like if you understand something it can't hurt you," I said.

"In a way," she said slowly. Then quickly she started to read again.

Some children coming home from school passed on the lower road. The little girls were walking quietly and the boys were darting about throwing stones and shouting at each other.

If I didn't have all these bandages on, I thought, I'd go and pick some flowers for Priscilla.

"Albert—Albert, I've been talking to you for the last five minutes."

"Oh, I'm sorry. . . ."

"Maybe I shouldn't bother to say it all over again. But it must be said now—in the beginning."

She was quiet, bending her head back to look up into the sky. There were three or four exciting shapes.

"What, Priscilla?" I asked, watching her face again.

"You're in love with me, aren't you, Albert?" she said very softly.

The book fell out of her lap and I picked it up. A tiny green worm was crawling along its edge.

"I can't tell you not to be—that would solve nothing, but you must try to understand."

The little worm arched up in a bow and pulled himself onto my thumb.

"It's hard to say without . . . without hurting you— And I'd rather die than hurt you. Only, if you aren't made to understand now, we'll both be hurt, terribly hurt later."

There were tears in her eyes and I stood up. I wanted to

say I'd go back on the next bus or anything if that would make her happy like I first saw her.

"For you see, Albert, I love you, too," she said.

"Then, why—why—"

"Because I . . . I'm a cripple—a hopeless cripple." And she was sobbing suddenly.

I got down on my knees and put my hands over her hands.

"Darling," I said. "Oh, darling, please don't cry."

She leaned forward into my arms. I pulled her close. . . .

A moment later she drew back and held my face in her soft, warm fingers.

"It was cruel of me to say that, Albert," she said.

I started to say something but she stopped my mouth with a quick little kiss.

"Let's think no more about it now, shall we?"

"I want to, Priscilla," I said, pulling free. "You don't understand me at all if you think your being a . . . a—"

"Do you see?" she said quickly. "It's even hard for you to say it. No, Albert, we must—"

"We must what, Priscilla? It's true that it's hard for me to say it—because I don't believe it—because it means absolutely nothing. All that I know and believe and hear in my heart is that we love each other. All that we are and—"

"But I shall never walk, Albert."

"How do *I* know that you'll never walk?"

I was standing up and almost shouting.

"Because the doctors—"

"The doctors don't love you!"

Then I felt strong and great. Something clicked into place.

"When you can walk," I said, "will you become my wife, Priscilla?"

"You are a strange man, Albert," she said softly.

4

There were little blue and white teacups and plates arranged in cupboards on either side of the shiny stove in the kitchen. And in the sitting room copper kettles and pots hung up over the fireplace so the whole house and the little room I slept in at the top of the stairs was all like you'd just walked in from an awful storm to find everything warm and clean and like people wanted you to sit down and talk about wonderful things with them.

They never seemed to hear enough stories about The Diver and Mr. Wan and My Agent, and as much as I told them of the parties they asked to hear over and over again.

But I couldn't somehow tell them very much about my job winding spools or how words had been left out of my book. Though one day after they had asked about it so often I sent in to the city for a copy and read it out loud to them in the evenings.

I just read all the right words in the places that had been filled with those funny little marks.

Both Priscilla and her mother cried in a few parts, and sometimes I had to wait a little while myself before I could go on reading.

Their three cats curled up in our laps and seemed very contented and happy.

"Even Smoky's got a lap now," Mrs. Cumberland said. "I'm afraid he used to feel a little out of it."

Now and then when neighbors dropped in we'd all sing old songs—sometimes to a fiddle somebody brought along, or an accordion, or even a mouth-organ. So I got to know most of the villagites by their first names and a great deal about them —just as everyone seemed to guess I was "sweet" on Miss Cumberland, as they called it.

Because I could never look at anything else when she was in the room, and I never heard what anybody else said when she spoke. And every time she laughed I wanted to put my arms around her.

One morning I was peeling potatoes for Mrs. Cumberland. It was looking very rainy outdoors and the wind was beginning to make the shutters bang.

"I want to talk with you about Priscilla, Albert," she said, looking at the gauge on the oven.

"Shouldn't she be home by now?" I said.

"She'll get back in good season—Priscilla is a sensible girl. Likely she couldn't tear away from Mrs. Ronkett . . . splendid one for a talk is Abigail Ronkett."

"Maybe I should just go to the head of the lane. . . ."

"You'll do no such thing. I've been starving-up for this chance to talk to you alone," she said, pushing some hair from her eyes, and leaving a little streak of flour on her forehead.

I reached for another potato but the wind was coming up so fast and the clouds so black I was getting the skins about an inch deep.

"I called Priscilla a sensible girl a minute ago," she said, "and she's neither. . . . How old are you, Albert?"

"Well, let's see, 1905—"

"My daughter's three years younger." She put some squash covered with anchovies and grated almonds into the oven. It's going to start raining any minute now, I thought, slicing into my finger. "That's not sensible, Albert . . . romance out of story books, day-dreams by two people almost into their middle-age—and one of them not able to get out of a wheelchair."

"It's starting to sprinkle," I said, getting up and upsetting the potatoes all over the floor.

"Well, let it sprinkle . . . and for heaven's sake let me

finish the peeling. I never in my life saw a man who— Albert Budd, come back here, I've got a lot more to say to you!"

"I'm sorry, Mrs. Cumberland," I said, putting my coat on and getting my arms in the wrong sleeves. "She may have started back and—"

"Fiddlesticks. Priscilla was not born in the country for nothing."

But I was already half out the door.

The rain was coming down in buckets before I got to the gate. I had trouble staying on my feet the wind was so hard and it was like it was night instead of the morning only half over. Twice I stumbled and fell in the thick mud of the road. I found her just the other side of the old mill, the wheels of her chair all clogged and stopped.

"Where can we go?" I shouted above the wind.

"There's a ledge in there among the rocks."

I bent down and picked her up, surprised that I could carry her so easily even against the storm.

"Just past the fallen tree. . . ."

It was like a small cave, full of dry leaves and smelling strangely like a stable.

"Gee, Albert—was I glad to see you!"

"Take your wet clothes off," I said, "while I build a fire."

"It won't do much good, I'm wet through."

"Take all of them off—" I began, then I remembered. "Lean against me. We'll get your coat off . . . now your dress. . . ."

"But, Albert—"

"Stop twisting. It slips over, doesn't it? Here, I'll hold your shoulders. . . . Just kick them down. We'll pick them up later. Now your stockings . . . I won't let you fall. Just sit here on my coat a minute. We'll have a nice fire in a jiffy."

"You don't smoke, do you, Albert?"

"No—why?"

"I don't either." I thought she might be laughing to herself in the dark.

"Two dry sticks," I said, finding them after a little hunting.

"Were you a Boy Scout?"

"No, I wasn't," I answered, rubbing like mad.

"Or an Indian . . . ?" Now, anyway, she was laughing.

Just then two or three sparks shot up and I moved the sticks in among the heap of leaves and rubbed until I felt dizzy.

A blaze. Out. Another. It went out too. But the next one caught the leaves.

I gathered all the heavy stuff I could find and the cave sprang to life. I could see that Priscilla had my coat wrapped around her.

"Are you trying to get pneumonia?" I asked, going over and lifting her to her feet. I cleared a space beside the fire. "Now sit down there and get warm while I hang your clothes up to dry."

"Mightn't this be considered just a bit, uh, primitive?" she asked, bending to the fire.

"I don't care what it's considered— You're not going to catch cold if I can help it," I said, placing her things on crossed sticks near the heat.

"Well, I certainly brought you to the right place today," she said, turning her stockings inside out and moving them back a little.

I never thought anything could rain harder than we'd come through, but when I looked out all I could see was a solid wall of water.

"Isn't there usually thunder and lightning?" I asked.

"Not always—particularly in cloud-bursts."

"Was that a cloud-burst?"

"It most certainly was . . . or is, I should say. But, Albert, what about you? Are you going to allow yourself to catch pneumonia?"

"Your stockings are still too close."

"They are not. And if you don't take those wet clothes off this minute I'm going to . . . I'll run outside."

I didn't want to answer anything and I hoped she wouldn't think of what she had said.

"Why, Albert—" And she turned her head around to look at me. "For one moment I thought . . . I thought I really could!"

"And when you do hard enough and—"

"Let's not think about that now," she said in a changed voice. "Please get out of those wet clothes and come near the fire, Albert."

"All right, Priscilla," I said.

I hung my things up beside hers.

"The children used to come here to play cops and robbers," she said, looking into the fire.

"Did you come here?"

"Yes. Yes, I used to come here. . . . Oh, it's no use! We can't stop thinking of it."

"I only—"

"It happened when I was twelve, Albert. I was picking apples in a tree . . . and I fell. At first I couldn't even sit up— Then, little by little, day after day, year after year— Oh, fiddle-dee-flab, as Mother would say. Let's see. What shall we talk about?"

"Why does it smell of horses in here?" I asked.

"Because of horses. They don't like to be out in bad weather any better than we do," she answered.

"Lucky all those leaves and dry sticks were handy."

"Albert . . ."

"Yes?"

"Look at me. No, not at my face. Look at my body."
She threw her arms wide.
"I'm not misshapen, am I? Am I?"
At last I could do as she wanted.
"It's beautiful," I said.
"And a man wouldn't—"
"I am a man, Priscilla."
"Then if you love me . . . What am I saying!" She lowered her arms, and stared into the fire again. "The rain should let up soon."
"It seems just about as bad as it was."
"My clothes are almost dry."
I had already put most of mine back on.
"You'll hate me for what I was going to ask you, Albert." She raised her eyes. Now for the first time there was a peal of thunder. "I was going to ask you to . . . to possess me."
Lightning lashed across the sky like a shaky hand writing some awful tiding.
"I knew that," I said.
"And—"
"I wanted to."
Her eyes seemed to fill with little whirling stars.
"I'm so glad. . . . Oh, I'm so terribly glad!" she said so softly I could hardly hear her.
And together we put her clothes on.

5

A few days later Mrs. Cumberland asked me to take some snapshot negatives over to Willie Shaun's to have them developed. I'd been there a couple times before and I didn't enjoy doing it because he was very grumpy and irritable about everything.
So I decided to walk down a few new roads before I went

there. Besides that way, alone and just looking at things which pleased me, I'd have an opportunity to think—never had I felt so near myself to try to understand how many different joys and pains could happen all at once.

Making me afraid and almost glad to be afraid.

I came to a sort of huge wooden box that had the whole roof glass and a narrow little porch running around it. Just wide boards overlapping one another—no paint or windows. A door about three feet high and on a long pole at the top a flag with green stripes and yellow stars with seven points.

When I knocked I heard like children scuffling inside and a man with a red beard leaned down in the opening and said:

"Fill up the other pitcher and tell the boys I died with a smile on their faces."

And he took hold of my arm and I bent as low as I could and went in. There were about fifty or sixty little men with dark, shiny hair doing all sorts of tricks and exercises on a big mat. One of them came over and handed me something that looked like a round cucumber.

"Eat it," he said, stepping quickly forward as two others came sailing through the air at him. They landed one on either of his shoulders—right away another of the same, which had been swinging back and forth on a rope, let go and landed on their shoulders.

I bit into it. It tasted like a piece of banana in orange juice.

"It's an old saw that can't see the prettiest girl at the fair," the man with the red beard said.

"He wants you to look in his pocket," the little one with the five—two more had landed on the first two by now—on his shoulders said.

I thought I might as well. Something grabbed hold of my finger and I came out with a tiny alligator.

"You can have it," the balancer said, "he has a lot more."

Just then I saw one of the little men diving up at me. In a

minute two more came down on him—and two more on those two.

"Having fun, Budd?" a voice said, and I tried to move around to see, but I was afraid my knees would give altogether. Even the alligator was beginning to feel heavy.

So it was a relief when Mr. McGranehan stepped around and said, "Build it some place else, boys, okay?" and they all jumped down.

"Hiyah, Glasshoe," he went on to the man with the red beard.

"May the best man win said the bridegroom as he slipped the ring on the preacher's finger," Mr. Glasshoe answered.

"What do you mean littering up these premises he declared sternly as he fixed the bitch with an eagle's eye just before it flew off," My Agent said, sidestepping so at least that little one couldn't start a pyramid.

I bit into it again. This time it was like a pineapple with cabbage flavoring.

"I want you to meet a friend of mine—Budd, Pinklady." We shook hands. My fingers all made noise like somebody tramping on dry sticks. "Pinklady," Mr. McGranehan went on to explain, "is probably the strongest man in the world— in his arms, anyway." Probably has no place in that sentence, I thought—even an alligator he could pull off, easy.

"I have something I have to do," I said, trying not to watch all of the tiny, dark-haired men building one together—now I knew why the shed had to be so high.

"On your way, then," My Agent said. "I want to take a few kinks out— See you at supper."

The whole thing was beginning to sway back and forth and I didn't stop to ask him anything about that supper part.

"——is such sweet sorrow that had I but one life to lose it would be thine, Horatio," Mr. Glasshoe said as we walked down the path.

Every few feet Mr. Pinklady would run into the bushes and come back with a log or an iron bar or something which he'd break into many pieces.

I had to lean very hard to keep Mr. Glasshoe from edging me off the road but when I got too tired for it I just let him and we went up the side of a hill and then down over it until we must have walked several hours that way. And all the time he continued telling me his anecdotes and Mr. Pinklady darted in and out finding things he could break.

So I finally managed that they walk together and as I ran back I saw Mr. Glasshoe edging Mr. Pinklady into what looked like a swamp.

It was gloaming when I got to Willie Shaun's house. He'd only been up in his dark-room a few minutes when the door opened and they came in. Mr. Pinklady started to look over the living-room chairs and tables and things very carefully, so I took him into the kitchen.

After a few minutes Willie Shaun clumped down and growled:

"I wish she'd learn not to over-expose them. A waste of developer and—"

Mr. Glasshoe, who had stepped behind the opening door, said right in his ear:

"O little star that shineth in the night tell me whither hast tomorrow gone."

Willie Shaun's upper teeth almost fell out.

"What's he doing here!" he demanded loudly.

Then Mr. Pinklady walked in and stated:

"We've just come from Chloe. She said to tell you everything's under control now, and until she sends in some definite orders just sit tight and keep your banjo tuned."

He was studying Willie Shaun's right leg with a great interest and I figured I'd have to get them out of there right away.

"I'll tell Mrs. Cumberland about too much exposing," I said, turning to the door.

But Mr. Glasshoe came alongside and the first thing I knew he was edging me into the kitchen. . . . The other two followed us in.

Willie Shaun started to yell at the top of his lungs and I didn't blame him because he didn't have much of a kitchen anymore.

"I never came up against a steel rolling pin before," Mr. Pinklady said, going over to bend it back the other way.

"And Marblebone . . . ah yes . . . that most repulsive Marblebone . . . all the toime taking his lips off and kissing his own behind," Mr. Glasshoe remarked, as we tore through a plowed field—and even at top speed like that he kept edging me right off in the direction of a place called Deadman's Bluff.

"The man's a fool," Mr. Pinklady said. "Everybody knows a person with a broken wooden leg's too jumpy to handle a shotgun that size."

It was almost dark when I arranged to get them walking together.

The last I saw of them Mr. Glasshoe was leaning in pretty hard and they were about two feet away from the edge of the cliff.

I wonder if his little jaws will open when he gets sleepy? I thought.

6

George Arliss and My Agent were waiting for me at the gate. The evening star looked pale and cold on the hill. A dog was barking off in the direction of the village.

"Why do they tumble around like that, Skujellifeddy?" I asked, as we walked along up to the house.

"You mean Wallcott's boys—that's Glasshoe—they're flies

from Puerto Rico. He brings them up here every summer."

"Flies?"

"You didn't think they were feathers, did you?"

"That's the weight they fight under," George Arliss explained. I noticed that he was limping very badly.

"The Juan Bacas are always getting doll trouble in the apple," Mr. McGranehan said.

"Doll trouble is doses," George Arliss explained again. "New York they call the apple."

"Are they brothers?" I asked.

"Nah, he books them all Juan Baca," Skujellifeddy said. "Why bother for a lot of names with flies?"

"Do you have athletic feet, Mr. Arliss?" I asked, as he stopped to take his shoes off and walk in his socks.

"George is Senior Counselor in Mrs. Narva Ziltainboorg's *Bideawhilugroandlaf Camp for Tiny Tots of Prosperous Parentage.*"

"Three to seven," Mr. Arliss said.

"I'll take that and raise you ten," My Agent said.

"That's how old the kiddies are," Mr. Arliss went on. "We just got back from a twenty-mile hike and I'm not as young as they are any more."

After supper Mrs. Cumberland said, "Don't you smoke cigars, Mr. McGranehan?"

"Why, yeah, I do—"

"Well, why don't you?"

My Agent took one out and snipped off the end.

"There's beer in the ice box," Priscilla said.

"Say, this is just like home," George Arliss said.

"That's what it's meant to be," Mrs. Cumberland said.

Skujellifeddy came back with a tray with bottles and glasses on it.

"Do you know Black Jack?" Mrs. Cumberland asked, putting a deck of cards out on the table in front of her.

"Lady, he's my brother," My Agent said, pulling his chair up and lighting his cigar.

"Well, we'll see how you get along with your family," Mrs. Cumberland said, as she pulled the cards out like an accordion and brought them together with a loud snap.

Mr. McGranehan looked over at Mr. Arliss.

"Think I'll try a couple hands myself," George said, taking his mole out of his pocket and rubbing it along the side of his nose.

"Give me a nice little one now," Skujellifeddy said. "D—n! Pardon the expression, but you knew G———ed well a nine would put me over."

"Hit me," George said. "Again. Oh, so easy now . . . just a pretty little deuce or trey like—"

He threw his cards in and drank a glass of beer in one gulp. Then he took out another mole and pushed their noses together before he rubbed them all over his face and even around on the back of his neck.

"Albert," Priscilla said, "let's you and I hold a couple hands out on the porch, shall we . . . ?"

They didn't even look up as I pushed her chair out. I sat down on the top step at her feet. She ran her fingers through my hair and I remembered I'd have to get another bottle of Wild Root first thing in the morning.

"Do you ever wonder why we were put here?" she asked.

"What do you mean, Priscilla?"

"Oh, all of it . . . being alive . . . having something that thinks in us, that makes us have silly and wonderful thoughts . . . like we were somehow important . . . like maybe what we do and can't do has an importance which if we understood or felt deeply enough about would bring us nearer to—"

I think she saw the star fall too.

"Men call that God," she went on softly. "That being near something so hard you're not . . . not afraid or lonely any more."

"Priscilla, I know that—"

"I know that when I'm with you I feel it. Just like what I was supposed to be is what you think I am, and in a funny way . . . oh, I can't say it, but like you understand why there are trees and flowers and houses and men who kill each other and men who give their lives for each other . . . and why we feel happy and sad and ashamed and proud— Did you ever want to be so great and strong that you could just say to one other human being, Somewhere, somehow, there is a place that is always pure and untouched, a place where all that is good and clean and beautiful in the world may live on forever. . . ."

"I believe there is such a place, Priscilla," I said. "And I believe it is in all of us—if only we knew how to know it's there."

A train whistled away down in the valley—lonely, sort of like it was telling the hills all about the sadness of the people who were riding along through the night in it.

"All over the world . . ." she said slowly, "everybody wondering where their own little destinies will lead them; into what quiet and safe haven, or into what undreamed-of land of speechless horror— Oh, Albert, there are times when I am so afraid, so desperately afraid. . . ."

"I won't ever leave you," I said, kneeling to hold her in my arms. "I'll always be with you, Priscilla."

She was trembling and her tears burnt my hands.

Footsteps sounded on the path behind me and as I turned around an old man walked into the light and said:

"Where can I find an Alvin Bludge?"

"You don't mean a Mr. Budd, do you?" Priscilla said.

"Mebba so. . . . Left my glasses in my other coat."

The telegram was for me. I gave him a quarter and tore it open.

"Missed by all," it read. "Hope come back city soon. Have new injection for you to try. Love."—and it was signed, Donald Wan, Inventor to the Universe.

"Isn't that sweet," Priscilla said. "What does he mean by your trying a new injection? Do you have some disease you didn't tell us about, Albert?"

"Oh, no, never had a sick day in my life— It's just something we do together. Maybe we'll find out something that will make it a little better for people."

"Well, you be careful, and don't get yourself in trouble trying to make things better for people," she said, taking both my hands and squeezing them. "Let's go in now and see who's got the shirt off whose back."

Mr. McGranehan had his cigar chewed up so it spread out over most of the bottom part of his face and George Arliss' nose had little pieces of mole hair stuck all over it.

"Mother!" Priscilla exclaimed.

"It was perfectly all right," Mrs. Cumberland said. "I suggested playing Strip myself—and they always went in the other room to change."

I was wondering why they had bathrobes on—and all their clothes piled up in front of Priscilla's mother.

"The only thing not all right was the kind of spots she slipped us," My Agent said. "Why, I'll swear there were some I never saw in a deck before tonight."

"Well, Skujellifeddy," George Arliss said, pushing his chair back, "I gotta take my little charges up a mountain at five tomorrow morning."

"Are you staying at the hotel?" Priscilla asked.

"Nah, George's got a tent down the road apiece," My Agent said. "Healthier he says."

"Where down the road?" Mrs. Cumberland asked.

"Near the snake farm," Mr. Arliss said.

"Oh," Priscilla said.

"What's the matter? They can't get out, can they?" Mr. McGranehan said.

"How are you on mosquitoes?" Priscilla asked.

"Mosquitoes? George, you told me that was the best camp site in Russell's Folly."

"Oh, keep your britches on," Mr. Arliss said. "They never bothered me none down there."

As they got up, Charcoal and Midnight jumped to the floor —sulky, their golden eyes half-closed against the light. Smoky still slept peacefully in Mrs. Cumberland's lap.

"Well, we sure had a fine session," My Agent said, his hand on the doorknob.

"Yeah, it was right in there," George Arliss said, starting to follow him out.

"Don't you think you'd better get some britches to keep on?" Mrs. Cumberland said.

"How do you like that! First thing you know, George, we'll be rummy enough to take that tent of yours right out in the middle of some swamp," My Agent said, starting to slip the robe off.

"Hold it!" Mr. Arliss said. "Don't you remember, we promised our mothers faithfully we wouldn't undress in public until after Passover?"

While they were in the other room changing I gathered up all the glasses and things and took them into the kitchen. There was a tap at the window and I looked out to see Mr. Pinklady holding up a big pump handle. He had a little trouble with it but finally got it bent double—then he bent the doubled-up part double, and for some reason he seemed to have an easier time doing it the second time. Mr. Glasshoe was smiling and since I could only see the lower part of one Juan Baca I couldn't tell how far up the pyramid went.

7

I had found the prettiest wild flowers I could and as Priscilla sat there in the sun with them pinned in her hair I thought it would be a sad thing to be dead.

Children's voices floated across to us like bright toys which the wind was amusing the angels with. Mr. Dickens was telling about how some poor people didn't have any fuel in their house and the snow drifting in on their beds at night. . . .

The little deer walked up and stood very quietly watching us. Its coat was yellow and it held a basket of white roses in its mouth.

"Priscilla . . ." I said softly.

"Yes, Albert, what is it?"

"Don't look up until I tell you to," I said.

"All right, but—"

"Do you believe I love you?"

"Why, yes, of course, Albert—"

"Do you believe I would lie to you?"

"No, Albert, I know you wouldn't."

"Do you believe in—" I was afraid to say what I wanted to say.

"Do I believe in what?"

"In us," I said.

"I do, Albert," she answered.

"Then believe as hard as you can now. Because . . . because there's something standing in front of us which no one else in the world has ever seen before."

"Something standing—"

"Lift your eyes, Priscilla."

As her head raised I tried to think of every beautiful thing I had ever heard of.

"Oh, Albert!" she said. "It's . . . it's . . . why, it's a lovely little faun bringing us flowers!"

"He wants you to go over and pick out the ones you like best," I said, wondering how long I could pray that hard.

She let the book fall to the grass and getting out of her wheel chair she started to walk over to him. . . .

He stood very still. And Priscilla took a rose out of the basket and held it up for me to see.

Then suddenly her eyes filled with terror.

"Priscilla," I called, "you've taken only for yourself. . . . Aren't you going to find one for me?"

Slowly she turned back and extended her hand again. This time he raised his head, shaking the basket gently back and forth.

"Why, he wants me to scratch his neck," she said, and she allowed him to nuzzle her fingers.

"Oh, Albert! Albert! He's real! He's real! His nose is all wet!"

I crossed over and put my arm around her, swinging her about so she faced me. . . . Then I pressed my mouth on her forehead.

"Promise me you'll never doubt again, Priscilla," I said.

"I can walk," she said softly. "Oh, Albert, I can walk! I can walk! I'll take all the roses now. . . ."

As she turned and found him gone her eyes filled again with terror.

"Look in your hand, Priscilla," I said, gripping her shoulders.

"The roses," she said. "I still have the roses. . . ."

"Of course," I said. "Would you like another one to come? Perhaps a green one this time."

And she flung out of my arms and ran down among the trees to meet him.

"Oh, this one has purple daffodils," she called, laughing and half-dancing in her excitement. "But where did the first one go, Albert?" she asked, as I came up to her.

"I just wished him away," I said.

She looked at me a long moment before she said slowly:

"Then it is through you they come—that I am able to walk?"

"No, Priscilla," I said, "not through me, but through our love."

"But it was you who believed enough—"

"And now you believe too."

"Yes, Albert, now I believe too," she said, taking another flower from the basket and smelling it.

Then we heard the voice of her mother calling from the house. . . .

And Priscilla sank to the ground, her legs twisting horribly under her.

"Oh, God! O my God!" she sobbed.

The little green deer was gone.

The roses and the daffodils were gone from her hand.

And something was dying away deep inside me.

8

On my way to get the developed pictures I turned down a lane and after a short while came to a big, swinging sign which read:

BIDEAWHILUGROANDLAF
Mrs. Ziltainboorg, O.B.S.

I walked up the walk and came to two large barns which had porches built on and maybe fifty windows in each. There were a lot of sad-faced, tiny boys and girls standing in rows on the lawn. I could see gardens with several men in overalls working in them, and two cows and seven bulls eating grass in a pasture.

George Arliss limped up and I asked him why all the children were standing so stiff and not singing or laughing as they played ball or some of them hide-and-seek or jumping rope.

"It's Parents' Day," he explained. "They're waiting around for their mamas and papas to show."

"I'd think they'd be happy to see them," I said.

"These are what you call Modern Parents," he said. "Little Davie and Mary Ann are being brought up scientifically—or in English, somebody else looks after them. Never let Junior know you love him, Mrs. Uppityblah—want him to get a fixation and end up a swish? and little sis a nasty Les with a handle-bar mustache? So said small-fry don't know whether it's h—l or breakfast or just something they Oedipus—and by the time they get to Princeton or Smith they think it's their elbow."

A lot of cars that seemed to just float without engines and with men in dark suits and caps at the wheel were turning in at the gate.

"What's Mr. Pinklady doing here?" I asked. He was standing in front of a phone booth near the tool house.

"That's how I got my job," George Arliss said. "The Breaker is The String's lamby-pie."

"The String . . . ?"

"That's Zilie."

"What is The Breaker's real name?"

"Shoals. He took his crib apart when he was two weeks old."

"Oh, Georgie!"

"Coming, Marster," Mr. Arliss called back, and I followed him as he went over to a woman who was just coming out of one of the barns in a silver-plated evening gown. A black ribbon about four inches wide came down from a little glass she held to her eye on a stick.

"Have you seen Mr. McGranehan this morning?" she asked. "He promised to deliver the flag-raising speech."

"I wouldn't get my milk all in a boil expecting him if I was you—"

"Impune not the virtue of my por' little dotter the salesman

said as he saw the farmer getting ready to make with the oat,"
Mr. Glasshoe said, emerging from one of the phone booths.

"Who is this bottom-drawer individual?" Mrs. Ziltainboorg
said, shifting the glass to her other eye.

"I demand my nickel back kindly because the party who
answered the phone don't know anybody there with that
gnome."

"I think he wants you to look in his pocket," I said, before
I could consider it much.

"Well—" she said, moving the glass back and forth a couple
of times.

I guess she thought it must be all right because finally she
put the hand with only five rings on it into his pocket and took
out a little rubber bag like the one The Diver gave me to keep
my fountain pen in. For some reason this made her very angry
and if Mr. McGranehan hadn't come up just then I think it
might have got the best of her.

"My God!" she said, "why did they ever bother to dig you
up again?"

And he was terrible to look at—like two faces on one, and
covered with big red welts.

"Did the snakes get out, Skujellifeddy?" I asked.

"Snakes h—l! I woulda kissed any snake that got through
them last night," he mumbled, what showed of his eyes looking at Mr. Arliss.

"How was I to know?" Mr. Arliss said. "I never knew they'd
take you like that—you gotta grant me that—"

"Like Richmond," My Agent said.

"Sit down here and let me think of something," I said.

"I must go now to officiate," Mrs. Ziltainboorg said, taking
out a new glass with a green ribbon about three inches wider.

"Before you go—" I said. "What does O.B.S. stand for?"

"What do you mean, stand for?" Mr. McGranehan mumbled.

"The Order of Beatific Savants," she explained. "Oh, there's the Mayor of Throgs Neck—I really must take a powder now, gentlemen."

Alone with My Agent on the steps I tried to watch as the children marched up and down in different formations and their parents on the platform now and then clapped their hands a little but without taking their white gloves off or smiling except in a polite way.

Yet I couldn't with the swelling going up all the time.

Not even Mrs. Ziltainboorg's green ribbon—

"What are you thinking of, Skujellifeddy?" I asked.

"Poison ivy," he answered.

"Isn't there something else?"

"Yeah, mosquitoes with their teeth filed, yet."

I'll do it anyway, I thought.

Its coat was an even prettier green than the one I brought Priscilla and in his basket were black lilies.

"Do you notice anything new, Skujellifeddy?" I asked.

"I think maybe I got a little poison oak mixed in," he said.

Then I realized that his eyes were all swollen closed so he wouldn't be able to see anything anyway.

I walked over and took one of the flowers.

"Here's a lily, Mr. McGranehan," I said.

"Just pin it on my bosom—because I'm gonna die laughing any minute now," he said. "What the h—l are them brats yelling about?"

I put it in his hand and turned around in time to see all the children flying past the grandstand in the direction of my tiny green deer. They threw their arms around him and all the little girls got flowers which they waved in the air. Then not afraid at all he started to trot off over the field and laughing and singing they ran along beside him.

I heard the parents shouting and making a great commotion and Mrs. Ziltainboorg saying:

"This is an outrage! A crime against the sanctity of progressive education everywhere!"

"What did those kids see?" Mr. McGranehan said in a quiet voice.

His eyes were sort of frightened-looking and all the swelling had left his hands and face.

"A little green deer with a basket of flowers in his mouth," I said.

"This kind?" he said, holding it out. The lily was now a hideous red and big drops of pus oozed down from its petals.

9

Everything had changed in the house. I would look up to find Mrs. Cumberland watching me like she was a little afraid to have me there anymore. Even Charcoal never jumped onto my lap in the evenings and when the neighbors dropped in there wasn't much laughing or singing—then after a few times they stopped coming altogether.

I'd see faces pulling back from the windows when I went anywhere along the roads.

Only Priscilla tried to make it seem as if it was the same as it had been before.

But her face was sad when she didn't know I was looking at her.

And I knew that the time had come for me to go away for a while.

She told me not to bring the little deer into the orchard again. The time had come for me to go. . . .

"I'll come back soon, Priscilla," I said.

"I'll be here waiting for you, darling," she said.

10

As I walked to the bus station I heard the children being very happy playing with something in the woods.

A little deer pranced across the lane in front of me.

Its coat was yellow— The first one I had brought for Priscilla. . . .

That is something to think about, I thought.

Then a huge bird circled around my head and as I bent back to watch, it flew straight up into the air and after a long time I couldn't see it anymore.

When I looked down again it seemed as though the whole world had grown giant wings which were carrying it away out of my sight.

DOES THE

FAMOUS DETECTIVE KNOW THAT LOVE IN A MIST IS ONLY THE GREAT WHITE WHALE GOING DOWN FOR THE FULL COUNT IN THAT OLD SEVENTH ROUND?

Donald Wan was dying.

The house was waiting and quiet.

His cheeks were flushed and his eyes bright-hot with fever.

He raised himself from the bank of pillows.

"Albert," he said softly, "I haven't long."

I took his hand in mine. It burned with a dry fire.

"I shall never know how my next-to-last injection works. This is what I have tried to do—I have tried to defeat all obstacles of time and space—I have tried to . . . well, you shall see—" He coughed. It hurt him terribly. The cloth he put to his lips came away vividly stained. "First you will become what will please you most in the world to be. Next, what the people in our house have voted as the most exciting thing anyone could be. Next, their second choice. And finally, your good friend The Diver's—" A spell of coughing took all the color out of his face, leaving his eyes like coals which have been blowed upon.

"The first you know," he said with great effort.

I thought I heard crying in the hall.

"Next you will become a little wild flower.

"Third, a great whale.

"And last, a boxer knocking out Joe Louis."

"Why didn't you choose something, Mr. Wan?"

"I have," he said. "But I hope you never have occasion to know what it is—"

Coughing stained his mouth again.

"My last injection is in this needle," he went on. And he handed me a little leather case. "If ever you have a trouble so great that there seems to be nothing whatever you can do to meet it, then—and only then—I want you to use it." (I put it away in an inside pocket.)

"Never allow it out of your hands.

"If events work out well for you, destroy it.

"It is a terrible and beautiful thing, Albert.

"And since if you do use it it will be after I am dead, there will be no way for you to ever go back to what you were—"

The violence of his coughing made him gasp for breath.

"This is my way of saying good-bye, Albert," he said, poising the next-to-last needle over my arm. "Please don't be sad. I have never consciously hurt anyone, and I am eager to see the other world—"

"Good-bye, Mr. Wan," I said. "I'll come to you there."

His eyes filled with tears.

"Never lose that faith, my dear friend," he said.

And he moved the needle into place and sent its charge into me.

2

"There are some people waiting to see you, Chief," Stella Discreet said, closing the door and leaning her trim shoulders back against it.

"What do they want?" I asked, returning the receiver to its cradle and quickly signing a stack of letters which required my signature.

Then the door was flung open, flinging Stella crazy-legged over my desk.

"What do you want?" I asked them without looking up.

"Are you Mr. Chasen?" a grim voice—whose owner was trying to suppress laughter—said.

"Yes, I am Berry Chasen," I answered easily. It was no trouble at all.

"There have been murders," a new voice went on, "Mr. Chasen."

"Murders!" I got some more ink on my pen and wrote rapidly on Stella's wrist: 'Get Mall Goose on the phone, Stella. Right away.' Her wrist had little pink hairs on it and an Elgin with a slightly bent minute hand.

"Yes,"—with a quick intake of breath—"Mr. Chasen. Murders!"

Stella had Mall on the phone now. "Mall? Stella. Berry wants you to check all buses and trains leaving Los Angeles during the next two hours. Put a shadow on any person seen loitering on Figueroa between Spring and Champion. Look for eye-shadow on the pair of red gloves you will find in a baby carriage in the lobby of Grauman's Chinese Theatre. What! You have? That's fine, Mall. Just sit tight on him until you hear from me in forty-one minutes." She returned the receiver to its cradle. I thought for a moment that she might slide off the desk; her right leg in its black, fish-net mesh stocking was bent awkwardly under her. "Chief," she said, "Mall said, Look out the window."

"Look out the what?" I demanded, my intent, level gaze not leaving her leg. It was a foot nine inches long.

"The window," she replied in a hoarse whisper.

I did. I looked out of the window as Mall Goose had told Stella to tell me to.

There was a huge eye in the sky.

It filled the sky.

It was a white eye.

As I looked, it winked, once—cagily.

"Whom did you tell Mall to sit tight on, Stella?" I asked, watching to see maybe it'd wink again.

"A little man in a yellow suit," she answered. I was surprised to see a tiny fish struggling in the net.

"In a yellow suit?" I breathed. I couldn't believe it.

"In a yellow suit?" I tried it again. I still couldn't believe it.

"Murder!" said one of the voices.

"Murders!" said yet another.

For the first time I looked at them. "Stella," I said in an intense, resourceful tone, "get out my files."

She slid down and crawled over to the files. Her right leg was broken in two places and the fish was still struggling to free himself.

"Yes, Chief?" she said not too easily.

"We will call this," I told her, as she waited with her shorthand pad ready, ". . ."

"Yes, Chief?"

"The Case Of The Eye That Could See Itself," I said remorselessly.

"Murders!" said one of the voices again.

Each of the twenty-three girls who were crowded up in front of my desk had a single eye in her forehead.

A white eye.

And quivering in each of their heaving chests was the handle of a long, jewel-encrusted knife.

"It's an evening primrose, Gertrude," a voice said near me.

"No, Ernest," a short, stubby woman declared, "a michaelmas daisy is a michaelmas daisy is a—"

"It's a gentian, I said," he said. "Look, Gert." And he ripped his shirt open.

"O what is hair hair is hair here or thar," she replied.

He tore out a handful and gazed at it fiercely.

"I wish I had a bull handy, I said," he said.

"O Toklas is not to talk when talking is—"

"Or an obscenity drink, I said," he interrupted. "Or just an obscenity obscenity, I said tersely."

I smiled to myself when they had gone. How could anyone fail to see that I was a little love-in-a-mist?

"That's an alpine forget-me-not, Cliff," a new voice said. "I want to kill a million—with my bare hands!"

"No, Rex, it's a wild geranium. I want to kill two million— watch them writhe, rip their guts out. What do you think, Quent?"

"You're both wrong. It's a gaillardia pinwheel. I want to dig up all the dead ones too—chew up their bones. D—m subhuman animals. Heine, Beethoven, Goethe— G———ed Huns!"

I could feel the warm, good earth pulsing up through me. I thought, God! how beautiful everything is.

"It's a silver tithonia, Archie," a woman in a long purple

robe said. "Every doggerel has its day because we gotta keep people posted there ain't no islands nomore."

"Dear Edna, it's so obviously a viola blue elf. And besides, America was promises to Standard Oil and those beautiful du Pont boys in the front room."

"I, Carl, speaking from Abraham's bosom," a second man with an accordion began, "do solemnly declare it to be a portulaca trimjane. And if we can continue to get the people to say yes to everything, how nice for us who are in the know."

I must have dozed because when I became aware again the darkness was falling and the evening star shone coldly on the hill.

My petals felt stiff and the warmth was leaving the ground.

A fox barked somewhere in the distance.

Then I sensed the shudder of approaching hoofs and soon the little glade danced ghost-like under torches held swaying aloft by silent riders on great black horses.

Black hoods hid their faces.

Black capes covered their broad shoulders.

They dismounted slowly. They dragged a young woman into the clearing among the trees.

The moon was like a white eye in the heavens.

While I watched they stripped the clothing from her back— She stood naked in the cold, soft light.

Then, one by one, without haste or anger, they—

I could hear the voice of my mother saying:

"You must learn to be snubbed and looked down on, because you're not like the rest, Moby."

That was many years ago and it's taken all this time to understand what she meant.

For, you see, while all the others were black, I was white.

And nobody likes you to be different.

So as I got older I thought, I'll show some of you boys what's what.

I had a whale of a time chasing those same black lads who had chased me because I was white.

It was fun fighting storms too.

The ocean'd dam up like a big angry gray giant and hit me right on the top of my wrinkled forehead—lightning like a fiery eye trying to see everything at once—bang! bang! like terrific guns aimed right at me—but I'd just lift my white hump that was shaped like a pyramid and tear in against it.

Then one day I met a man who hated me.

I think he also loved me.

Fool! Throwing himself out of a boat into my face— Naturally I snipped his leg off.

That was my first taste of long pig.

I got madder and madder— At the sky and the far-off earth, at the wind and the stars, at the night and the day— and especially at that crazy man who clumped the decks above my head.

Trying to find me, was he!

Well! I'll take him this round. He bobbed and weaved in an effort to stay away from my left.

I shot my right in. He rode with it.

Then he caught me with a short, jolting left. Jesus! What a kick he's got in that left, I thought.

I tied him up.

Donavan broke us.

Louis shuffled his feet in a slow little dance.

My arms were getting tired.

Shoot it now, boy, I thought.

I put my right out. He shoved at it with his left.

His right was cocked but he was off balance.

I ripped my left into his ribs. That hurt—

The right got him on the button!

I saw his legs start to go.

I hit him with left and right—

He started down.

The Garden was nuts. When that bell comes, we won't hear it, I thought.

Louis was on one knee, his gloves on the canvas—keeping him up.

Then he pushed to his feet.

I hit him with a right. His eyes looked glazed.

He shuffled away. I followed him, trying to set him up.

His left shot out. I felt my head leaving my shoulders.

I tried to keep him off. He got that left in again. Red was pouring down over my chin.

His glove was dripping with it.

Always that left—

My knees started to buckle.

I put all I had into a right upper-cut.

I saw the look come back on his face.

I doubled him with one to the basket.

As he bent, I chopped him. And again. Again.

All I've got, O God!

He wouldn't go down.

I can't do it, Mr. Wan!

His left had my head off again.

He was stalking me around the ring.

There was a funny, absent-minded look on his face.

Rights and those quick, chopping lefts.

He had me. That left exploding on my chin—

The last thing I thought was: You didn't put enough in again, Mr. Wan.

THE DEER ARE ENTERING THIS BEAUTIFUL FOREST

As I got off the train a man came up to me and said:
"Do you want to buy an automobile, Budd?"
How did you know? I thought. "Yes, I do," I said.
He led me out to a car parked in an alley.
"Nice bus, hunh?"
It was pretty dark in there and I couldn't see it very well.
"What color is it?" I asked.
"Robin's egg blue," he told me.
"What are you asking for it, Mr. . . ."
"Two hundred fish. My name's Karl C. Lyon."

"All right, Mr. Lyon, I'll buy it. Let's go somewhere so I can see to write out a check—"

"Nah, Budd. Look, I'm in a hurry. Just slip me the happy paper and we're all set."

"But what about the bill of sale?"

"We'll cement the deal with a kiss."

"I can't even see to count the money in here."

"I can. Give me your wallet."

I gave it to him.

He sort of sighed as he handed it back.

"How will I get gasoline?" I asked.

"Every hundred miles drop one of these pills in the tank," he said, pushing a little box into my hand.

"What condition are the tires in?" I asked.

He didn't answer.

"What condition are the tires in?"

Then I realized he wasn't there anymore.

I opened the door and climbed in. I felt around for the light switch and the keys. Then I realized I was in the back seat instead of the front. So I opened that door again. I climbed out and opened the other door. I felt around and found the light switch. There weren't any keys.

I pressed a couple buttons and the motor started up. I pushed at a lever and the car started to back. I pushed another lever when I got to the middle of the street. It started right up again. There was a truck coming along and when I didn't turn in time it ran up over the curb and into a little stand which had pottery for sale. In a little mirror I saw the driver get out and wave his arms around—I also saw that the truck had a W. Virginia license plate.

But perhaps I hadn't better try to add that one to my collection, I thought.

Past the tiny cemetery, past the red barn, past the old mill wheel, past the general store—down the lane and up to the little white gate.

And there was Priscilla waiting for me.

"I was afraid you wouldn't get my letter," I said, as I carried her out and lifted her into the front seat.

"That wasn't the thing to be afraid of, Albert," she said, laughing. "You should have had some doubt at least that I would be able to make the trip."

"Oh, Mabelle Frances will be happy to see you," I said. "I wrote her all about us."

"I have a mother, you know," she said, leaning forward as I fixed pillows around her.

"Didn't she want you to go?"

"Oh, sure, she was crazy about the idea—absolutely mad about it."

I pressed a couple buttons and pushed a lever.

"Wait, Albert," she said. "You've forgotten to take my wheel chair."

"No, I haven't, Priscilla," I said, turning in at the lane. "You won't need it."

"Well, all right, but your sister's going to think it a bit unusual when she sees you carrying me around."

"I won't have to. Just wait and see."

"I hope you're right, darling."

I stopped the car and kissed her.

"Darling," she said.

I kissed her again. "My little darling," I said.

I pressed a couple buttons and the radio came on:

"Flash! Flash! What light blue car on what lonely New England road has what mutilated body of what beautiful young lady in what trunk compartment—"

I snapped it off and pushed the starting lever.

"It's certainly a beautiful day," I said.

"How long will it take us to get there?"

"We should be there by dark."

"Have you had this car very long, Albert?"

"No, not very."

"Have you been driving very long?"

"No, not very."

I didn't think it would be wise to tell her that I'd never been in a car before.

"It's a nice color blue."

"Robin's egg," I said.

"What do you keep in it?"

"In what?"

"Why, the trunk."

"Oh, the trunk. Oh, this and that—wrenches, hammers, glue, spark plugs, gauze—the usual things."

"Would you say this was a lonely road, Albert?"

"Lonely? Not at all. Why, look over there—just beside the tree with the vine growing out of it—"

"It looks like a totem pole. And that isn't a vine, it's a rope. But what I meant was, we haven't passed a house for more than an hour now," she said.

"They probably build them back off the highway," I said.

"Where are the mail boxes? And how could anybody get in through those trees?"

The trees were pretty close together. "Has your mother been more careful with her exposure?"

"What? Yes, I guess so. Albert, are you sure we're on the right road?"

"The right road . . . ? Oh, sure. Sure I'm sure."

"There's another totem pole."

"Farmers probably scare crows with them."

The motor started to sort of cough—then it stopped.

"Just needs a little more gas," I said, getting out and going around back to the tank. I took the lid off and looked in but I couldn't see anything.

"Use a stick," a voice said.

I looked around. There was nobody there but a totem pole. I lowered my necktie into the tank.

"That won't work. Get a stick," the voice said.

Then I noticed the lips moving on the third face from the top of the pole. It was a pretty awful-looking face with big green bumps all over it.

"Where would I get a stick?" I asked.

"Here's one," said the next face down, holding it out.

I took it and shoved it in as far as it would go.

"Empty?" another face asked. It had little golden toads all over its upper lip.

"Yes, it is," I said, taking out a pill and dropping it in. Then I dropped in another just to make sure.

All at once gasoline started to gush up out of the tank and I got my feet wet before I could get out of the way.

I put the cap back on. "Well, thank you very much," I said, starting to walk around.

"Watch out for hot foots," one of the faces said.

"What you got in the trunk?" another asked.

I looked at the trunk. "Oh, just tools and wrenches and things," I said.

"Open it up."

Something red was seeping out around the edges. "I'm sort of in a hurry," I said. "Good-bye—and thanks again."

"So long, Budd," all the faces said. "Let us know when you get ready to open it."

Priscilla said: "I could have sworn I heard people talking somewhere near here."

"Probably just somebody trying to scare crows," I said, pushing down the lever.

"Well, it certainly succeeded in scaring me," she said. "Albert, have you noticed that there don't seem to be any roads turning off anywhere?"

I had noticed it. "We'll come to something soon," I said.

We rode for about two hours. The trees seemed to get closer and closer together. Now and then we heard strange sounds off in the distance.

"Albert, I'm frightened."

"There's nothing to be frightened of, Priscilla."

It was getting dark.

Like great owls swooped down around us.

I pushed all the buttons but the lights wouldn't come on. The radio did:

"What robin's egg blue sedan is at this moment driving along what lonely country road with what—"

"Oh, Albert . . ." Priscilla was starting to cry.

"Everything will work out all right," I said.

The moon was making ghosts of the trees.

I tried to whistle something but it didn't sound very good. Then the motor began to cough again—and it went dead.

As I looked in the little mirror I saw the cover of the trunk slowly lifting. . . .

The hair on the back of my neck started up too.

Somehow I got out of the car and went around back.

Priscilla will hear my knees, I thought.

There was just light enough to see.

I managed to look in.

The trunk was empty.

There wasn't anything in it.

And then I saw the label from a bottle of Wild Root.

There was writing on the other side. It said:

'Your hat's on Backwards.'

I ran around to Priscilla. "They're wrong this time!" I said.

"Who is? What are you talking about, Albert?"

"I don't have a hat on," I said.

"Poor darling," she said. "Oh, you precious sweet, pretending all this time that you weren't afraid— There . . . there . . . It'll turn out all right."

I tried to start the car. It wouldn't start.

The trees seemed to be leaning in on us.

"Albert! What's that . . . ?"

Something walking in the road toward us. . . .

The moon suddenly swung clear of the highest tree.

"Why, it's one of our little deer!" she said with a sigh of joy and relief.

Then she opened the door and ran over to him.

"Oh, how pretty!" she said, as I came up. "This one is just like striped candy—and what beautiful lilies-of-the-valley!"

As she reached out her hand to take one from the basket, the little candy-stick deer retreated a few steps, paused, looked back at us, and then trotted on a little farther through the trees.

"He wants us to follow him, Albert."

"Aren't you afraid to go into the forest, Priscilla?"

"Of course I'm not afraid," she said. "Hurry, we'll lose him."

But he was waiting. He pranced on ahead of us, the orange flowers in his basket dancing like velvet flames.

And we followed him into the forest.

2

It was like walking through a great church. The trees, marbled white and purple in the light of the full moon, stood like pillars holding the sky up. And the trees seemed to sing when we waited silent a moment. I had never known that there were so many trees in the world. Somehow it made me happy to know there were so many trees.

Trees are good things to be with.

"Aren't the trees wonderful, Priscilla?"

"They are wonderful, Albert."

The little red-and-yellow striped deer turned down another soft aisle. Everything seemed bewitched—I said to myself: O God! how beautiful it is here!

The trees sang and the trees were beautiful.

Then the little deer stopped with lifted foot.

It listened to something we couldn't hear.

It turned to look at us— Then it sped away through the trees, scattering flowers as it ran.

A voice said near us: "Will you come with me, please."

Priscilla gave a little startled cry and sank to the ground. I bent beside her and lifted her in my arms.

"Who are you and what do you want?" I said.

A man stepped into the moonlight. He smiled pleasantly at us. "I am your friend. Since it is night and the lanes of the forest are at best difficult to follow, we were worried that you would lose your way."

"We haven't much choice," Priscilla whispered in my ear, "except to go with him."

"That is the only sensible attitude, my dear," the man said. "Surely you will admit that your present position is not an enviable one— Why, you could wander in this wood until you hadn't strength to go another step, and not find one recognizable landmark, not one suggestion that you were not the only man and woman left alive on the earth." His voice changed in a strange way. "You have nothing to fear as long as I am with you. And now, please follow me. We haven't far to go."

"I wonder who the others are?" Priscilla whispered so softly I could hardly hear her.

"Your curiosity on that score will be satisfied very shortly," he said.

I stumbled over a root and almost fell down.

"May I give you a hand with her?" he asked.

"No!" I said. "No, thank you."

We walked for about half an hour. I finally had to admit to myself that I couldn't keep it up much longer.

"Here we are," he said, stepping aside and beckoning me to walk past him. I did and a door swung open and we were in an immense room. It was the biggest room I had ever seen. Candles six feet high were placed in rows about twenty feet apart. I counted eleven rows before my attention was drawn to a group of men who were walking towards us.

"How do you do," one of them said. "We are honored to welcome you to our house."

I lowered Priscilla to a little couch. "Hello," I said.

"Would you like a drink?"

"We don't drink," I said.

"Of course, quite right."

"We are very puzzled by all this," Priscilla said.

"Puzzled? But why, dear lady?"

All but one man suddenly walked down between the rows of yellow candles and disappeared.

"What is there to puzzle you?" he went on. "You had lost your way—your friend Charles Elton had the happy fortune to encounter you, and . . . well, here you are."

"Who is Charles Elton?" I asked.

He looked at me for a long moment. "Quite right," he said. "I can understand why you would want to play it that way."

"What are you going to do to us?" Priscilla asked.

"Do to you? Why—" He spread his hands and smiled in a sort of sad way. "Ours is indeed a difficult world, isn't it?"

"Will you have one of your men direct us to the road?" I said.

"To the road? What road would you have us direct you to?"

"Why, the one off there." I pointed where I thought it might be. "We left the car there."

"Quite so." He clapped his hands together.

Right away the group of men walked towards us, this time through the rows of red candles.

"Is everything ready?" the man asked.

"Everything's ready, Chief," one of them answered. He had on a huge yellow hat.

"Stuff get through to McKeesport?"

"Right."

"Any trouble with Corvollis?"

"Squawked a bit, Chief."

"What happened?"

"Corvollis is just a memory."

"Quite so. Chattanooga lined-up?"

"She's set, Chief."

"And Daytona Beach?"

"Daytona's in."

"Did Willy get what he wanted in Lodi?"

"He certainly did. Why, Chief—"

"Quite right. Where's Yazoo City stand?"

"Well, you see—that is—"

"Well?"

"She's making it a contest."

"Oh, she is, eh!" He whammed his hands together. "Get Tony on the phone first thing in the morning. I want her smashed—but good!"

"Don't worry, Chief."

"I don't. Any report from Sulphur Springs?"

"She was easy."

The door opened and a slim youth in white clothes came in. He said, "Chief, can I see you a minute?"

"Certainly. Your eyes are open, aren't they?"

"We got Eddie out there."

"Windsor?"

"Sure."

"Frankie out there?"

"Frankie—Winnie and Joey too."

"Joey, too, hunh?"

"Sure, Boss."

"Shave off his mustache. Who else you got?"

"We got the Van Dorens—"

"What! Not all of them?"

"Sure. We got the Farrars, the Harcourts, the Duttons, the Macmillans, the Holts, the Schusters, the Harpers, the Mifflins—"

"You got Bennett?"

"No Bennett, Boss."

"Good! You got Elsa?"

"Sure."

"You got Dot?"

"Sure. We got Danton, Walter, Eugene—"

"Which Walter? the Brain or the Mouth?"

"Both of them. We got Greta, Rita, Greer, Carol, Rosalind, Betty, Marlene—"

"Bette the Grimace, or Betty the Cheesecake?"

"With the 'y.' We got Tyrone, Robert, Clark, Dennis, William, Franchot, Errol, Joel—"

"Is that Errol the Wobble-legs, or Errol the Young Woman's Home Companion?"

"I'll have to check that. We got Metro, Paramount, Universal—"

He broke off as another, slimmer youth in even whiter clothes came in. This one said, "We got Columbia University away all right."

"Was Nick in his office?"

"Sure. We just took him along."

"What next, the Chrysler?"

"No, probably the Palmer House in Chi."

"Sort of small, isn't it?"

"It's got a lot of old iron in the frame. Old iron's hard to get these days."

"Quite right. Tell Wilbur to come in, will you?"

Wilbur was so slim I wondered how he could stand up, and his clothes were so white it hurt to look at them.

"Bring Charles Elton in," the Chief told him.

When he went out through the candles, Priscilla said, "Oh, please. . . . Please stop this nonsense, and let us go."

He looked at her for a long moment. Then he said sort of sadly, "Quite so. I have been rude keeping you waiting so long."

The man who had led us through the forest came down the rows of candles, Wilbur following with a revolver pressed into his back.

"Good evening, Charles," the Chief said.

"Good evening, Thomas."

"Are you quite ready, Charles?"

"Yes, I am quite ready, Thomas J."

"Very well." The Chief took a revolver out of his pocket.

Then the Chief raised the revolver and fired. The whole face of the other man seemed to spring into a bloody flower.

"Sorry, Charles," the Chief said softly, as the other crumbled to the floor.

There were tears in his eyes as he turned to us.

Priscilla had lowered her face into her hands. She was trembling as I knelt beside her.

Quietly the three slim young men in white crossed until they stood before us. "We will take you to your car," one of them said.

"Oh, just one moment, Mr. Budd," the Chief said. "I believe this is your hat."

The one who had the big yellow sombrero on took it off and handed it to me. It was mine all right.

"It may amuse you to know the name of the man who has

been wearing your hat," the Chief went on. "May I present Herman Y. Backwards—Mr. Budd, Mr. Backwards."

As I picked up Priscilla I remembered the note on the Wild Root label.

Then I followed the three in white out through the lanes of terrible, man-high candles. At the door I looked back— I could have sworn that the one called Charles Elton was rising slowly to his feet.

3

The stars were like pale eyes looking out of the sky at us. The three walked in front, their narrow shoulders just touching.

The three in white.

Like one broad man in white.

The forest was greenish white under the great heads of the trees.

Heads which sang softly to the white moon.

The moon.

Moon.

The gentle and terrible moon.

The three did not talk together.

Great white moon.

Whitemoon.

MOON. moon. mOOOOOON. . . .

What is the moon?

The moon is in the sky.

What is the sky?

The sky is above the earth.

What is the earth?

The earth is where people live and die.

What does it mean to live?

What does it mean to die?

WHAT DOES IT MEAN TO LIVE!
WHAT DOES IT MEAN TO DIE!
"Where are they taking us, Albert?"
"I don't know, Priscilla."
Where are we being taken, dear unknown friend?
Do you sorrow?
Do you know your way?
Have you found what you were seeking?
What is it that has meaning for you?
WHAT DOES IT MEAN TO LIVE!
WHAT DOES IT MEAN TO DIE!
The three led us through the white forest.
The three whose touching was one.
The three led us under a lost moon.
We who are lost speak to the lost.
We who are afraid speak to those who are afraid.
We who are alive speak to the living.
We who are dying speak to the dead.
"What are you saying, Albert?"
"Saying . . . ?"
"I never heard you speak like this before."
"It's as though somebody else was inside me, Priscilla."
"You are probably too tired, Albert."
"I never felt so strong—so sure of everything."
"Have you noticed how strange the moon looks, Albert?"
"Yes, Priscilla."
"Something seems to be . . . to be watching us. . . ."
"Don't be afraid, Priscilla."
"I'm not afraid— It's just that I *feel* my eyes seeing something that I can't see. . . ."
Suddenly an awful cry stabbed through the white forest—
The scream of a woman in horrible pain or fear.
"Mountain lion," said one of the three.
"Her love cry," said another.

"Or hunting," the other said.

"Are we near the road now?" Priscilla asked.

"In a little while, Miss."

Then one of them started to sing. He sang of a girl named Pretty Polly.

I felt Priscilla tremble in my arms.

We came to an open clearing.

They halted, turned to us.

"We have reached what we were seeking," said one of the three.

"Soon you shall see beyond the little meanings," said another.

The moon seemed to draw nearer.

"There is more than just to live—and to die," the other said.

The moon seemed to get bigger in the sky.

One of them took Priscilla out of my arms and laid her gently on a bank of moss and flowers.

I could not move to stop him.

Priscilla's golden hair looked like pale fire in the cold, dead light.

Her eyes were very wide—without fear.

I tried to speak—to move my arms and legs. I couldn't.

The moon seemed to be an eye.

The moon was a great white eye.

The three bent above her.

I saw the knives in their hands.

I saw one of them grasp her golden hair and bend her head back.

Her throat looked warm and pure in the cold, dead light.

They bent slowly toward her.

I saw them lift their knives.

I saw Priscilla smile up at them. . . .

I tried to speak. I tried to move my legs to walk upon them —to lift my arms to strike them to the ground. I couldn't!

And I was smiling.
And I was smiling at them too!
What is a knife?
A knife is used to kill.
Why should anyone kill?
WHY SHOULD ANYONE KILL!
Because that is the way the world was made.
Who made the world in this way?
You speak like a stupid child.
You speak like a vicious fool.
WHY SHOULD ANYONE KILL!
WHO MADE THE WORLD IN THIS WAY!
O warm pure throat—
The long thirsting knives—
What is madness but this!
Aren't all sane evils a madness like this?
Whence the terrible seed—
The white voice—
What is madness if not this world?
Aren't all their sane evils a kind of madness!
Is it sane to lie when that lie kills?
Is it sane to accept evil when that evil brings death?
Is it sane for man to murder himself!
Why should we kill each other?
WHY SHOULD WE KILL EACH OTHER!
And you are smiling at them too. . . .
I saw the knives moving down.
The knives are moving down.
They are long and cruel-looking in the cold, dead light.
Then my little green deer came into the clearing.
His coat was matted with burrs—muddy water dripped
from his heaving sides.
His basket was torn—and there were no flowers in it.
At once I rushed upon the three.

They made no move to hold me off.

I knocked them to the ground.

I would have kicked their faces in.

I would have stamped their faces to a pulp.

But Priscilla rose to her feet and said:

"Don't, Albert! Please don't. They can't harm me now."

I took her hand in mine.

I kissed her sweet mouth.

Then, making a sort of bed out of our coats, we carried our little green friend out of the clearing.

4

After we had gone a short way we came to a beautiful place where the trees had stood aside to make a field. A gentle hill rose to our left, a pretty little river to our right. Here a soft wind brought the scent of curious flowers. And the stars were clearer, the moon less cruel. The stars looked like tiny pieces of paper burning on the table of the sky. The moon looked like a friendly butcher leaning over his counter of clouds.

We laid the little deer in the fragrant grass.

"How are we ever going to find the road, Albert?"

I was trying to think of something else.

I thought as hard as I could.

"Perhaps we can find some of the things we want here, Priscilla," I said.

"Like a nice juicy steak maybe," she said, laughing.

"What would you like with it?"

"Isn't that a wee bit cruel, Albert?"

"No, I've been thinking. What would you—"

"Well, shoestring potatoes—just loads and loads— some nice crisp leaves of Boston lettuce, ice cold tomatoes—sliced paper-thin, a loaf of French bread—heated for one minute in a hot oven, and, of course, gallons of piping hot coffee—good, strong, boiled coffee."

"And your steak? How would you like it?"

"Three inches thick—sirloin or porterhouse—broiled under a high flame just long enough to really sear it. . . ." She sighed wistfully. "Yum yum! But you stop it now, Albert Budd— Why, you've got me so I can almost smell it!"

"You do smell it, Priscilla." As I spoke a man appeared pushing a small cart which was covered with a snowy cloth. He pushed it to within reach of her "Oh! Oh's!", bowed from the waist, and deftly snapped the covering off.

"But how! Where!" she said in a sort of choked way.

"I advise eating it while it's still hot, madam," the man said.

"I didn't realize I was so hungry myself," I said, forking a very plump veal chop onto my plate. It didn't have so much as a fleck of fat on it.

"I'll believe anything now," Priscilla said, between mouthfuls of steak.

"And why shouldn't it be easier to believe than to doubt?" I said, biting into my piece of whole-wheat bread which was covered with buckwheat honey.

The deer was quietly cropping tender shoots on the river bank. He'd had a nice swim and his coat shone beautifully in the moonlight.

"Well . . . !" Priscilla said, settling her third cup of coffee back into its saucer. "I'd be willing to invest in a few more shares of this little old world right at this minute."

"It's a wonderful world," I said. "Only sometimes people forget that almost everything has a side they can't see unless they—"

"Unless they what, Albert?"

"Unless they believe it's there."

The man was putting the used things back in the cart.

"That makes some sense," she said, "and then again—it doesn't make any sense at all."

I watched her face in the moonlight.

"How can you believe in something you have no reason to think exists?" she went on slowly.

"Have you any reason to think it doesn't?" I asked.

"Why, yes—of course. All things, admittedly, must conform to certain, fundamental logics—to what the scientists call 'the pattern of natural laws'—"

"Is it a natural law to believe in God?"

"Yes, I think it is," she answered slowly. "Man is a rational animal whose setting, cycle, life—what you want to call it—has mainly been determined in an irrational way. Therefore, ipso facto, or flibberty-flab, he tries to account for what is unaccountable around him by imagining that somewhere there is a pristine, infallible, predictable intelligence which—where am I?—at any rate, the natural law here is that man needs more to weather the kind of world he lives in than anything he can summon up out of himself."

"And that more is God?"

"Yes."

"Doesn't the man who believes in God have God?"

"I don't quite know what you mean, Albert. You must have somebody else inside you again." She was leaning back, smiling contentedly at me.

"I mean that the man who understands God is capable of being God." What does that mean?

"What on earth does that mean, Albert? You speak of understanding God as though it were . . . were either something very mysterious or something very easy."

"It is both, I think, Priscilla. How can anyone talk of faith or belief except in terms of what is mysterious? We don't say we have faith in a pumpkin pie—or that we believe in a snow storm. The thing which interests man most is to believe in something—to have faith in something—and we can only believe in what we do not understand, for the rest of it requires no belief—but only an acceptance of what we already know."

"That's a nice little idea, all fattened up by sleight-of-hand with words—"

"What does God mean?"

"Whatever you like, I suppose."

"You're dodging away now, Priscilla. If you tell me that God is an abstract idea, I can always ask you, an abstract idea of what?"

"Of God—let's say."

"Then truth is an idea of truth?"

"Not at all—except maybe for a Harvard prof—. Truth is examinable, finite, predictable—like puppies, it may romp and cavort, but the same, certain things may always be said of it."

"Would you say that there is truth in the idea of God?"

"Certainly. It is true that there is an idea or imagining which is called God."

"That's no answer, Priscilla."

"I know it isn't. What do you want me to say?—that I do or that I do not believe in God . . . ?"

"Yes."

"Why?"

"Because I want you to believe in God."

"Why?"

"Because then you would understand what I mean when I say that there is no God."

"And what would you mean!"

"That if there is a God, then there isn't a God—because there'd be no need for one."

"Ask your little inside friend to come again with that one, Albert." But she was listening very carefully.

"Who truly believes that God is standing before him?"

"Why, a lot of people, I suppose—"

"No, they believe that God is somewhere everywhere—even in the sky."

"Especially in the sky."

"But how can he be if he is standing before you?"

"That—if you will excuse me, little inside friend—sounds childish."

"But think about it for a moment."

"I have."

"No, you haven't. Because if you believe that God is standing before you, then you must know that everything which you want to happen, must happen."

"What if it's something bad . . . ?"

"With God standing before you? The moment a man believes in a sky-God or in a God who is off somewhere everywhere, then he does not sense the God who is standing before him."

"And what would you say the God who stands before you is?"

"Everything."

"That's certainly narrowing it down."

"Everything which man can imagine, dream or conceivably want to exist—"

"Will exist?"

"Does exist. How else could we conceive of them? It amazes me to think that there are people who suppose they believe in God, and yet won't believe that there are butterflies bigger than the earth, that there are fires raging at the bottom of the sea, that there are leopards made of golden wire circling the sun—"

"And these things prove there is a God?"

"Prove there isn't—because there's no need for one. On the score of being childish . . . I think it's childish to imagine that somewhere somehow is something that will punish us if we do evil, reward us if we do good. That is a monstrous idea of God. It means we can cheat, lie and kill each other with the nice comforting thought that we're stepping on the toes of something that someday maybe perhaps will fix us for it. No. God stands before everyman. When you cheat, you cheat him —when you lie, you lie to him—and when you kill, you kill him. Not in some nebulous hereafter, but at this moment, now."

"I still can't figure out who this God who stands before you is."

"He is everyman. What we do, we can only do for each other. Any dream we have, is a dream which all must share in. Any goal we set for ourselves, must be a goal for all—"

"That's kind of mushy— A kiss in time saves Diane sort of thing. The whole business gets foggier by the minute. I'm leary of this dewy-eyed lion and lamb notion—any lion I'd have any respect for would sit right down and have himself a nice dinner."

"That's beside the point."

"All right, what's the point?"

"That any man is capable of anything."

"Y.M.C.A. booklet no. 27."

"That man is the strangest thing in the world."

"No. 28."

"That man has possibles greater than anyone has imagined for God."

"Please, Albert—I don't know your little insider's name— let's talk about something else. We can't be stuck out here in the middle of the woods all our lives—though I must admit you did all right with our supper."

THE GOD WHO STANDS BEFORE YOU. . . .

Who is the God who stands before you?

Everyman is.

Everyman is that God.

EVERYMAN IS THE GOD WHO STANDS BEFORE YOU.

"Albert. . . ."

"Yes, Priscilla."

"Are we alone now?"

"Alone?"

"All right. I guess we are," she said. "What are we going to do?"

"Wait for daylight, I guess."

"Yes, I guess we'll have to." She yawned, stretching her legs out.

"Are you getting chilly?"

"A little. . . ."

I put my coat over her.

"You go to sleep for a while," I said. "I'll sit up and watch."

"Watch what?" she asked sleepily.

Then she was asleep.

I wondered about things.

She was beautiful in the soft light.

I heard a noise in back of me.

I turned around.

There was nothing there.

And I couldn't see our little deer anymore.

5

A voice said: "Don't go too near."

I looked about me but could see no one.

"There is a place you may not enter.

"There is a gate which is not to be opened, a throne where only the damned may sit, a city from which no traveler may ever return."

"Who are you?" I asked, hoping Priscilla would not awaken.

There was no answer.
WHO ARE YOU?
What is the answer to that!

6

While Priscilla slept I sat and wondered about the world. I wondered what the stars were. I wondered what the life of man on this earth was supposed to be.

I wondered whether the life of man might not be a separate thing—a thing which would live on when he was dead.

I wondered where the life of man on this earth went when it was no longer what we think it is.

I wondered why the life of man on this earth had never been understood by anyone.

I wondered why what being dead was had never been understood by anyone alive.

I wondered if the dead knew.

Where are the dead?

I wondered what the trees were thinking.

I wondered if the trees knew something we do not know.

I wondered if Priscilla was asleep—or if rather it wasn't myself who stood unwaking there in the cold, dead light of the watching moon.

I wondered if perhaps we both were not asleep—because it might be that in her dreams she imagined me, and in doing so gave herself a life in what I was dreaming.

I wondered if Priscilla dreaming was not a Priscilla who tasted death.

I wondered if to dream was not to have knowledge of death.

I wondered if what we consider life may not in reality be death.

I wondered if perhaps when we 'die' we will not come into our real life.

WHERE ARE THE 'DEAD'?

Why must man believe that first there is life, and then there is being dead?

Isn't it more logical to think that first there is death—and then we shall be alive?

What would be the purpose of living if we had only to die?

How can life become death?

I wondered if Priscilla dreaming was not a Priscilla who tasted what being alive meant.

I wondered if to dream was not to have knowledge of life.

Is it not obvious that the purpose of 'dying' is that we may live?

Is it not obvious that the purpose in all things is to bring to life?

Is it not obvious that it is death which is not understood?

Is it not obvious that when we shall live we shall have understanding of all things?

Is it not logical that we should go from death into life?

What would be the purpose of living if we had only to die?

Who shall say that there is no purpose in being what we are on this earth?

Who shall say that the purpose of God is to bring death?

In the halls of eternity what noise does the little minute which has passed make?

In the cathedrals of space what murmur reaches the ears of the awesome runners who wait there?

Not what shall we do.

Not what shall we think, or feel, or want.

But what are we?

Whence do we come?

Whither are we going?

What are we?

What does being a man mean?

What does it mean to live?

What does it mean to die?

WHAT DOES BEING A MAN MEAN!

Then I felt sort of tired. There was a numbness in my fore-head and I had the strange feeling that someone was going to sleep there—that someone I had never seen had been talking to me.

It must be a million miles to Visalia and Fairwood, I thought sleepily.

It must have been a million years ago that I snatched the last glass of water out of Medrid's fat little hand.

It must have . . .

"Are you asleep, Albert?"

"What— Oh, why, no— No, I'm not, Priscilla."

"Aren't you getting very tired doubled-up in that tiny cart?"

I crawled out of it. Very quickly the man appeared and started to push it off.

"Mister . . . !" Priscilla called after him.

"Yes, madam?" he answered.

"Can you tell us how we can reach the road?"

"The road?"

"Yes, the highway to Shrewsbury. We have our car parked on it," I said.

"The highway to Shrewsbury?"

"That's right." Priscilla said.

"Is it macadam, madam?"

"No, concrete."

"Then what?"

"What do you mean— Then what?" Priscilla asked.

"If it isn't concrete?"

"But it is concrete."

"I thought I heard you say no concrete."

"I said, No comma concrete. . . ."

"That's what I thought— No comma concrete. No concrete, right?"

"Oh—" Priscilla said.

"Do you live around here?" I asked.

"No. Just now I'm sleeping in a car down the road a-piece—"

"What color?"

"Orange—with maybe a little mocha in it."

"Oh—" I said.

"What's the matter? Prejudiced?"

"No, not at all. It's probably very nice."

"It was good enough for my father," he said loudly.

"Was his that color, too?"

"Was his what that color?"

"Why, his car, of course."

"He never had a car. What would he be doing with a car down in the water?" And he started to push off again. Just then a bush broke into flame and we could see what he meant by his father being satisfied with that color too.

"Oh—" Priscilla said.

I felt like saying, Make that two 'ohs.'

"Up in the north of Ireland," he explained, "my great, great ancestors lived on nothing but chocolate bars for many generations—"

"But what color is the car?" I asked hopefully.

"One failure of the potato crop after another," he said. "There was some talk that the keening of the kümmelbesotted colleens who klegged in the cordavasated fields made the eyes of the potatoes run so with tears that they couldn't see to grow, though those which did come up were a big saving on salt. Father still never had a car, mate."

"But the car you're sleeping in . . . ?"

"Oh, that car! I told you once."

"Please tell us again!" Priscilla said.

"I think it has something in the trunk."

"Robin's egg?"

"No, I think it's a brutally dismembered body—"

"But what color is it?"

"I tink it's a white goil from up Newport way—there's something blue seeping out around de edges." And he put the blazing bush into his cart and made off whistling 'An old flame never dies.'

"Sometimes I get a little weary of this sort of thing," Priscilla said wearily.

"What do you mean, Priscilla?"

"What under heaven shouldn't I mean! If mother could only see me now! stuck out in the middle of the woods a thousand miles from nowhere watching an orange-colored man hauling a burning bush around— Oh . . . !"

"Don't forget he brought us our suppers, Priscilla," I reminded her.

"That's another thing I want to talk to you about, Mr. Albert Hubert Leander Cauldwaller Budd," she said. She wasn't so weary-sounding now. "How do you get me to believe such things? You know as well as I do that it's ridiculous. Why is it that when I'm with you—and these preposterous things are happening—that I hardly notice how preposterous they are?"

"You enjoyed your steak, didn't you?" I asked.

She burst out laughing. "Somehow that's the funniest thing —*your* bringing *me* back to earth."

I went over and sat down beside her. "Are you sure you're not getting cold, Priscilla?" I said.

"Yes, I'm sure, but put your arms around me anyway." She snuggled up against me. Her hair smelled like orchids look. "Albert—sometimes I'm afraid. I'm almost as afraid as mother was when I told her about the green deer. . . ."

"But why should he frighten anyone?"

"Because—well, because it isn't possible for anything like that to happen, Albert," she said slowly.

I watched a star fall.

How can a star 'fall'?

"Because, Albert, it's . . . it's sort of crazy."

Why are you crying, Priscilla!

"I mean I'm afraid," she said, and I sensed that something in her was moving away from me.

Suddenly I felt angry. I don't know why I did. It was a kind of anger I had never felt before. "Of course you're afraid," I said. "Why shouldn't you be afraid? Why shouldn't you think it's crazy to believe in a green deer? All your life you have been taught to believe in only what you can use—to set on the table, to put in the bank, to build a house with. What possible use would a green deer be to anyone? Who would believe in a man with a blazing bush in his cart? Then let me tell you that it is beliefs just such as these that are the only hope of the world. Let me tell you that until men are ready to believe in the green deer and the strange carter, we shall not lift our noses above the bloody mess we have made of our living. No man who honors Caesar but dishonors God. No man who wilfully snuffles and roots in the slimy rubble of this hatred and greed but shall be stained beyond the idiot dog which slobbers up his own filth. Let me tell you that it is not getting along in the world to eat when your neighbor is hungry; to add to your income when he has nothing; to build a new house when he is homeless. There is no bread but the bread which shall feed your least neighbor; there is no possession but the possession which you shall share in common with him; there is no dwelling but the dwelling whose doors shall be opened joyfully to him.

"Wars and the plague-sores left by wars shall not be ended until mankind turns from the murder *which is practiced every day by everyone.*"

"Albert, please— You're just getting yourself all upset. . . ."

"It's crazy to believe, is it? Let me tell you that it exceeds the wildest insanity to accept some of the things which the world takes for granted—

"That men should starve each other.

"That men should hate one another because their skins are of a different color.

"That men should hate one another because their races are not the same.

"That men should kill one another!"

I didn't feel angry anymore. I felt very strong and at peace with myself.

"If to believe in what is good and beautiful is a crime in the eyes of the world, then, why . . ." That's enough of that.

"That's enough now, Albert."

"I'm sorry, Priscilla—I don't know what gets into me."

"Your little friend, obviously," she said, cuddling up again.

It was very still. Even the trees had stopped singing. There was stillness over everything. The stars bent low to watch. I could hear the beating of our two hearts.

"Are you going to marry me, Priscilla?" I asked.

She was silent for a long moment.

"I don't know," she answered softly. "I really don't know, Albert."

"We could be very happy together," I said.

She kissed me on the cheek. "You're the nicest person in the world," she said.

"You're the nicest person in the world," I said, putting my lips on her forehead.

"Then we're the nicest persons in the world," she said. "Maybe . . . maybe that's what frightens me, Albert." She was quiet. The trees were not singing. "Oh, Albert . . . ! we're so defenseless— What weapons have we? What could we do to fight against them?"

"Fight against who, Priscilla?"

"My mother, your sister—even the strangers in the house we'd live in. Maybe if we were ten years younger— Maybe if . . . well, maybe if it were possible for us to have a normal life together." She was crying now.

"But none of that means anything, Priscilla. Won't it be normal to be happy? Won't people love us when they see how happy we are with each other? Don't forget that you are able to walk now, darling."

"Oh, you sweet! It seems that everything I do must end by hurting you in some way. You see— O how can I say it? how can I make you understand?—Albert, I . . . I don't want to walk ever again."

"But why? I thought—"

"I know, my love. You thought that when I could walk I would feel whole again. But I don't! It's . . . it's hideous that I should be able to walk. There's something monstrous, something unclean about it— Because . . . because a cripple should not walk— Because only something I can't understand in me can walk now. My body is still crippled. Oh, Albert, can't you see that one of the least things a cripple would want is to be able to walk? Oh, don't you see that for me to walk is only to flaunt my deformity like a prostitute her paint—like uncovering a horrible cancer in order to convince someone that I am without disease. . . ."

"We can make your body well again, Priscilla," I said, trying hard to keep her from knowing that I was crying too.

"No, Albert," she said softly. "Perhaps, if I had your faith —but I haven't."

"Then it won't make any difference. I love you, Priscilla. I would love you if you were—if you were a tree or a leper."

She cried in a funny little almost happy way.

"I would love you if you were a stone in this field—or a toad croaking on the bank of that river."

"Albert. . . ."

"Yes, Priscilla?"

"We . . . we would never be able to sleep together."

"Then I'll move my bed up just as close as it'll go—"

"Sweet!" And she managed a choked laugh. "We shall never be able to do what people do who want children."

"Then we'll adopt some— First a little girl, then . . . well, maybe another little girl— Oh, please, please, Priscilla . . . !"

She put her salty-tasting lips against mine.

Then she said very softly:

"I shall be happy and proud to be your wife, Albert."

7

Now a beautiful singing filled the forest. I stood up and raised my face to the stars. How wonderful it is to be alive! I thought.

I reached up and picked a star out of the sky.

It felt smooth and cold in my hand.

It looked very pretty in Priscilla's hair.

I got a bad itch under my left arm-pit. When I scratched it only seemed to make the itching worse.

"It'll be daylight in another minute, Al," Priscilla said.

Al!

She took the star from her hair. The glow was beginning to fade out of it.

"Make a wish," I said.

"I wish," she said softly, "that we might be together here like this forever."

"I'm very sleepy," the star said. "Put me back now."

I put it back.

"Thanks, Budd," it said, starting to snore at once.

Like a dim, green gate opening . . . the trees swung back and the clearing filled with girls in blue, transparent dresses

who danced in the most lovely way for us. Each led a grace-
ful animal on a golden chain . . . white lions with red wings,
green bears with yellow faces, purple leopards spotted with
silver, black tigers with orange stripes. And each of the animals had a boy-angel riding on its back. And the angels were
laughing and talking together, waving their little suitcases
about like boxes of happiness.

The more I scratched the more I had to scratch. I'd already
worn a hole in my shirt.

Then the girls formed in a great line. Standing on each
other's shoulders. Still dancing. (Or dancing still, rather).

"What in the world are they doing?" Priscilla asked.

"Building a pyramid," I answered.

They had it up higher than the trees now.

Their dresses fluttered like the hands of the sky reaching
down to touch them.

Then the whole thing just started to float up. . . . The lions
and bears and tigers and leopards singing about a Child of
Wondrous Design, and the angels hopping from back to back
in their excitement at going home.

Came the dawn.

We started to leave the woods.

"Al, there's the car!"

It was just around a bush.

"Why, it was just around this bush," I said, "the whole
time."

"You should have beat around a bit more," the bush said.

8

"Hiyuh, folks," My Agent said.

" 'Lo there," George Arliss said.

"Top of the morning," the stranger said.

The three of them were sitting in the back seat of the car.

"Meet our friend Liederkranz," Skujellifeddy said.

We accepted the introduction. I pushed the lever and we were on our way again.

"What are you doing way out here?" I asked.

"Thumbing up to Liedy's farm," My Agent explained.

"I've got a gland farm," Mr. Liederkranz said.

"A simply gland farm. Ha. Ha," Mr. Arliss said.

"Rejuvenation," Skujellifeddy said.

"Anyway, that explains the monkey," Priscilla said.

It was sitting on Mr. Liederkranz' knee.

"Nice country," My Agent said.

"Lot of nice trees," George Arliss said.

"Master Bates likes trees," Mr. Liederkranz said.

"Who's Master Bates?" I asked.

"Look back here and you'll soon find out," Skujellifeddy said. "For Christ's sake, Liedy, can't you get him to stop for a minute?"

I almost ran off the road when I saw what he was doing in the mirror.

"All night long," George Arliss said sadly.

"It's the smell of that mole excites him," Mr. Liederkranz said. "Here's where we take our short-cut."

I stopped the car. They got out.

"Ah," My Agent said. He scratched himself very hard all over.

"Make that two 'ahs,'" George Arliss said. He also scratched himself very hard all over. Then he took his mole out and scratched it too.

"Well, so long, kids," Skujellifeddy said.

"Many happy returns," George Arliss said.

"If you're ever in the market for a gland," Mr. Liederkranz said, "just think of me."

They walked off into the woods. Mr. Liederkranz, with the monkey perched on his shoulder, reached up and grabbed a branch and started to swing up. My Agent quickly grabbed the farmer's tail, George Arliss grabbed My Agent's hand, and they swung up through the trees.

Master Bates was taking up where he had left off.

I got out and went around and opened the trunk.

It was empty. Except that on the bottom was the imprint of a giant half-pear.

9

When we finally got to Mabelle Frances', there was a poster tacked to the door. It read: CHICKEN POX.

Medrid's face in the window explained why they needed the sign. As we drove off, he waved his glass of water at me. I pushed the gas-feed to the floor and held it there.

"Al."

"Yes, honey."

"Love me?"

"I love you with all my heart."

"Do you love me as much as—"

"As what?"

"As a hungry boy eating mince pie?"

"I love you as much as ten hungry boys eating pumpkin pie."

"Don't you like mince?"

"No, not very. Do you?"

"Mmm. Do you like sawdust?"

"I suppose so. Do you?"

"I'm crazy about it for some reason."

"Where did you have sawdust?"

"I didn't. Read a story in *Mademoiselle* once, about a lumber camp out in Oregon somewhere. I don't know why—somehow I could just smell that wonderful smell of sawdust."

"How do you know it's wonderful if you never actually smelled it?"

"Oh, I've smelled itsy-bitsy sawdust here and there—the little you get in a woodpile."

I pushed her chair around an old sheep that was sleeping under a tree. We still had about two miles to the place I'd picked for our picnic.

"Al."

"Yes, Cludgy."

"Cludgy?"

"I sorta made it up. Don't you want me to call you Cludgy?"

"No."

"Boody?"

"No."

"Deggy?"

"No."

"Piddy?"

"I should say not! What ever possessed you to think up such ridiculous names?"

"I don't know. Sometimes when I'm thinking about you, I just sort of . . . sort of—"

"Sort of what?"

"Just sort of."

"Oh, you sweet silly!" She raised her face and I bent over. When our lips parted, she said, "Call me whatever you like—they're all lovely names."

"Are you getting tired?"

"Of course not. Do you love me as much as . . . as a big bunch of nice, fresh watercress?"

"I love you as much as a brown puppy with a white star on his forehead."

"Do you have a favorite dog?"

"The Seeing-Eye kind."

"They are wonderful, aren't they? I like cats better."

"I'm a little afraid of cats."

"You're just not used to them."

"I never had a dog either."

"We'll have seven dogs, Al. And we'll name them after the days of the week."

"You can have all the cats you want, Boody."

"Make that Cludgy."

"All right. Cludgy."

"No. What was that other one?"

"Piddy?"

"No, that's not it."

"Deggy?"

"No. Didn't you have another?"

"Mimi?"

"Mimi! Good heavens! Where'd you get that?"

"It just sort of—"

"Call me . . . let's see . . . call me . . . I know, call me Chaleen."

"Chaleen!"

"Why, what's the matter, Albert?"

"Oh, nothing. I just—"

"You just sort of, hunh?"

"I guess so."

"Don't you like it?"

"What?"

"To call me Chaleen?"

"No, I don't."

"Why not?"

"I just—"

"Okay. If you did like sawdust, Al, what would your favorite tree for sawdust be?"

"The willow, I guess."

"How nice! The willow's my favorite too."

"Which would be Tuesday?"

"Tuesday?"

"Which dog."

"Oh. Well, let's name our water spaniel Tuesday."

"I want him named Saturday."

"Why Saturday?"

"They're sort of sad like."

"I get it. What day will your airedale be?"

"I don't like airedales."

"Shall I wear my hair short?"

"Long!"

"Okay. Okay. Do you like cottage cheese and peaches?"

"No. Cream."

"Cottage cheese and cream?"

"No. Peaches."

"Peaches and cream."

A cow walked up and sniffed the back of my neck. She had very long, hard horns. I scratched her forehead. She snorted, almost blowing my red scarf off. As we went over the hill, she was digging her feet into the ground.

"Too bad we didn't have a bucket," I said.

"Why? Did you want to kick it?" she asked, letting her breath out in a deep sigh.

"No, we could have milked that cow."

"Mr. Cow, you mean. Isn't that that Glasshoe over there?"

"Yes, I think it is," I said. "Hello, Mr. Glasshoe."

He raised his head from his work to smile at us.

"I've just figured out a way to invent a bass drum," he said. "After you have stretched your skin up good, hit anything that is big enough hard enough and if your idea is sound you'll get it."

He dabbed some more gilt paint on the stump. There were about twenty already painted, and maybe twice that many still to be painted.

"Why are you putting gold paint on these stumps, Mr. Glasshoe?" I asked.

"If murder can be thought a breach of manners," he answered, "what excuse then for Eustace O'Gruell who kindled a fire under his aged ma. . . . Yet as he said she was just an old pot anyway and if the rabbit hadn't barked we'da got that darn hound."

A tree fell near us. Mr. Pinklady had taken only three swings with the ax to get it down.

If these two really put their minds to it, I thought, America will look like a place where a couple giants up overhead in the sky were having a fistfight—and knocking one another's gold teeth out.

As I shoved off again, Mr. Glasshoe called after us: "For the fuddle is an appalling beast who assumes that the world is full of elbows whereas we assert the reverse to be true. . . . So why be fuddles? Are you?"

I pushed her chair around a young man who was sitting in the middle of the path. A very beautiful woman was standing beside him, her hand on his bent shoulder.

"Tell me what to do, mister," he said in a funny, choked voice.

"I'll be glad to if I can," I said, stopping the chair.

"I'm going to kill her," he said.

"Shush, Philip," she said soothingly.

"Shush, is it!" He sprang to his feet and struck her in the face. She slumped to the ground, a red stain appearing at the corners of her mouth. "You dirty, vicious bitch! You stinking, rotten slut!"

I threw my arms around him. He did not struggle, instead he went so limp and trembling I felt somehow ashamed to be stopping him from doing what he wanted to do.

"You can let him go now," the woman said, getting up off the ground. "He won't hurt me again."

She was the most beautiful woman I had ever seen. There was so much purity and—there isn't any word—that I felt like dropping to my knees.

I let Philip go.

"Oh, I won't, eh!" he shouted. And he ran over like someone possessed and hit her another savage blow in the face. This time she didn't go down. He hit her again. Her nose was bleeding now.

"Albert! For God's sake! stop him!" Priscilla cried.

Before I could do anything, the woman took a tiny gun from her blouse and shot him. As he sank down, she fired again.

She turned to face us. She was smiling.

"Nothing very serious," she said. "Just his legs—he'll be walking again in a few days."

"Slimy,——, decayed,—— snotty-pig," Philip said. "Sure. Sure, I'll be walking again in a few days. Tell them where you'll have me walking to. Go on! I dare you to tell them!"

"Certainly I'll tell them, Philip—if you really want me to," she said in a low, lovely voice.

Blood was dripping down into his shoe tops, but he didn't seem to notice. His face looked like a piece of sick wood.

"She makes me rape women," he said in a cold, dead voice. "She makes me rape them—while she watches. Then . . . then—"

"Yes, Philip," she said, smiling. "Then?"

"Then she chokes them to death," he said.

He was beginning to sob in a hopeless way.

She still had the gun in her hand.

Her eyes turned to look at Priscilla.

"This might be interesting, Philip," she said so softly I wondered if she had really said it.

Philip turned to look at Priscilla.

"She's a cripple, Helen!"

"I know," she whispered. "Yes, I know."

The young man pushed himself onto his hands and knees —then he started to crawl toward her.

It seemed to take hours. Then he was putting his arms around her legs—

He pulled her down. Blood smeared her dress from his wounded legs.

She allowed the gun to drop out of her fingers.

"Oh, Philip . . . Philip . . ." she moaned. "Oh, my poor darling. . . ." Then she gave a little scream. "You're hurting me, Philip! Please, Philip, please!"

"Dirty filthy bitch— You dirty slimy bitch— It's your turn now."

Her eyes were looking up at us. They were like strange sins. They were full of pain. They were full of tears.

I pushed the chair a little while in silence.

Finally I said, "We're almost there, Priscilla."

"I don't feel much like it now," she said.

"Oh, we shouldn't worry too much about them," I said. "He should have taken his problem to Mr. Anthony when it first started—saved himself a lot of trouble now."

"I'm surprised to hear that you listen to the radio," she said.

"Oh, I don't—when I can help it, anyway. When I lived with my sister, I couldn't help it. Mabelle Frances thought of taking the problem of Leroy to the Good Will Court at one time."

"And why didn't she?"

"Mike fright, I think," I said. I could have said that it ran in the family—when I thought of Karlanne's little playmate.

I lifted her out and placed her on my coat.

"Al."

"Yes, Prill."

"Prill. I like that—Prill. Do you remember when we were in the cave?"

I took out all the picnic things and arranged them nicely in front of her.

"Yes. I remember."

"When you saw me naked . . . ?"

"Yes, Priscilla, I remember."

"Did you . . . did you really want me, Albert?"

I started to unwrap the sandwiches.

"I don't know," I said.

"Have you ever been with a woman?"

"Why, yes, lots of times."

"No, I mean, have you ever had one in the Biblical sense?"

"I never got beyond the first few chapters," I said.

"Uh. . . . How did you know what I meant when I asked you if you wanted me?"

"I don't know," I said.

"But you did?"

I got up and went after one of the sandwiches the ants were carrying away. "Yes, I did."

"And you know what I'm talking about now?"

"Yes."

"Then why do you pretend not to?"

"I don't. I don't know how to talk about it."

"But we must talk about it."

"You said in the forest that we couldn't be together like that."

"I lied to you. I don't really know."

"Why?"

"I don't know. Ever since that first day in the orchard, I've . . . I've been afraid . . . afraid to face it."

"Face it how? I don't know what you mean, Priscilla."

"I . . . I thought that if we did it—you might hate me."

"Hate you? Why would I hate you?"

"Because it might not be nice for you," she said in a whisper.

"We'll just forget about it— We won't have to do it."

"But I'll want to. Oh, Albert, until we do . . . until I know whether—"

A bird called up in a tree somewhere and the ants were back for the sandwich.

"Until I know whether we can really be husband and wife, I'll always be . . . so terribly afraid."

"Then we'll do it now," I said.

2

I watched a cloud. It had the shape of a tall-headed child sitting in a high chair. Another floated up—it hadn't much of a shape at all.

"I'll come for you a week from next Wednesday," I said.

"Mother is home all day Wednesdays. Would Friday do as well for you?"

"I don't like Friday much," I said.

"Then, Saturday."

"Saturday will be fine, Priscilla."

"Oh, Albert—"

I sealed her mouth with a kiss.

"We'll have no trouble at all," I said. "People are eloping every day."

"I wasn't thinking of that—"

"Bivalve is just the place for a honeymoon. It was just made for honeymooning."

A man walked up and said: "Can you tell me how to get to— Say, what's been going on here? What have you been doing to her anyway?"

"It's all right. We were just having a picnic," Priscilla said.

"You don't look as though you'd been having a picnic," he said. "You look more as though you'd just seen a ghost."

"Where was it you wanted to go?" I asked.

"I'll find it," he said, walking away quickly. He stopped some distance away and watched us.

"Albert," Priscilla said quietly.

"Yes, darling," I said.

"I wish I could believe in God," she said.

"We'll have lots of time to think of that later on," I said. "Just now we must think of our elopement— The greatest and most wonderful plan on earth!"

"I love you, Albert," Priscilla said. "I love you with all my heart."

HOUSE OF THE FROWNING HEART

Saturday had the slowest coming of any day since the world began.

At one point I thought that it wouldn't come at all—that in some way time had gone to sleep.

But at last it did come.

And it was very beautiful.

The sun shone.

The air was clean.

How nice it must be in Bivalve now! I thought.

My scalp tingled at the notion of *our being in Bivalve together!*

I started to walk down the street to the train.

We'd worked everything out to the last detail.

I'd gone over every detail a thousand times. Not that anything could possibly go wrong.

Priscilla waiting beside the white gate in the orchard—It was as simple as that. *Priscilla waiting to become Mrs. Budd.*

Hello, Mr. Saturday!

Boy! am I glad to see you!

I started to run to Grand Central. Turning a sudden corner I ran into a fat man carrying a lot of bundles. There was a great breaking of glass and a terrible whiskey smell.

There wasn't anything to pick up and it was pretty bad to see a grown man crying in the street like that. Right away some bellhops with sponges came up and set to work. As I turned the next corner, I saw that they had the fat man's pants off and were wringing them out into a bucket.

I reached in my pocket for the ring. Not in the side, not in the hip, breast, watch— Wait a minute! I started to run back. I had gone about ten blocks when I found the ring. It was in my hand.

The hair settled down on my head again.

Well, anyway, I've got plenty of time.

My train wouldn't be leaving for six hours.

Take it easy.

I went into a bookstore and asked for *Spill of Desire.* The clerk leered and reached under the counter.

"That will be twenty dollars," he said shiftyeyedly.

"Why, this is an outrage," I said, reaching for the wallet which I hadn't opened since Mr. Lyon returned it to me in the dark alley.

"It's an outrageous book," the clerk said lecherously.

"It is not," I told him. "And I should know—I wrote it."

There were five women in the shop.

When I came to in the store room, I seemed all right except

for some bluish bruises on my shoulders and hips. It wasn't until later I discovered that my zipper wouldn't work anymore.

"That will be 672 dollars," the clerk said bad-humoredly.

"The O.P.A.'ll fix you," I said, taking out my billfold.

"I'll need the W.P.A. to fix up the store," he said shifty-blackeyedly.

As I gave him the money, a note fell out of the wallet. It read:

'Your underwear's on backwards.'

And when I looked, it was.

The store looked like Mr. Pinklady had been around.

I started off to the train again. I better just get my ticket and wait in the station, I thought.

And this time I'll take a taxi.

I went into a stationery store and bought a little flag. I waved it at the first taxi that went by. It went by. I waved it at the next one. It went by too.

I sat down on the steps of a house to wait for another. The door of the house opened, and a voice said:

"Won't you come in for a minute, Mr. Budd?"

Well, all right, but only for a minute, I thought.

2

The door opened on a room full of people sitting at long tables eating clams. I walked over to a man in a checked suit and said: "Who was it wanted to see me?" He put a knife under a shell and twisted, then he swished the knife around inside the half-shell. "They're Little Necks," he said, holding it out to me. "Go ahead—try one." I put it in my mouth. Oh. Oh! I looked all around. There weren't any potted trees here. I'd certainly hate to get one with a big neck, I thought, as I nearly choked to death swallowing it. The man was busy with his knife again and nobody else paid any attention to me. I guess they changed their mind about wanting to see me—I'll just slip out again. It's obvious that whoever it was changed their mind about wanting to see me. I opened the door. I held it open. The door opened on a room full of little girls sitting on three-legged stools making artificial flowers. But I just walked through that door from the street. I walked over to a little girl with black hair. "Who is in charge here?" I asked. "Somebody wanted to see me." She didn't lift her eyes from her work. "You see, little girl, I have a train to catch. Somebody here wanted to see me. I just now walked in that door from the street. Only—" She pressed a white rose into my hand. "My name is Winifred," she said. "I am twelve years old. My favorite actor is Anthony Eden. I can't bear some of these new luxury taxes. My favorite state is suspended animation. My favorite bliss is wedded. I sleep in my pajama bottoms." I walked over to another little girl with red hair. She handed me the purple daffodil she had been working on. "I'll be eleven next Wednesday," she said. "My real name is Marceen, but anybody I'm really fond of calls me B.T.—and since I like you oh so desperately you may call me Lucille. Mama says if I drink up all my Ovaltine, I'll get nice big strong teeth like Eleanor R.'s and go all over the world rubbing noses with people. My favorite, ex-living-president is Herbert Hoover. My favorite bull-writer is Hemingway. I slumber in the raw." The next child handed me a black lily. "Princess Michael is my title-o," she said. "I bed in my robes of rayon-o. I want to be a poet when I grow up-o, and work for the O.W.I.-o— and lick every reactionary boot in sight-o. Don't you just adore people with nice, weather-cock integrity-o?" It didn't even surprise me that the flowers they made were real ones. The girl with the golden hair held the door open for me. Just as I passed her she gave me something which surprised me not a little. "You'll have to learn to take a goose better than that," the man sitting under a naked, two-hundred watt bulb stripped

to the waist and bleeding at the corners of his mouth said. The
three young men standing over him began to sing O Susanna
and every time they said banjo they slashed him across the
face with a cat-o-nine-tails. They said it twenty-one times.
Their white suits were immaculate. "Please help me," I said.
"I have to catch a train."—"You won't like it," the young man
under the light said. "I thought I would—once."—"What
won't I like?" I asked. "Being introduced to the most beautiful woman in the world. She'll make you want to go out and
change everything—destroy all that's degraded and vicious
and shoddy. She'll make you want to go out and fight against
oppression and evil and sloth and cruelty—batter down all
that's smug and vain and petty. Oh she's the spiritual type all
right." He had to stop because they had begun to sing O We're
the Jolly Lads of the Writers' War Board and every time they
said kill 'em or cash-register they slashed him. The cat was
beginning to miaow and one of its tails was working loose. I
opened the door and walked into a room where a lot of people
were waiting in queue in front of a booth with black silk cur-
tains. I got in queue and said to the man in front of me: "How
do you get out of here?" He looked at me a long time, then
he answered. "You're afraid, aren't you?"—"No, I'm not,"
I said. "It's just that I've an important appointment to keep."
He looked at me a long time again, then he said: "I wouldn't
worry too much about it if I were you."—"But I've got to get
away from here," I told him. "This is the most important day
in my life." He bit into his sandwich. "I don't doubt that," he
said. "Have a bite." I took as small a one as I could and still
be polite. It tasted like cantaloupe and rice pudding. "My wife
makes a pretty good sandwich, hunh?" he said. "I've got three
grown children. All in the old swim for themselves. My oldest
boy, Snowden, is a green grocer, but he'll get on to it in time.
Werner, he's a Yale man, is writing a novel about two men
who are in love with the same woman. He gives it a couple

unusual twists—because one of the men is in love with the other man too, and the woman is in love with a policeman's horse. My youngest, Thomas Myles Hessian Joseph, writes reviews for *The Nation*—got off to a bad start by falling on his head when he was three weeks old—though I will say this for him, he refused to study the mating habits of the Afghanistan glow worm for the Guggenheims. Why don't you put it on a chair somewhere?" I had to admit that the goose which the golden haired girl had given me was getting pretty heavy. "I think I will," I said. I put it down on a chair near a small boy who was fondling a dead cockroach with his thumb. I'll bet you can't wait until you're old enough for a mole, I thought. The goose cackled and the boy quickly put his hand under it and pulled out an egg. "Oh, mama!" he called, scampering off, "this is the one! This is the one you wanted papa to find!" I couldn't blame him for being excited —it's not every day you find a goose laying golden eggs. But now it was my turn. I walked into the booth. It was too dark in there to see much of anything, but I heard something breathing on the other side of a latticed partition. It was just light enough to see that I was supposed to kneel on a stool beside the tiny, window-like opening. After a while a voice said: "Well?" I said: "I hope you can tell me how to get out of this place. It's terribly important that I catch a train."— "Where had you planned to go?" the muffled voice asked. "Into the country. The woman I love is waiting there for me to carry her off," I told it. "To carry her off where?"—"To Bivalve—that's in New Jersey—I was born there—so we can get married." There was a little pause. "I see," it said slowly. "You plan to make this woman your wife. Have you . . . uh, ever had impure thoughts of her? Have you ever pictured in the cesspool of your mind . . . uh, actions which are not calculated to advance what we may term . . . uh, the spiritual—as opposed to the basely carnal? Have you ever . . .

uh—"—"I don't know what you're talking about," I interrupted. "All I know right now is that I must go to her—she'll
be waiting for me—and neither you nor anybody else can stop
me."—"I see," it said after a moment. "Yours is an excit-
able nature. You must try not to disturb yourself more than
events indicate. Is this . . . uh, woman one who would wait
for you if it should chance that you are . . . uh, delayed in
coming to her?"—"Of course Priscilla would wait!" I said.
"But I have no intention of making her."—"You haven't? A
strange attitude for a bridegroom to take," it said. "Have you
ever wondered about life? About why there is no—ah, but I
better not phrase it that way. Let me ask you some personal
questions. Answer them silently, in your own heart. Have you
ever felt so lonely that you wanted to run into the street and
implore the first person you met to say one comforting word
to you?"—"I have to catch that train, I tell you—"—"Have
you ever been so afraid that you awakened screaming in the
grim, pallid hours of the night? Have you ever felt so sickened
by what you saw around you that you wanted to vomit on the
brightest and most pristine of their altars?"—"Please! You
don't understand—Priscilla believes in me! Priscilla is waiting by the little white gate—"—"Have you ever felt so an-
gered by the merciless butchery of human beings that you
wanted to tear the throats out of these pious liars who perpetu-
ate it in the name of country or flag or some other d—n fraud?"
—"They even bring God into it," I said. "Have you forgotten
that you have a train to catch?" the voice said. "Ha. Ha. We
are trivial fools, aren't we?"—"No, I haven't forgotten," I answered. "But I don't believe you will help me—"—"Pompous
little fools who imagine that because we denounce the guilt
and madness of others, we are not equally guilty and mad
ourselves. Let me tell you—let me warn you—we are going
into a time of blackness and evil beyond the power of any living man to imagine. Those around you aren't cruel and de-

based because they are poor or misled or afraid or ignorant of the light—not for a moment—to h—l with the nonsense! They are as they are because they are mad, insane, teched in the haid, looney, loco, batty as a bird dog. And, my fine-feathered little friend, that's exactly the way they were meant to be. That's the lay, the leed, the precious loot—for the rest of it, molasses and an angel with the mumps. Most folks—ladies and gentlemen, fellow countermen, wearers of the striped drawers with the drop-leaf bottom, eaters of the lazy mordus fly, sleepers in those spoodunalized beds with the kerbas attachment—O mourners. . . . (Are you listening out there in Detroit!) O ulitenous lice on the big flabby fanny of the universe, do you heah me!—Most folks imagine that up on top somewhere, maybe picking their proud noses on a cloud, are a few brave souls who are someday, somehow, somefun, sometimes I'm happy, somebody stole my quail, summer is acumin in, some are fat and some are lean, but my pigeon Sarah's jest downright mean, in some manner, by some method, device, waying, baying, faying maneuver going to bring everybody up to their level. Didn't I tell you! Who could ever dream up a crazier idea? Who in the name of God wants any but the most filthy, sordid, useless, sloppy, depraved and wretched of levels to live on? How could we breathe otherwise? What ever in the world could we take pleasure in? or be proud of? or find to hate or love or weep over or get hot-pants about? Where is this stinking higher realm of life I've heard so much mooning over? Who ever lived with more grace or to a surer design than the mud-caked sow which gorges herself until her legs buckle under her—and so sinks to blissful sleep? For isn't the aim of life to drop our young into the near-est bog-hole, and so fulfilled and fulfilling, pursue our way into the soft, embracing shadow—where there is no desire or pain or remembering?" It stopped for a minute, but I didn't see any point in my saying anything. "It is a mess, isn't it?"

the voice went on. "If you want a tip right out of the horse's mouth—go dab-smack home and blow your brains out. That's —and what a quaint word for any of us!—the only honorable thing to do." Then it started a sort of laughing sing-song: "O spirit with the elepatted bejus, pray for us. O mother of the whirlwind and the ulcerated wootis, pray for us. O semper fidelis with the nickel-plated deekas, pray for us. O e pluribus unibus, O star of plunder, stare of the benighted, pray for us. O speelshanked clown with the fiery tights, pray for us. O vunegrinned leper with the sparkling sores of horror, pray for us. O O, pray for us, O O-O, pray for us, O O-O-O, pray for us. O febbulated donkey of imperishable mien and meth, bray for us. O wind and sand and wave and ethus—" I didn't see much point in my staying there any longer, so I walked out. It took a minute to get used to the light again. The room was empty except for some little golden goslings playing behind the sofa. Probably eggs that rolled under out of sight—but at any rate, that's pretty fast incubation, I thought. I opened the door. The first thing I saw in the next room was a great grandfather's clock standing under a painting of an old man with a long white beard kneading clay into what looked like a young woman in a nightgown just getting out of or into bed. The next thing I saw was a group of men in white smocks standing beside an operating table. "You're next," one of them said to me. That seemed to touch off a spring in the others because before I could more than yell a half dozen times I found myself strapped down breathing into a little cloth cup that smelled like a piece of fudge looks. Then I started to float up around the ceiling somewhere. I bit into one of the pink balloons—it tasted like a sewing machine salad with oil of tender moongrass dressing parturient. I came to on a huge bed in an empty room. The bed was about twelve feet across, and at least twenty long. So I was lying there wonderfully comfortable, not thinking, not at all anxious, strangely unafraid—with no thought, without anxiety, without fear of any kind—Boy! it's nice here, peaceful, I'm beginning to fall asl—WHEN I felt a hand on my . . . . "Stop it!" . . . . All right. *All right.* Half an hour later she crawled out of the covers and adjusted her nightgown around ankles which flashed like tiny silver fish. "Gee! that was horrible," she said, scratching under her left armpit. "I don't know when I've enjoyed anything so much"—"Do you know what time it is?" I asked. "No, I don't," she answered, "but I must have been waiting hours under those heavy covers for you to come—wonder I didn't smother."—"There's something I'm supposed to do—" I said, sinking back into the pillows. "Yes," she said, beginning to comb her luxuriant, golden hair with an Ogilvie Super-Special, "you're supposed to get married today." I sprang up and ran to the door. I wrenched at it so hard the knob came off in my hand. But it wouldn't open. "They'll unlock it in due season," she said, turning on the five-legged stool to face me. I suddenly felt so miserable and helpless I wanted to scream, to tear my hair out—well, maybe not quite that, but I did feel that things couldn't get much worse if they really sat down and spent a lifetime trying. "I'd give a lot to know what time it is," I said. "You can still make your train," she said, handing me the brush. "But how am I to get out of this terrible house?" I asked. "What did it cost?" I'd never felt a bristle so strong and massageable. "That was a Christmas present from Mr. Hall," she said, pleased. "Mr. Hall!"—"Why, yes. Do you know him? He has blue hairs growing out of his nose," she informed me. I could breathe again. "No, the Mr. Hall I have in mind had red hairs growing out of his nose," I informed her, sitting down on the edge of the bed. "What's the matter with your stomach?" she said. I looked down at it. It was swaying back and forth. "I don't know what that can be," I said. "I feel all right."—"You don't swallow live little pigs or anything, do you?" she asked, laughing prettily. "After what just happened to me, I wouldn't be at all surprised."—"I'd give a lot to know what time it is," I said. Just then a voice somewhere boomed: "Bong. Bong. Bong. Bong."—"That's four o'clock," I said. "Thank goodness, I still have an hour.—Why what's the matter, Miss? You look as though you'd seen a ghost."—"I just heard one," she said. "That was my grandfather doing that bonging." She started to watch my stomach again. "The swaying seems to be right in the pit," I said. "Like a pendulum, yet," she said. The door swung open and I looked into another room. I hurried in and asked one of the men sitting in the front row if he could tell me how I could get out of the house. He scribbled something on a paper and handed it to the man beside him. The paper started to circulate back and forth through the nineteen rows. After they had all seen it, the first man took off his white bow tie and put a black one in its place. Everybody did the same. They looked like fat little penguins sitting there in their tuxedos. "Here's Anatole now," one of them said. Anatole cleared his throat and smiled at me. He was a very young man with a sad face. "Sit down, Budd," somebody barked at me. All the chairs were taken, so I sat down on the floor. The young man said: "We shall not have the piece which surpasseth all understanding until some one of us is able to determine (by whatever means may seem expedient at this time and under these and other unrelated circumstances) an avenue or kindred aperture to the problem and hazard of once and for all time (as it was in the beginning or is now at this very moment) under these heavens (in whose dire compass those stalactite maidens known to our poor senses as the stars) and to establish whether her name is Beatreen or Marganne (or Michael Fabbicio Susan) and whether her temporal abode is Ashtabula or Hardscrabble or Deever City and gentlemen in the name of that God whose beneficent example (and chalteen omniprelipuddanumentaclikerized elfedineddy) discover whether her number is WA-9-5473 or EL-5-1892—" Here he was interrupted by loud applause. This is something which doesn't concern me very much personally, I thought; so I'll just leave quietly. But when I tried to stand up I discovered that the bottom of my pants was glued to the floor. There was no help for it—I got up anyway. As I reached the door somebody handed me the paper. It read: HUMILITY IS THE BEST POLICY. I stepped into the next room—or, I should say, shallow tank, for I found myself wading through about three feet of water. Something long and black started to wriggle toward me. . . . Then I felt my legs go all numb and I almost fell down. So that's what an electric eel is, I thought, flinging out of the glass-lined tank. The next room had a woman stretched out on a cot in it. "That must have been a shocking experience for you," she said, smiling up at me. She had nothing on except an American Indian with long green feathers in his war-bonnet. In the next room was the most beautiful woman in the world. Nobody had to tell me. She said, "Take them off and I'll patch them up for you." I couldn't do anything for looking at her. "There's a blue robe in the closet you can put on," she continued. Finally I managed to come back to earth. The robe had Maxie Baer lettered on the back of it. It was a little big in the shoulders and about three yards too long. "I'm afraid you'll have to fix my shorts too," I said, sitting down in a chair with orange dragons on a white slipcase. "Just pull it up around the front of you—I'm too busy to peek anyway." The slipcase felt a little rough on my bare skin. "Does it cost much to have a slipcase like this made?" I asked. "That slipcase cost sixty-five dollars for the material alone—but since I got exactly what I wanted, that was immaterial to me," she said. "I'm in awful trouble," I said. "You are? I'm terribly sorry. What sort of trouble? Perhaps I can help you."—"My fiancée is waiting for me beside a little white gate in the country. We are to be married today—"—"Oh, how nice! My warmest congratulations."—"Thank you. But you don't understand! I'll miss my train, and Priscilla will think I've deserted her," I said, getting up in my eagerness to make her understand and help me. "Oh!" she said. "Why, what's the matter, Miss?"— "What's the matter! Just you look at my new slipcase!" It had the imprint of a giant half-pear on its seat. I put my hand on mine—ink. "Gee I'm sorry," I said. "Put your arms around me," she said. "Well, I—" —"Do as I tell you," she ordered. "If it's all right, I'd like to put my pants on first," I said. She flung them across to me and I slipped into them. The zipper wasn't there at all anymore. "Hurry up," she said. "I want to help you—but I have to feel you first."—"What do you mean, feel me first?" I asked, backing away. "Oh, don't be a tiresome child," she admonished me. "Haven't you ever heard that a woman thinks with her feelings?"—"Well, all right," I said, allowing her to pull me down on the bed beside her. "Hold me tight," she said. I did as little of it as I could and still be polite. "Tell me about yourself now," she said, putting her hand on my knee. "I am to be married today," I told her. "I know—you said that before. Tell me . . . umm, do you like sex?"—"It's important in its place," I said, pushing her hand back to my knee. "What isn't its place?" she asked, starting to unbutton the top of her dress. "Please," I said.—"Yes, I know, you have a train to catch." She unbuttoned some more buttons. "Touch them," she said. I had a hard time getting my breath. "I shouldn't—" I said. "Don't be afraid," she said softly. "There, isn't that nice?"—"It's more than nice," I managed to say. I felt my fingers caressing them. "I think they're beautiful," she said. "I know I like to touch them myself." She leaned back on the bed and parted her dress all the way down. They were rising and falling evenly with her breath. She had dainty little pink panties on—above them, she was naked. I put my hand on her soft belly. It quivered

slightly. O my God! I wanted to say. "Shall I take them off?"
she asked in a whisper. "Yes," I heard myself say. She raised
her legs and kicked them off. "O my God!" I said. She had
blue eyes, a tiny, straight nose, full, beautifully modelled lips,
and golden hair which fell around her like the silken ropes
of paradise. "Put your hand there, Albert," she said. "I—I
couldn't—" But I did. I moved it along the warm curving of
her thighs. I was sure my heart would stop. "What did you
say your trouble was?" she asked. I felt all at once so tender
and brutal I wanted to touch her in the softest way my fingers
could—and I wanted to tear her to pieces with my teeth. "Perhaps you'd better go now," she said. "Priscilla is probably
getting worried that you won't come at all." I don't know how
I got my clothes off. She squiggled like a paper match under a
tonguing flame—oh so gently, so cruelly—I thought the top
of my head would blow off. . . .

GEE!

Then she lay in the crook of my arm. "Al," she said. "Yes—
what is your name?"—"Mrs. Potter. Do you ever wonder why
it feels that good? Nature's purpose would get solved just as
well if it felt, say, just half that good." I got up on my elbow.
"Mrs.?" I said. "Yes, but you needn't be alarmed—Seymour
doesn't mind. Do you, dear?"—"Quite all right," a voice said
behind me. I wheeled around. "Gosh!" I said, jumping up
and reaching for my pants. "Don't rush off on my account,
old fellow," the man said, crossing over and sinking down
beside his wife. "I thought I heard you come in just as we
finished," she said. "Oh, no—I was born with a horseshoe in
my mouth—I saw a lot more than that," he said. "Oh, Seymour," she said, as he ran his hairy hands over her heaving
bosoms. I stumbled out of the room—I'd never known anything like that before—and my eyes were so full of tears I
nearly fell over the lion which was standing just inside the

next room. His great golden eyes fixed on my knees—and for a little while there he looked as though he was at a very fast tennis match. When I could take my eyes off him, I saw that there were nineteen other lions sitting around on six-legged stools and an even thirty-one tigers sitting around on purple hassocks as big as giant toadstools. I wiped the sweat off my forehead. "Yessir," I muttered, "trains just don't wait for nobody—"—edging away to the door. Every one of them jumped down—there wasn't a sound (and I think that frightened me more than anything else frightened me). Like one mouth they all opened their mouths—and they started to pad nearer . . . one inch, two, three, pretty kitties, five, six, such nice clean teeth, ate—I could feel the design of the wallpaper against my shoulder blades. How is it again you make a yell? All right, throat, what are you waiting for! I could smell lion and tiger breaths on their breath. "Boys and girls!" a deep voice boomed in the doorway. They swung around meekly and went back to their places. "Are you all right, sir?" the animal-trainer asked me. "I think some of my teeth have melted together," I said. "You can't blame my babies," he said. "I forgot to feed them this week."—"No, I suppose you can't blame your babies," I agreed. "They're sure hungry," he said. He had on a red cloak, yellow pants, blue boots, a green, handle-bar mustache which was looped through his brass earrings, and he carried copies of *American Harvest, This Is My Best* and *New Poems: 1944* in his lavender sash. "Are they favorites of yours?" I asked. "These books, you mean—" He paused to look very pleased with himself. "We live in the country," he said; "and back at our house the mail order catalogues aren't as easy to get as they used to be—so I just mosey into a second-hand store everytime I get down this way." I noticed that the lions and tigers hadn't quite given up the first idea they had. One by one they were jumping down again. "They certainly have worked themselves up an appetite," he said pensively.

"By the way, are you a Christian?" I had my hand on the doorknob. "I think I'll just look around the rest of the house while I'm here," I said. I turned the knob. "They're very catholic in their taste," he said. "Would you believe it, these big cats eat nothing but fish on Friday."—"But this isn't Friday," I said, wrenching the door almost off its hinges as I made it into the next room. "Who said it was?" a pleasant voice asked. "Oh, I was just talking to somebody," I told her. "It must have been a nifty somebody all right," she said—"thinking Tuesday is Friday."—"What do you mean, Tuesday?" I asked. She lifted the lid off the box. "Okay by me. What day do you want it to be?"—"I like it to go right on being Saturday," I said. "Why, is Saturday the day you picked to go around with your pants unbuttoned?" she asked. "It's the zipper—or rather, it's because I haven't a zipper anymore," I explained. She took a man about six inches tall out of the box. "I want you to meet Mr. Budd, Izzy," she said. "Mr. Budd, Mr. Index." He held his hand out and I shook his arm. "Izzy fancies himself as a tough guy," she explained. "I can lick anybody my size in this room," he said. They laughed as though it was a favorite joke of theirs—but I didn't laugh—my ears were still ringing from the boom of his voice. I'd never heard such a deep, rich voice in all my life. The girl had on a very attractive peasant blouse, a full, flounced, fluted, blue-and-red striped corduroy skirt with pleats, green cotton stockings, orange patent leather pumps, size $2\frac{1}{2}$ A—"$3\frac{1}{4}$ B," Mr. Index said—size $3\frac{1}{4}$ B, and a yellow fur hat with a tiny silver wagon wheel on its side. It made me dizzy to watch the flashing revolutions of the wheel, so I turned to an examination of the room itself. Simple to the extreme, it yet radiated a quiet grace. The milky tan of the walls and counterpointing tones of dead beige in the damask draperies, motifed in the Aubusson rug and the vermilion camel-belly covering of the Margot Kye panelling, were repeated with indifferent effect in the paintings by Lancret, Huet, Boucher, Mondrian and Nattier. Elaborate care had been expended in achieving a harmony of mood and affinity in the furniture—in the one hurried glance I threw at them, I noticed a downholstered Regency sofa (holding a 32.20 Colt Automatic), a commode desk with pseudo-plaster moldings of lacerated copper, a Carfax fruitwood cabinet (pear, quince, plum, coconut husk and stromberry), an Hepplewhite hunt rack, a Sheraton cocktail dispenser in zinc and etched glass on diamond casters, a brocatelle Guidotti Directoire 'Migrating' short stool, an appliqued Meyer-Ganther-Marsini lowboy, an early Chippendale armchair with hand-woven sorrel bark back, a Louis XVIII tufted bergere and pipe stand (carved to simulate bamboo), a Knapp and Tubbs breakfront dishcase, a Duncan Phyfe gaming table of cobald ivory and wroughtgut, a Grinling Gibbons provincial rosewood mantel upon which sat a crystal sunburst clock with white holly trim, a figure (called *The Baptism*) of partially glazed terra cotta by Vicktor Schreckengost, a wey and conis soda-glaze bowl by Whitney Atchley, a red clay giraffe with a small colored boy on his back by Miss Mathilde Parmelee, and a mouth-organ of enameled wool (labeled: *Treitel Gratz, his organ*). "I wonder who's gotten into you now?" the girl interjected. "I'm getting hungry, Velmo Lucy Schmiez&katzian," Mr. Index declared. "I'm sort of hungry myself," I jected. "I see you found your car all right," the man who wheeled the cart in interposed. "Yes, thanks, I did," I posed. "Bring some wine too," Mr. Index said disgruntledly. "I shall be delighted, sire," the man answered gruntledly. We had onion soup au pige, chestnut-tomato madrilene, gelvish clam chowder (with raisins soaked in squab blood), noodle zoop, and lima bean-and-apricot pie for a first course. Mr. Index and Miss Schmiez&katzian each had a bottle each of Coronet Sherry, Noilly Prat Vermouth and Serial Madeira. I contented myself with a large glass of water. Next we had toast

and lime marmalade, poached eggs, boiled hominy with sour
cream, Turkish pilaf (with sweetbreads Monroe), weakfish
(with mussels in pigs feet allemande sauce), roast saddle of
pinto pony (still smelling of cowboy), spaghetti with goose
liver sauce, ros bif with Yorkshire puddin', broiled lobster
with Rhum Negrita, chicken fricasseed with reindeer suet,
baked wild duck, buttered celery, endive, lettuce and pineapple salad with Rueld olive oil and the juice of black rhu-
barb, mashed potato, winter squash and cherry pie, fried duck,
little broiled pig, and smorgasbord. Mr. Index also had a bottle of Graves, Côtes Cremant, Chablis, Kaveau Montrachet,
Sylander Reserve, Champagne Brut, Sauterne (Barsac), Do-
maines Dopff (Alsatian), Burgundy (one each of Maçon and
Pommard), Claret (one each of Medoc, St. Julien, Margaux),
and Haut Sauterne (Chateau Latour-Blanche). Velmo Lucy
contented herself with scotch whiskey and I had another glass
of water. Next we had Maryland beaten biscuits, watermelon
pickle, boned mink stew (with toasted almonds and craybill
kidneys), Swedish scones, shrimp and peanut butter sandwiches on pumperdime bread, riced boiled hickorynuts with
punished cream, antipasto, sauteed lark's eyeballs in Gonzales
sauce, marguerite squares, palm leaves, ginger doughnuts,
chocolate dominoes, grapeskins with powdered lilac petal, za-
baglione-and-deep-dish-apple pie, sponge cake with mayon-
naise, fried tame rice, scallops Oldberg, and tiny broiled sau-
sages and macaroni (with wilted cucumber leaves drowned in
alligator pear vinegar). Mr. Isidore Index drank a bottle each
of Palugyay Tokay, Champagne (Charles Heidsieck-1837),
Diamond Jubilee Port, Crema Sherry and Malmsey Madeira.
Miss V.L. soberly stuck to her whiskey, and I to my water.
"Why does the water have such a strange taste?" I asked.
"Pluto," Mr. Index said. "What does that mean?" I asked.
"You'll see," he said enigmatically. Time passed—probably
forty seconds. "I'll see you in a few minutes," I said automati-

cally. "Third door to your left," Miss V.L. said. When I got back all the dinner things had been cleared away and Mr. Index was smoking a cigar an inch longer than himself. "Ah, for a moment there I almost imagined myself at an official banquet in the Workers' State—and it sure would have pleased the biggest writer this country ever had too," he said. "He means Tom," Miss Schmiez&katzian explained. "Oh, by the by, Budd," the tiny one said, "there was somebody here asking after you."—"There was! Who? Who was it? Did he say what he wanted to see me about?" I asked eagerly. "She," he said. "I think she's waiting in the other room there." But there were so many people in the next room that I thought I'd never be able to find the woman who wanted to see me. First of all, in a corner near a majestic, marble stairway, a group of beautiful young women were lying on gray velvet couches, their naked bodies glowing like white, soft flames in the strange, withdrawn and dream-like light. I felt a great sense of awe as I walked toward them. It seemed that I moved in a world where everything was beautiful and horrible. I sank down on one of the couches. "There is no reason at all to lose heart," she said. She had golden hair and eyes. "Sometimes it's hard not to," I said. "That's because you don't understand the potentials and scope of this life," she continued. "What man can do and think and feel are of such enormous compass that were you to even imagine one thousandth part of them, your brain would turn to jelly." She smiled at me, stretching out her arms. As I settled into them, I said, "But why has so little been done and thought and felt?" Her hair smelled like an appletree in flower. "How do you know how much has been done and thought and felt?" she said softly. "The great and wonderful are ever at work—preparing the earth for that God which is everyone." I rose to my feet and walked among the maidens. There is no reason at all to lose heart. Potentials. Scope. *To think. To feel. To live. To die.* O spirits of the sky! O Love waiting on the roads of the world! Whence this darkness, this pain, this doubt, which have turned my soul to water—whither is the light, the sweet rest, the radiant merging of brother with brother— O where is the answer to my life! What am I to do! What am I! O God what am I and what am I to do! O thrones of the earth and the waters which surround the earth! O throat of mercy and everlasting wisdom! in what desert do I walk, in whose hands shall I commit this legacy of drought and white terror—! I walk across to a man who is standing in a corner of mirrors, and his seventy images are all doing a different thing—some with hatred, others in fear and vengeance, but none in love— O some with a knife, others with a fistful of bloody money, but none with the word of God, O none at all with the wish or desire or will to look upon the face of another human being. Now people were approaching very near me. They stood in a little circle around me. I said: "How am I to get out of this house!" and they bent their heads back and laughed at me. In what dread cave, in what ghost-fouled trench are we held, my dear friends? What is meaning . . . *when there is no meaning*— What is to be understood . . . *when there is nothing at all to understand*— What are we to say . . . *when there is nothing at all to be said*— What are we to live . . . *when there is no life*— How are we going to die . . . *when we can't even believe in death*—

WHAT DOES IT MEAN TO LIVE!
WHAT DOES IT MEAN TO DIE!
I am standing here looking at you.
Why do you laugh at me?
Why are you afraid of me?
WHY SHOULD WE LOVE EACH OTHER!
Who are you?
Who am I?
What are you going to do?
WHAT ARE YOU GOING TO DO!

What are you doing to prepare the way to God?

What can I do to prepare a way to you?

What can you do to prepare a way to me?

Why do we stand apart from one another?

O WHY DO WE STAND LONELY CRYING IN THIS NIGHT?

And they bent their heads back and laughed at me.

I walked over to the foot of the great stairway.

"You can't go up there, Budd," somebody said; and they ringed me round.

"I had an appointment to meet somebody," I told them.

"He says he had an appointment to meet somebody," one of them said.

"Can you tell me how I may find a door that will lead out of this house?" I asked.

"He says he wants to find a door that will lead out of this house," they said, padding in closer around me.

Somewhere I heard a voice calling my name.

"Somewhere he hears a voice calling his name," they chanted, and their golden eyes danced with a sad joy.

"But you don't understand!" I shouted. "She may be in trouble."

"And now we don't understand," they said. "For sure and she may be in trouble, yet."

I started to try the doors.

"Ah, now he's trying the doors."

This was to have been the most wonderful day in my life.

"—The most *wonderful* day in his whole life!"

The last door opened.

All was quiet now.

I stepped out of the house.

And a pair of white eyes was staring into mine.

A RADIANT TEMPLE STANDS ABOVE THE WATERS

I got off the train. The sun was shining. The air was warm and gentle on my face. It was a beautiful day. It was a day for the doing of wonderful and peaceful things.

I had never been so afraid in all my life.

2

Priscilla . . . Priscilla! *O my darling, my darling.* . . .

3

A big black and white dog ran down from a farmhouse and sniffed at my legs. I moved to touch him and he sank his teeth into my hand. He followed me for more than a mile, growling deep in his throat, ever on the alert for another chance to attack me.

As I passed the little cemetery in the valley, a man lurched to his feet from behind a headstone. His face was dark and evil, and menacing green eyes bit into mine. He cursed, waving a huge, hairy fist at me.

Where the red barn had been, a pile of charred timbers smoldered like bad-tempered crocodiles, their heavy, pocked thighs locked in an obscene embrace.

The old mill wheel was still—and in the barbed wire enclosure around it, sick-looking foxes padded in hopeless, forlorn parade. Bloated bodies stirred in the slimy pool—and the stench was that of the rotting, blasphemous mouth of death itself.

In front of the general store, shining like gloating bugs, a group of long, black Cadillacs was drawn-up. Slim young men, their eyes hideous with a new knowledge, were slouched at the polished wheels. Cigarettes, looking like leprous fangs, dangled from their ravaged, thin-fleshed jaws. As I walked past, they leaned toward me, and pointing yellowed fingers, sang out:

"Aah- Aah- Aah- Aah- Aah- Aah- Aah- Aah- Bing. Bing. Bing. Bing. Aah- Aah- Aah- You're dead."

When I got to the orchard, the first thing I saw was that the little white gate was down. Somehow, without it, the orchard looked like a blind, green idiot—holding gnarled, puny arms in front of its vacant, sad face.

I had never felt so alone in all my life.

4

O my little darling, my darling . . . *Priscilla! Priscilla.* . . .

5

I knelt on the ground in that garden of flowering trees.

6

O I sank to the cold ground in that jungle of horror.

7

And I wept.

8

For I saw that weeds grew in the yard of her house.
O I saw that boards were nailed over every window.

9

Boards were nailed over my heart.

10

HOW CAN I TELL IT!
O how can I tell it!

11

How can I say that—
O I sank to the earth in that pretty forest of terror . . . and
I could hear the boards being nailed over my life.
How can I tell it. . . .
O how am I to say that—

12

That the world had broken to pieces in my hands.
That I didn't know where to go.
And I had no one to go with me.

13

I heard something moving behind me in the road and turned
to see a man standing there.

"Nice orchard," he said.

"Yes, it is a nice orchard."

"Could stand a little pruning though."

"Yes, I guess it could."

"Say, maybe you can tell me something," he said, coming
up to where I knelt. "What'd you lose?" And he started to look
around.

"Nothing," I said, getting up. "I didn't lose anything. What
was it you wanted to find out?"

"I'm an agent," he explained, "a publicity agent—and I'm
up in these parts on business. I was told I might find the fellow I'm looking for up here—a dizzy bozo named Budd, Albert Budd."

I brushed my right knee off. "What did you want with him?"
I asked, brushing my left knee off.

"I wanta sign him up—ten year contract if I can rope the
dope right," he said, taking a lot of papers out of his pocket.
I helped him pick them up off the ground. His hands were
shaking so hard that he no sooner got them all together than
he dropped them again. "Here, you hold them," he said.

"You should do something about your nerves," I said.

"Yeah, I'd like to— Haven't got a needle on you by any
chance?"

"Why, yes, I have," I said.

"Brother!" He threw his arms around me. "You know, I'd never lamp you as a junkie. Where do you get it?"

"From a man called Donald Wan—he's dead now," I said.

"Never heard of him. Here, give me a shot—"

"I couldn't do that."

"Whattayuhmean, you couldn't do that? Why, a little guy like you—I'll roll you into a ball, and throw you at the moon!"

He tried to snatch the case out of my hand.

"I'm Albert Budd," I said.

He let go of my throat and stepped back. "You're—! Well whyinh—l didn't you say so!" He took a fountain pen out of his pocket. He dropped it too. "Guess you better hold it," he said. "Look, boy—I like you. You're my kind of people, see. We talk the same language. That's why I'm not going to ask you to read a lotta dull, technical stuff in that contract. Come 'ere, A.B., let's you and me lick this little proposition together—whattayuhsay? That's it! That's the old college try! Right on that dotted line. Hunh-uh, no outcry, chum— It's all down there in basic English . . . how much money I get, how much whiz whiz you get, and exactly how much money I get—"

"I appreciate your interest in me," I said, putting his papers and fountain pen back in his pocket—which was not an easy thing to do because he was shaking like he had an outboard motor or a grandfather's clock in his stomach.

"I'll only charge you five hundred for every Winchell I put over," he said, trying to get the papers out again.

"What's a Winchell?" I asked out of curiosity.

"What's a Winchell! Look—gather in close now. No shoving back there! I'm sure glad you asked me that. Whattayuhwant? you wanta get put over—am I right? Right. You wanta get your lousy name smeared around everywhere, hunh? You wanta think you're better than the next guy, hunh? Well let me just give you a tuneful little earful— Who the h—l do you figure you are anyway? Coming around here handing me a line like that. Hey! Wait a minute. . . . Who wrote this speech for me anyhow—?"

"You were only going to charge five hundred for a Winchell," I said.

"Right. Well, just because it's you—for the sake of all the good times we had together in— Where was it we had all them good times together?"

"I was raised in Bivalve."

"No foolin'! Good old Bivalve! How well I remember the railroad tracks—me on one side, and that nifty dish, the Mayor's daughter, on the other—"

"Bivalve has a City Manager."

"Right. The City Manager's daughter on one side and—"

"He didn't have a daughter."

"Look, Buddy, don't you want me to help you? Where was I? Oh, yes, the part where you pay me the five hundred."

"I can't do it," I said, starting to walk away.

"I'll throw Lyons in too. Maybe even get Maxwell to slip in a 'And as I said to my dear friend, Albert' now and then."

"No," I said.

When I looked back, he was leaning up against a tree—and apples were raining down all around him.

14

I stood in the field with the hypodermic case in my hand. If ever you have a trouble so great that there seems to be nothing whatever you can do to meet it, then I want you to use this needle, Donald Wan had said.

Priscilla . . . *Priscilla* . . . !

15

I plunged the needle into my wrist.

16

I can't tell this.
The voice said, "Cry!"
And he said, "What shall I cry?
All flesh is grass,
And all the goodliness thereof is as the flower of the field:
The grass withereth, the flower fadeth:
Because the spirit of the Lord bloweth upon it:
Surely the people is grass.
The grass withereth, the flower fadeth:
But the word of our God shall stand for ever."
I don't know how to tell you this.
Who hath measured the waters in the hollow of his hand,
And meted out heaven with the span,
And comprehended the dust of the earth in a measure,
And weighed the mountains in scales,
And the hills in a balance?
How can I tell you how it was with me then. . . .
Who hath directed the Spirit of the Lord,
Or being his counsellor hath taught him?
With whom took he council,
And who instructed him,
And taught him in the path of judgment,
And taught him knowledge,
And showed to him the way of understanding?
That beautiful and terrible stirring in my heart. . . .
That living which was as a flame,
And an awakening into flame. . . .
All nations before him are as nothing;
And they are counted to him less than nothing, and vanity.
And I move upon the roads of the world,
And upon those roads come I to this dread place—
Come I, O my brothers—an avenger

Whose vengeance shall be love for every man. . . .
Have ye not known? have ye not heard?
Hath it not been told you from the beginning?
Have ye not understood from the foundations of the earth?
Come I with the stern and beautiful engines of a new war.
He am I that sitteth upon the circle of the earth,
And the inhabitants thereof are as grasshoppers;
That stretcheth out the heavens as a curtain,
And spreadeth them out as a tent to dwell in;
That bringeth the princes to nothing;
He maketh the judges of the earth as vanity.
Yea, they shall not be planted;
Yea, they shall not be sown;
Yea, their stock shall not take root in the earth;
And he shall also blow upon them, and they shall wither,
And the whirlwind shall take them away as the stubble.

Even now, curious and watchful, they follow me—
They follow me into the heart of Times Square.
"No man can serve two masters," I tell them: "for either
he will hate the one, and love the other; or else he will hold
to the one, and despise the other. You cannot serve God and
Mammon."

"*Kill the dirty bastard!*" *one of them shouts.* "*Just let me*
get my mitts on him."

"A good tree cannot bring forth evil fruit," I go on, "neither
can a corrupt tree bring forth good fruit. Every tree that bringeth not forth good fruit is hewn down, and cast into the fire.
Whereof by their fruits shall you know them."

"*Just one moment, Mr. Christ, please— Would you mind*
speaking up just a little? All this racket and confusion— We
pride ourselves that ours is the most complete and accurate
news reel service in the country. . . ."

"Enter you in at the strait gate: for wide is the gate, and

broad is the way, that leadeth to destruction, and many there be which go in thereat: because strait is the gate, and narrow is the way, which leadeth unto life—"

"Ladies and gentlemen, this is your announcer, Warren Monger, bringing you a hammer by hammer description of a most interesting event which is now taking place in Times Square. Oh, oh—someone in the crowd—one of the largest I've ever seen here, by the way—is tearing the robe off his shoulders— Ha, ha, that was funny— Several people got hold of it at the same time, and it's in half a dozen pieces already— Wait now! Hold everything! They've got the cross up—I may interrupt to say that I've never, never at least since I've been with my present sponsor, seen a more glorious day for a crucifixion—everybody of any note at all seems to be here—right over there is my good friend, that great public-spirited— Hold it! Hold it! There she goes, folks!—They've just pounded the first nail in—and, yup, there goes another—"

"And I say unto you:
THOU SHALT NOT KILL."
"Waaa! Waaa!"
"Waaa! Waaa!"
"Waaaaaa! Waaaaaaaaaaa!"
"That does the stinking sonofabitch—"

And I had a great thirst.
And pain melted the marrow of my bones.

And a voice said:
Come unto me now, my son.
"Waaa! Waaa! Waaaaaaaaaaa!"
And I went unto Him.

WHAT BECAME OF ME

Now I'll try to tell you something about the other world.

In the first place—and this was pretty hard for me to get used to—there isn't any ground.

That probably doesn't seem like much of a problem to you, I suppose—and it wouldn't be if when you got there you knew how to fly.

I'd always thought, naturally enough, that all an angel had to do was spread his wings and coast around wherever he wanted to—but it's not as simple as that. . . .

The trouble with a new angel is, he's got to learn to fly— and that's not as easy as you might think.

One of the things wrong is, there's nothing to stand on.

I spent most of the first day just falling.

It's amazing what a speed you can work up after you've fallen a couple thousand miles. If I open a wing now, I thought, it'll just get torn off.

(I forgot to say that you fall upwards. In heaven they have a saying: Anything that goes up, must come up.)

So, after I'd just about reconciled myself to it, I felt an arm grab round my waist. I must have pulled him up a thousand yards or so before he could get me stopped.

"Welcome to heaven, Budd," he said in a very cheerful way.

Husky is not a word you think of in connection with angels, but he had muscles like big vines growing all over him.

"The trouble is, I can't fly yet," I panted.

"Why don't you take the cellophane off your wings, yet?" he said.

"Oh," I said.

He helped me unwrap them.

"Now let's see what you can do," he said, letting go of me.

"Oh! Oh!" I said—because what I could do was right away start falling again.

He flew up after me and grabbed my arm.

"Don't fight it!" he said. "Let it come to you. Let your wings do the work."

Well, that went on for a couple hours. We were both sweating like mad and he didn't look so cheerful anymore.

"I'm beginning to think you just like being a fall-guy," he grumbled. "Here. Watch me close this time. First the right wing, now the left— One, two, one, two— That's it! You've got the right down pat—but I never in my after-life saw such a sloppy left."

Gee! what a top I would have made for somebody!

"Get that left in! Throw that left in there!"

Well, that went on for a couple more hours. How can any-body get this dizzy and live? I thought. Even putting the 'live' in there. . . .

"Now you're getting it, kid," he said. "That left's all you got to worry about."

Just then a voice from somewhere called:

"Willl-berrr . . . Supper's ready."

"Coming, Hubertetta," he called back. "That's the wifie— See you around, pal."

"You have wives up here?" I called after him.

"Wifes, you mean— What'd you think we'd have?"

"I didn't think there'd be any sex in heaven," I said lamely —or, I should say, dizzily.

"There isn't," he yelled back. "Here we got seben."

Maybe I got more to worry about than my left, I thought, as I flew over and sat up on a little cloud.

Now I could see what sort of a place I'd come to.

The first thing I noticed was the sky. It had a lot of drawings of birds and fishes and funny little trees on it. But I should have saved funny to say that these drawings were flying around and swimming and had real apples and pears and oranges on them.

Also there was a big golden ball with lines shooting out from it. That must be the sun, I thought—and just then one of the lines reached down and touched my sandal—it was the sun all right.

Far below I could see thousands of pretty houses. They looked like a crazy-quilt a wonderful giant might have for his bed. Just scattered all about like they were beautiful blocks a child had got tired of playing with. Then I saw that they were moving around. One would shove its front door up against the front door of the next. It took me a little while to realize that what they were doing was kissing each other.

Reaching up as high as I could see, were huge *scenes*—a very weak word in this case—"scenes" (landscapes, sky-scapes, peoplescapes, whateveryouwantscapes) which looked something like paintings . . . sort of withdrawn-like and making you say: I wonder what that means? . . . only everything in them was REAL, *and I knew what the one who had put them there intended me to think they meant.*

Maybe they really meant something very different; but somehow I didn't worry about it.

This is what I saw on the walls of heaven.

The First Picture (or Whathaveyou). In a round frame. Two tiny men digging into the side of a rock with silver spades. Rock—glowing like an over-heated electric iron—shaped like a woman having a striped jockey's cap on her head. Some smaller rocks around . . . white, but getting green at the tops like asparagus. A pool of yellow water with the toe of a rubber boot sticking up out of it. Beneath—still in the frame —a group of people in old-fashioned clothes sitting quietly on a pile of discarded children. Up in *its* sky, the word POODLE . . . surrounded by a circle of little blue cupids holding goblets of oatmeal and ground desire.

The Second Picture. Two old men, nude as doorknobs, standing at the foot of a tree. A boy in a lounging robe made of postage stamps is picking crowns from the boughs and dropping them down on the heads of seven women who are bathing in a marble tub which stands between four pillars made of snakes. One of the latter is staring sadly at a saloon full of gay people which floats soothingly by. One of the old men takes the shoe off the tree's foot and drinks a toast to quail all toasts out of it. Framed by clocks all telling a different time.

The Third Picture. A black angel with two glowing heads. Holds a diamond-shaped shield upon which is etched *The Parable Of The Subtle Shepherd Who Is Watched Over By His*

Sheep. In the foreground, a hill of peacocks struts in the golden air. No frame.

The Fourth Picture. Framed in a frieze of little orange-and-green spotted puppies wading dolefully through a snowstorm. Shows a man with a long sword in one hand and a severed head in the other. Limbless body of victim is lying on a tiled floor—this out in a field. The head is smiling in a satisfied sort of way. The body is of a sex new to me. The standing man has a better than average supply of hair.

I was drifting along with my cloud. What a fine way to travel, I thought. Through a lovely village—where all the houses were in the shape of letters. I'd gone almost through it before I realized that the houses spelt:

THE REASON WHY ALL BEINGS ARE SETTLED IN A SINGLE BODY, IS THAT THERE MAY BE A UNITED COMPOSITION—WHICH IS THE SECRET OF ALL BEAUTIFUL THINGS.

Next I floated into what was like a big tent. Seven or eight—seven—quite tall men were standing in front of a stove watching a pot.

"A watch-pot never boils," I said to be sociable.

They smiled down at me; and one of them said:

"Take 8 Loth (4 ozs.) calcined Alum, 8 Loth calkifferated Pepperpetre, and 6 Doap Lilysalt, and triturate with 23 Gubbs Corrosive Sublimate, and sublimate in a proper Subliming Vessel.

"Carefully take out the Sublimate and resublimate it with 18 Rohrschach fresh Eagle Blood. During this operation it will be advisable, on account of the poisonous fumes, to eat levee-wellies thickly spread with a butter made from the oil of jaundiced parsnips."

Then one of them reached in the pot. "Yep—just as I figured —mine's an Elgin," he announced, holding up the dripping time-piece.

"Bulova here," said another, lifting his out.

"Waltham," said another happily.

"Oh, oh—an Ingersoll," said another unhappily.

"You didn't put enough Leopard Snot in, Mr. P," the first another declared.

"Ah, you fellows probably gummed it up on me," Mr. P said sourly, taking another bite of his levee-welly.

"What would you do if you had a pot of your own, P?" the second another asked.

I floated out before I could hear the answer.

And I better get back to telling you about the pictures. There are forty-one yet to be told about.

The Fifth Picture. Shows a Sun just arising out of a gray sea. His eyes look around like stones about to be thrown at everything evil. A city sleeps at his chin. There is no life stirring in any of the houses. It's as though the Sun had COME UPON THE PEOPLE UNAWARES—and nothing he could do would wake them.

The Sixth Picture. Shows a sad-looking old woman sitting near a waterfall holding a very tiny baby on her lap. Three crows as big as dogs hop about a short distance away. A butterfly in a red coat walks in with a basin of dirty water. One of the crows gets his beak caught in a crack in the floor, and a lion with a flaming mane swallows him. Framed with little figures of various thoughts—for instance, the figure for Unless It's Endorsed By Our Leading (sic) Critics, You Can't Get Me To Have Anything To Do With It is a large hole full of the ghosts of yesterday's remisses. And the figure for The American Writer Must First Of All Become A Real (!) American is a man in a black shirt with his hand lifted stiffly out in front of him.

The Seventh Picture. Strolling groups of young men and women. Laughing and talking together. *I certainly am getting lonesome, I thought, as I watched them.* Up above, a chariot pulled by two big birds with feathers made of split-up shoe-laces. Right in the middle—with a frame of its own inside the outer one—a very enormous glass thing shaped like a teardrop. And standing inside it was . . . well, I don't know how to tell you about that. *I don't know a soul up here, I thought. All this is going to get pretty tiresome if I never bump into any of my friends from the world or New Jersey.* Up front were some men playing strange-looking instruments and singing. There wasn't a single song I knew. *Boy! lonesome is a very puny word for the way I feel right now. I was beginning to think that maybe all my friends had gone to the other place, when my cloud floated right in*TO THE PICTURE.

"Albert!"

"Priscilla!"

I was in heaven all right.

Our house was built with nothing but windows. It sat on a little hill overlooking a river. The water in the river was white. Black boats sailed along it.

But I better tell you something of what went on back there a bit. I don't have to tell you how happy I was to see Priscilla again. She'd put on some weight and she looked wonderful.

As we walked along, she said, "Albert, don't you want to know what I died from?"

"Oh, why, yes—I'm so happy to see you that—"

"I died having our baby," she said.

"Our *baby!*" I said, getting my wings in such a tangle that their tips nearly knocked my beret around backwards.

"Yes, Albert. Our little boy."

"Our little—!" I yelled so loud that a big bell hanging up in the air started to ring and a little angel near us started to shuffle around—boxing his shadow. I didn't have time to tell him to keep that left up— and then the shadow was standing over him, a satisfied gray smudge giving it like a smile would be on something you can see better.

"He died, too," Priscilla said.

I wanted to cry. I started to cry.

She started to laugh.

"Oh—" I said in the middle of crying.

"You're an old silly," she said.

"That means he's—!" I couldn't get the words out.

"Certainly it does, Albert."

"Where is he? Where's my son!"

She called after me, "Wait! Wait! You're flying in the wrong direction."

Even in the wrong direction I could get there before anybody else could.

He was the most wonderful little boy that had ever been born into . . .

"Into heaven," Priscilla said softly.

"He's got hands," I said.

"And feet too," his mother said, laughing.

"He has your eyes, I think, Priscilla."

"And your hair—so far anyway."

"Don't you worry about his hair," I told her, taking a brush out of my robe pocket.

"Oh no you don't!— You put that right back, Albert Alltherestofit Budd."

He said something. "Wasn't that papa he just said—!"

"No. It was oobegoobie— Wasn't it, Michael?"

"Wasn't it *what!*"

"Shush! Do you want to give him an ear-splitting shout complex? What would you have named him?"

"Alcillafeddy," I said quickly.

"For that little baby!" She laughed until she could hardly get her breath; then she stopped laughing and gave me a stern look. "Well, don't let me hear you calling my half of him that," she said like the look.

Death went on very happily in our little house. It's wonderful to be dead and at peace, and not to have to bother about money and evils and all the rest of it.

Then one day when I was flying over to watch some baseballs playing people, a boy yelled after me:

"How about a shine, Budd?"

I looked down at my beaded moccasins. Maybe they could stand a bit of brightening up—

"Don't mind if I do," I said, sinking back on a rainbow that some little angel-children were repainting.

So right away he whipped out a big towel-like and started to shine like mad.

"Hey! Wait a minute—"

"Whatsa mattah? Hoit yereppedoimus?"

"No, it isn't that," I panted, as he worked in under my robe to get at my wing-blades. "It's just that I thought you were a shoe-shine boy."

"Naah—I'm an angel-shine boy. Gotta keep God's chillun all fresh and perty— There yuh are, Mazda. Yer a sight to make sore eyes."

"Well, what do I owe you?"

He grinned. "Oh, me," he said.

"Yes," I said, "owe you."

"You got that wrong," he said. "It's—'Oh, you.' "

"Do you happen to know anybody by the name of Donald Wan?" I asked, thinking I wouldn't get far going on with that.

"Yeah, I do— I know a Donald Wan by that name," he said, biting into a worm. He made a face and spit it out. "Fooey! that's an apple-y worm."

"You do! Where is he?"

"Right over thar— He dies in that house right next to the ferris-wheel."

Flew is a pathetic word for what I did then.

"Mr. Wan!"

"Albert Budd!"

I was still in heaven all right.

The first thing I saw when I walked into The Inventor's house were five men playing three-handed Stud Poker. It's a much faster game that way. The stakes were off to one side eating hay.

"Nice red horses," I said.

"Yeah, these boys are pretty good stallionists," Mr. Wan said, starting to lead me through the rooms. They didn't have any walls. "Simplifies things," Mr. Wan told me, as we passed a man made of water.

Off somewhere a voice said in a stage whisper: . . . . "please believe me, darling—I wouldn't trade all the gold in the world for you."

Water-man jetted up and flowed off. "That's my cue," he gurgled.

"Great one for his pool," Donald said, walking carefully around a woman made of pins and needles.

Then we passed some men singing 'We've got a right to sing the blues.' One of them said to me: "Not prejudiced, are you?"

"It's as good a color as any to be," I said.

"What's the trouble with you, Xogar?" Mr. Wan asked a man who was standing beside a huge book. "You look all cut up about something."

"I'VE BEEN ON PINS AND NEEDLES ALL AFTER-NOON," Mr. Xogar answered.

"Meet a good friend of mine," Donald said.

"GLAD TO MAKE YOUR ACQUAINTANCE, I'M SURE,"
—you don't have to be told who said—shaking my hand.

"Ouch!" I said.

"SORRY—I THOUGHT I'D GOT THEM ALL OUT."

"How's the people coming along?" Mr. Wan asked the huge book.

"Oh, not too bad. I've still got one chap ta finish—takes a lad of manipopulation," the book said.

Mr. Xogar followed us into a corner where some men with horns and forked tails were sticking red-hot spears into each other.

"Devils in heaven!" I couldn't help saying.

"WHY NOT?" Mr. Xogar said. "CAN YOU IMAGINE GOD SAYING TO HELL WITH THEM?"

We stopped near a little man who was sneezing violently. "Meet Morris," Donald said.

The little man took his nose off and pulled a fresh one out of his pocket. As he put it in place, he looked over at me and said:

"1-8——8-1!   23-1-19-20-9-14-7   25-15-21-18   20-9-13-5   1-20   20-8-9-19 —— 4-15-14'-20   25-15-21   11-14-15-23   20-8-5-18'-19   1   23-1-18   15-14?"

"YOU BETTER DO SOMETHING FOR THAT CODE OF YOURS,"—you know who said—and he started to follow a pretty girl-angel through a group of men made of lavender grass, barnswallows, paving bricks, golden shingles, balls full of colored enterprises, and one with a sort of bayer look made of aspirin tablets.

"Why does he talk like that?" I asked.

"Oh, Xogar's a capital fellow really— It's just his upper-case background," Mr. Wan said.

We stood a while watching a man make w's. He had quite a lot of trouble around the loops, but finally got them the way he wanted. Standing back aways, he said proudly, "Well, how do you like my

Then he stood on his head and added: "Mmmm."

We crossed over to a man sitting at a high desk who was making furious lines up and down the pages of a book with a blue pencil.

"Hey! Wait a minute—" I said. "That's my book you're making furious lines up and down the pages of!"

"Why not, pally—?" he said. "What would be the sense of my translating it if I left all those dull words in? Up here all we want are the ones they left out down there— Just let me tell you, The Four Letter Press's going to come through with a simply heavenly edition."

"I don't think you'll get far going into that either," Mr. Wan said, taking my arm. Then I felt his fingers tighten on it. "Oh, oh," he said. "Hold everything— Here comes Horace the I-Couldn't-Help-It."

He looked like a very mild, nice little angel. "What does he do?" I asked.

"It'll be a nuisance for you if you find out," The Inventor said, watching him sit down on a pile of worn-out sunbeams near us.

"Are you doing much inventing, Mr. Wan?" I asked, as we leaned back against a wall of green ducks.

"Yes and no," he answered. "You see, to speak very frankly,

this is about the worst possible place for me to come to."

"Heaven—!"

"That's right." He sighed. "What in the h—l—I mean heaven—is there to invent! For a while there I worked on a thing called 'Nothing For Nobody'—but it was no good. You can even have nothing if you want it up here—everything is taken for granted."

"What are you going to do?" I asked.

"Well . . . I don't know. I may try to get a transfer to The Other Place for a while."

"What could you do there?"

"Who can say? . . . Maybe rig something up so they can use fewer people to stoke the furnaces—"

Right at that point I found myself flying like mad off over the airscape. After a bit I zoomed down and into a cottage where a very large woman-angel was standing waiting with a rolling-pin in her hand.

"Who are you?" she demanded.

Then I heard a voice say: "Now, apple-cake, don't be angry with me. I had some urgent business to attend to—"

Hey! wait a minute— That voice came out of me!

"Apple-cake, is it, yet?" she said. "I'll give you the business! Now you fly right back with him—do you hear me! And then get straight on home here if you know what's bad for you."

Then I was beside Mr. Wan again.

"What was that!" I asked him.

"Who was that, you mean," he said. "Tell him you're sorry, Horace."

Horace, looking very sheepish, said, "Ah, I couldn't help it." And he whizzed off, his baa-baa's getting fainter and fainter.

"What he does," Mr. Wan explained, "is every so often fly off in somebody else's body."

"One thing I can't understand is why his wife should get so angry just because he stayed out a little late," I said.

"It's 4 A.M." Mr. Wan remarked, yawning. "I wonder how that does as a piece of dialogue to get you out of here and back to your house again."

"Now, Priscilla—"

"Don't you Priscilla me! Coming home here at all hours of the morning with your clothes all covered with gold paint— Where have you been—?"

"Oh, just visiting. . . ."

"Visiting who? Not some gilded lily from the carnival, I hope."

"Carnival? I didn't know there was one. Where is—"

"It'll be right here if you don't start explaining—and explaining fast. Where were you?"

"At Donald Wan's."

"If he gave you another injection I'm going to—"

"No, Priscilla. We just talked—and looked at people and things."

"Then how'd you get that gold paint all over your best robe?"

"Well, you see . . . There was a little man there. . . ."

"Yes, I see. There was a little man there."

"And he has a good reason for painting people."

"Umm . . . ?"

"Well. . . ."

"Ummm . . . ?"

"He's working off a guilt complex."

"Oh!"

She sort of groaned and started into the other room.

"Cludgy . . ." I called.

"*What!*"

"Is Alcillafeddy awake?"

"Is—OH!" And she closed the door with a bang that split it into two 'ohs.'

After a couple weeks I thought I'd fly down to the earth and see how things were doing with my sister. It was a strange sensation skimming along over the streets and nobody seeing you at all. It's a popular thing with angels, I found out—a lot of them were skimming along with me.

When I got up above their house the first thing I saw was Medrid standing out on the lawn drinking from a watering-hose. That grass is going to die of thirst with him there, I thought. Then I heard Mabelle Frances complaining to some-body about something. . . .

And suddenly I realized that I didn't care anything at all about seeing them or knowing what they were doing.

Of all the people in the world, I thought, they probably interest me less than anybody else.

It was so dark in Skujellifeddy's bedroom that I couldn't see anything—and coming from an angel, that's dark. Then I heard his voice:

"Babe. . . ."

"Whut . . . ?"

"Asleep?"

"Not now I ain't."

"Shall we have another one?"

"No, I'm tired— You've had enough for tonight."

This is the place where nobody said anything.

"Hon. . . ."

"What do you want now?"

"The same thing."

"I tell you I'm worn out."

"It won't take long."

"That's what you said the fifth time."

"Ah, Babe. . . ."

"Ah, Babe—nuts!"

"It'll only take a minute. . . ."

"No! I'm worn to a frazzle already."

This is the second place where nobody said anything.

"The answer is no, eh?"

"The answer is no—with neons around it."

I heard the bedsprings creak.

"A fine thing when a man has to go all the way downstairs and make his own sandwich. . . ."

"Oh, stop grumbling— You've pulled in all the suckers you're going to tonight with that line."

"Ouch!"

"Now what?"

"Chair."

"Why don't you put the light on?"

"Somebody's moved the d—n switch— Ah, here it is."

He looked just about the same. Though I'd always seen him with clothes on before.

"Any butter left?" he asked, as he started down the stairs.

"A little. Sckuggie. . . ."

"What?"

"Make me one."

"No. I don't like that 'one' in there."

"All right for you."

"Get used to that no. My conversation with you is going to be full of it from now on."

"Even if I . . ."

"If you what?"

"You know. . . . When we get through with our sandwiches."

"That, hunh?"

"Uh hunh. . . ."

"What kind?"

"Ham."

"Cheese?"

"Maybe a little."

"Lettuce?"

"No lettuce."

"White?"

"Rye."

"Say, that reminds me— What happened to that bottle I brought home a couple days ago?"

"That was a couple days ago."

"I'll couple days ago you. Want a dill?"

"I don't like pickles."

"Uh hunh."

"Put maybe a little mustard . . ."

"A little mustard after all, eh?"

"And not too thick the bread, Sckuggie."

"It's the thickness of my head I'm worried about— How do I know you'll go through with your promise to skratch my back?"

"I did last night."

"That was last night."

A little more of nobody saying anything.

"Last night was nice," she said.

"Yeah," My Agent said, "and it was nice having these eavesdropping people in too. So long, Budd, old boy. So long, folks—don't forget to lend your copy around."

". . . . treblA"

"?allicsirP, seY"

Our eyes met in the mirror and, as we turned away from it, I took her in my arms.

"Who was that pretty young woman I saw you skating with this afternoon?" she asked, drawing back a little.

I held her tighter. "That was a girl I was raised with— Chaleen Hall. I think a lot of her."

"Yes . . ." she said sort of dreamy-like. "I can understand how you would. She's very lovely."

"And she's intelligent too," I said.

"I don't doubt it at all." She pulled away and went over to stand in front of the window. "Albert . . . I . . . I haven't been very nice to you lately. I . . ."

"Oh, that's all right, Priscilla," I said, crossing over and trying to put my arms around her once more—but she drew back again.

"No, it isn't all right, Albert. I'm getting to be a real nag—"

"Oh, that doesn't matter."

"Honey," she said, turning to face me, "help me to be the sort of wife you think I am. Oh, please help me. . . ."

She was crying and I felt very awkward.

"There. . . . There. . . ." I said. "I've got to try to be nicer too."

I kissed her wet cheek. It had a cool, dewy smell—like the cheek of an angel.

"And Albert . . . I . . . I want you to promise me something," she whispered— "Don't see that girl again."

After a little while I said, "All right, Priscilla. I promise not to see her again."

We were standing at the window looking up into the heavens.

"Levels on top of levels," my wife said. "It's staggering . . . so enormous . . . so beautiful . . . so sort of making you want to kneel down like . . ."

"I wonder how soon we'll move up to the next level," I said.

"When we understand this one, I guess," she said.

"And on the highest level—is God. . . ."

"And on the highest level is God," she repeated.

"I know what I want our son to be," I said, looking up through that beauty and wonder.

"What, Albert?"

"A sort of detective. . . ."

"Oh, no, darling."

"To search out the ways of the Mystery— To hunt down all clues which may lead man to that level where the Answer is— where God is—and where everything is done in purity and innocence to the end that all men may live in peace and love the Beautiful together," I said, lowering my eyes from the light which I could not see—but which I knew was there.

"A sort of Public Detective . . ." she said softly.

Our son cried in his sleep and we went in together to comfort him.

Then I thought I'd just fly down to the earth for one last time. You'd think they'd be more careful with the spelling of street signs—but he didn't live in Patchin Place anyway.

Though he did live within very easy winging distance of it.

He was sitting in a big chair drinking beer.

"Hello, Budd," he said. "Sit down."

I sat down.

We looked at each other for a minute.

"How do you like it up there?" he asked.

"I don't understand a lot of it," I said.

"Yes, I know." He took another drink of beer. "Tell me something— What is life exactly, Mr. Budd? What's it all about?"

". . . ."

"And while you're at it— What is death?"

". . . ." I said.

"They're about as good answers as I've heard," he said, pouring himself some more beer.

We looked at each other for a minute again.

"Well, here's an eye in your mud," he said, lifting his glass.

"I think I better be going now," I said, shifting my wings

to limber them. "Priscilla gets pretty upset when I'm late."

"Yes, I guess you better."

"Well . . . Good-bye then."

He stood up and gripped my hand.

"So-long, Budd. Take care of yourself— You're on your own now."

"I'll do my best," I said.

"How are you going to end the book?" he asked.

"I haven't thought much about that."

"This might be a pretty good time to think about it."

"Well . . ." I said, getting my wings all set, and tossing my new hair back out of my eyes—"I guess maybe the best way would be to fly right up out of it."

Like this.

New Directions Paperbooks—a partial listing

Martín Adán, The Cardboard House

César Aira
  An Episode in the Life of a Landscape Painter
  Ghosts
  The Literary Conference

Will Alexander, The Sri Lankan Loxodrome

Paul Auster, The Red Notebook

Gennady Aygi, Child-and-Rose

Honoré de Balzac, Colonel Chabert

Djuna Barnes, Nightwood

Charles Baudelaire, The Flowers of Evil*

Bei Dao, The Rose of Time: New & Selected Poems*

Nina Berberova, The Ladies From St. Petersburg

Roberto Bolaño, By Night in Chile
  Distant Star
  Last Evenings on Earth
  Nazi Literature in the Americas
  Jorge Luis Borges, Labyrinths
  Seven Nights

Coral Bracho, Firefly Under the Tongue*

Kamau Brathwaite, Ancestors

Sir Thomas Browne, Urn Burial

Basil Bunting, Complete Poems

Anne Carson, Glass, Irony & God

Horacio Castellanos Moya, Senselessness
  The She-Devil in the Mirror

Louis-Ferdinand Céline
  Death on the Installment Plan
  Journey to the End of the Night

René Char, Selected Poems

Inger Christensen, alphabet

Jean Cocteau, The Holy Terrors

Peter Cole, Things on Which I've Stumbled

Julio Cortázar, Cronopios & Famas

Albert Cossery, The Colors of Infamy

Robert Creeley, If I Were Writing This
  Life and Death

Guy Davenport, 7 Greeks

Osamu Dazai, The Setting Sun

H.D., Tribute to Freud
  Trilogy

Helen DeWitt, Lightning Rods

Robert Duncan, Groundwork
  Selected Poems

Eça de Queirós, The Maias

William Empson, 7 Types of Ambiguity

Shusaku Endo, Deep River
  The Samurai

Jenny Erpenbeck, Visitation

Lawrence Ferlinghetti
  A Coney Island of the Mind
  Time of Useful Consciousness

Thalia Field, Bird Lovers, Backyard

F. Scott Fitzgerald, The Crack-Up
  On Booze

Forrest Gander, As a Friend
  Core Samples From the World

Romain Gary, The Life Before Us (Mme. Rosa)

Henry Green, Pack My Bag

Allen Grossman, Descartes' Loneliness

John Hawkes, The Lime Twig
  Felisberto Hernández, Lands of Memory

Hermann Hesse, Siddhartha

Takashi Hiraide
  For the Fighting Spirit of the Walnut*

Yoel Hoffman, The Christ of Fish

Susan Howe, My Emily Dickinson
  That This

Bohumil Hrabal, I Served the King of England

Christopher Isherwood, The Berlin Stories

Fleur Jaeggy, Sweet Days of Discipline

Gustav Janouch, Conversations With Kafka

Alfred Jarry, Ubu Roi

B.S. Johnson, House Mother Normal

Franz Kafka, Amerika: The Man Who Disappeared

Alexander Kluge, Cinema Stories

Laszlo Krasznahorkai
  The Melancholy of Resistance
  Satantango

Mme. de Lafayette, The Princess of Clèves

Lautréamont, Maldoror

Denise Levertov, Selected Poems
  Tesserae

Li Po, Selected Poems

Clarice Lispector, The Hour of the Star
  Near to the Wild Heart
  The Passion According to G. H.

Luljeta Lleshanaku, Child of Nature

Federico García Lorca, Selected Poems*
  Three Tragedies

Nathaniel Mackey, Splay Anthem

Stéphane Mallarmé, Selected Poetry and Prose*

Javier Marías, Your Face Tomorrow (3 volumes)
  While the Women Are Sleeping

Thomas Merton, New Seeds of Contemplation
  The Way of Chuang Tzu

Henri Michaux, Selected Writings
Dunya Mikhail, Diary of a Wave Outside the Sea
Henry Miller, The Air-Conditioned Nightmare
  Big Sur & The Oranges of Hieronymus Bosch
  The Colossus of Maroussi
Yukio Mishima, Confessions of a Mask
  Death in Midsummer
Eugenio Montale, Selected Poems*
Vladimir Nabokov, Laughter in the Dark
  Nikolai Gogol
  The Real Life of Sebastian Knight
Pablo Neruda, The Captain's Verses*
  Love Poems*
  Residence on Earth*
Charles Olson, Selected Writings
George Oppen, New Collected Poems (with CD)
Wilfred Owen, Collected Poems
Michael Palmer, Thread
Nicanor Parra, Antipoems*
Boris Pasternak, Safe Conduct
Kenneth Patchen
  Memoirs of a Shy Pornographer
Octavio Paz, Selected Poems
  A Tale of Two Gardens
Victor Pelevin
  The Hall of the Singing Caryatids
  Omon Ra
Saint-John Perse, Selected Poems
Ezra Pound, The Cantos
  New Selected Poems and Translations
  Personae
Raymond Queneau, Exercises in Style
Qian Zhongshu, Fortress Besieged
Raja Rao, Kanthapura
Herbert Read, The Green Child
Kenneth Rexroth, Songs of Love, Moon & Wind
  Written on the Sky: Poems from the Japanese
Rainer Maria Rilke
  Poems from the Book of Hours
  The Possibility of Being
Arthur Rimbaud, Illuminations*
  A Season in Hell and The Drunken Boat*
Guillermo Rosales, The Halfway House
Evelio Rosero, The Armies
  Good Offices
Joseph Roth, The Leviathan
Jerome Rothenberg, Triptych
Ihara Saikaku, The Life of an Amorous Woman
William Saroyan
  The Daring Young Man on the Flying Trapeze

Jean-Paul Sartre, Nausea
  The Wall
Delmore Schwartz
  In Dreams Begin Responsibilities
W.G. Sebald, The Emigrants
  The Rings of Saturn
  Vertigo
Aharon Shabtai, J'accuse
Hasan Shah, The Dancing Girl
C.H. Sisson, Selected Poems
Gary Snyder, Turtle Island
Muriel Spark, The Ballad of Peckham Rye
  A Far Cry From Kensington
  Memento Mori
George Steiner, My Unwritten Books
Antonio Tabucchi, Indian Nocturne
  Pereira Declares
Yoko Tawada, The Bridegroom Was a Dog
  The Naked Eye
Dylan Thomas, A Child's Christmas in Wales
  Collected Poems
  Under Milk Wood
Uwe Timm, The Invention of Curried Sausage
Charles Tomlinson, Selected Poems
Tomas Tranströmer
  The Great Enigma: New Collected Poems
Leonid Tsypkin, Summer in Baden-Baden
Tu Fu, Selected Poems
Frederic Tuten, The Adventures of Mao
Paul Valéry, Selected Writings
Enrique Vila-Matas, Bartleby & Co.
  Dublinesque
Elio Vittorini, Conversations in Sicily
Rosmarie Waldrop, Driven to Abstraction
Robert Walser, The Assistant
  Microscripts
  The Tanners
Eliot Weinberger, An Elemental Thing
  Oranges and Peanuts for Sale
Nathanael West
  Miss Lonelyhearts & The Day of the Locust
Tennessee Williams, Cat on a Hot Tin Roof
  The Glass Menagerie
  A Streetcar Named Desire
William Carlos Williams, In the American Grain
  Paterson
  Selected Poems
  Spring and All
Louis Zukofsky, "A"
  Anew

*BILINGUAL EDITION

For a complete listing, request a free catalog from New Directions, 80 8th Avenue, NY NY 10011 or visit us online at www.ndpublishing.com